BOOK OF
MURDER

BY
FREDERICK IRVING ANDERSON

DOVER PUBLICATIONS, INC.
NEW YORK

Published in Canada by General Publishing Company, Ltd., 30 Lesmill Road, Don Mills, Toronto, Ontario.

Published in the United Kingdom by Constable and Company, Ltd., 10 Orange Street, London WC2H 7EG.

This Dover edition, first published in 1988, is an unabridged, unaltered republication of the work first published by E. P. Dutton, New York, 1930.

Manufactured in the United States of America
Dover Publications, Inc., 31 East 2nd Street, Mineola, N.Y. 11501

Library of Congress Cataloging-in-Publication Data

Anderson, Frederick Irving, 1877–1947.
　　Book of murder / by Frederick Irving Anderson.
　　　　p.　　cm.
　　　　Contents: Beyond all conjecture—The wedding gift—The Japanese parasol—The dead end—The magician—A start in life—Big time—The recoil—Gulf Stream green—The door key.
　　ISBN 0-486-25630-8 (pbk.)
　　1. Crime and criminals—Fiction.　2. Detective and mystery stories, American.　I. Title.
PS3501.N2265B66　　1988
813'.52—dc19　　　　　　　　　　　　　　　　　　87-34570
　　　　　　　　　　　　　　　　　　　　　　　　　　　CIP

S
501
2265
66
788

CONTENTS

I

BEYOND ALL CONJECTURE

TO DIE at a ripe old age in the same house where you were born—on the Island of Manhattan—one must either be very, very rich or very, very poor. For a person in ordinary circumstances the wish is a good deal like reaching for the moon on a particularly bright night—it seems possible, but one gradually grows up and forgets about it. For the ground underfoot is like a precious palimpsest of many erasures. In other parts of the world it is humdrum enough.

For instance, Cornelius Vlemynck's remotest progenitors had made it a practice for uncounted generations to die in the same delft cottage they were born in, on the delft banks of the Schie; until that historic Vlemynck with a wandering foot put that fatal feather bed behind him and cast his lot with those adventurous souls within the stockade known as Nieuw Amsterdam at the confluence of the North and East rivers, in the New World. Later there was to emerge a Cornelius Vlemynck—through a constantly descending line of devisees—of Number — Fifth Avenue, which number, containing only one figure and that a very small one, would be south of the Brevoort and north of the Arch—a very desirable place indeed, located on the first page, near the top, of the old, old bluebooks.

On the evening Cornelius Vlemynck died he had occupied this house, a four-story brownstone from which the high stoop had been removed in later times, just sixty-five years lacking a few days, which was enough to insure him a good obituary even though he had not possessed other distinctions. People passed by in crowds when the fact was printed, many simply to see for themselves a New York house in which one man could live so elegantly for so many years.

There had always been a white-shirted manservant standing inside the vestibule door waiting for people to come up the steps, though the only callers Cornelius Vlemynck had, of later years, were real-estate brokers, to buy the ground lease. To each of them he related, with great dignity, his ambition in life—to die in the house he was born in—and since he had the means to indulge himself, and was so adamantine in his purpose, they all departed finally wishing him luck. No argument moved him. He was lonely in his old age; otherwise he wouldn't even have consented to see them.

"You can't stand in the path of a glacier," they would say. "The private house is too regal for one man in a democracy. It has to go. You dam progress."

"I do, indeed!" agreed the old gentleman fervently, with a final *n*.

"Look at So-and-So, who left a lumberyard in the middle of Broadway—he drove retail trade over to Fifth Avenue—and left his heirs whistling up a hollow tree!" The real-estate men said: "We are assemblers of parcels. If you won't sell we will build around you and use you for permanent light and air."

In the end that is what they had to do; and before its owner died this historic mansion of old New York was boxed in at the bottom of a well by skyscraping apartment hotels.

Mr. Vlemynck was very vain of his slender height. He was given to bright colors and *outré* effects, and his abundant hair—kept snowy by bluing—showed under his hat brim like lumps of freshly ginned cotton. He did his own marketing, taking with him his fat cook, Martha, who had teeth like pearls and a smooth skin as clear as skimmed chocolate.

At one in the morning on May twenty-first, having written with a bold hand that never quavered the last superscription of his correspondence and affixed the necessary stamps thereunto, he took his hat and his cloak and his stick and went softly down the padded hall and out, being careful, in the kindness of his heart, not to waken the manservant, who, as the hour waxed late, had finally fallen asleep at his empty post. Cornelius Vlemynck drew the vestibule door shut behind him and listened for the click of the spring lock. Crossing the broad sidewalk, he moved diagonally over the velvety asphalt, a safe enough procedure at this hour, for the buses had stopped running and the Avenue was deserted, and the only signs of life were porters of the tall apartment hotels, dusting out the interstices of the rubber hall strips at the edge of the sidewalk. A mail box stood on the corner below, but the night being fine, Cornelius Vlemynck squared his shoulders and passed it by. He walked to the east, then southerly through the park, passing some raucous pothouses on the southern rim, which still thrived in spite of—or maybe because of—the law at this ungodly hour of the morning.

Something led him into Sullivan Street, where the descent from polished door knockers is very rapid. There was a mail box at the first intersection, and he was in the act of counting his letters and wondering if he had cross-hitched any of his missives—that is, put any inclosure in a wrong envelope; that would be awkward, but it is an extremely human failing—when the languid footfall of a patrolling policeman, probably on his first tour through the side street to the river and back, attracted his attention. The policeman, a young fellow, crossing the street, noticed the very tall old gentleman standing there with a handful of letters he was holding up to the light of the street lamp; he noted with a smile the extravagant white hair hanging in cottony lumps under the broad-brimmed hat; he noted the florid face, the bright tie, the flowing cloak and the general carnival effect of the whole outfit.

And he said, nodding, "Where is the party tonight?" He thought Mr. Vlemynck was in costume. But he saw his mistake instantly in the surprised countenance of the old man. "It's beautiful tonight, isn't it, sir?" he added hastily.

"Indeed, yes, it is!" agreed Cornelius Vlemynck with grave courtesy. The policeman, amused, cast a last look over his shoulder at the old gentleman. Mr. Vlemynck had discovered one envelope to be unsealed. Summoning his courage—for he disliked the taste of dextrin, even when flavored with some essential oil—he liberally moistened the flap with the tip of his tongue and pressed it down, making a wry face over the thought of the millions of germs he must be ingesting. The policeman passed on.

"Seven," counted the old man, paying in the letters, "eight, nine——"

The mail box shut with a surly clang. He hung there for a moment. He turned himself toward home, as an old man will, before relinquishing his support. But he had scarcely crossed the first flag of the sidewalk when an odd surprised look shot across his face and he reached out quickly for a staircase balustrade. He tugged at his collar to loosen his gaudy cravat; his hand went to his heart and he tugged there, too, as if to loosen something inside. He tried to cry out, but his knees sagged and he sank gently to earth, clenching his fingers. He slipped down the single step into a little areaway and rested there in the shadow against the high stoop. A little later an unlucky nightbird came prowling along in his regular quest for some blind drunk out of the pothouses. Skilfully he went through Cornelius Vlemynck and took everything—his bill fold, his watch and his keys; there was nothing left but an empty hulk.

The night wore on, the stars moved to the other side of the little street; Antares blinked itself out against the ridge-pole of a roof and Vega came to the zenith. Passersby who saw the reclining figure did not pause to inquire, but shaking their heads, gave it a wide berth; it is always best—these shadows that sleep in doorways.

A little after two there was a police whistle, some windows went up and heads came out; a small group accumulated about the high stoop and waited in silence. After an interminable delay an ambulance rolled into the street, its bell tapering off to nothing as the wheels stopped at the curb. A young interne pushed his way through the crowd, his white uniform glowing in the night light.

He said, after a single look, "Another thick cop! Do you think I'm a hearse?"

"Ain't you going to take him?" said the policeman.

"You know damned well I'm not!" returned the shaveling medico as he swung on his seat again, twisting a wrist through the safety loop. He lighted a cigarette; they wound up the bell and started back home.

It was not until daylight that the scuttled hulk that had been Cornelius Vlemynck found a temporary resting place on a marble slab that pulled in and out on rollers, his fine clothes hung in a bag. North of the Square everybody knew the gay old beau with his cottony white hair, his florid countenance, his lurid ties, his spats and the affected cut of his clothes. South of the Square nobody knew him.

"He is somebody," said the gatekeeper at the foot of East Twenty-sixth Street, the pier of outgoing souls. But that was as far as his curiosity went. His whole life, passed on the River Styx, made him keen in allotting caste to his guests.

The medical examiner, passing down the aisle after a look, said, out of his complex experience:

"That was either prussic acid or nitrobenzol. There is a very pretty differentiation under certain conditions, and it takes a good man, well grounded in his toxicology, to discover it. We'll do that the first thing in the morning."

Nobody, of course, would inquire at the police station for the absent Cornelius Vlemynck, much less at the morgue. It simply was not done in his circle. Toward noon Martha took off her gay bandanna and kerchief which he insisted she wear when she accompanied him to market. The second man brought word downstairs that neither the tepid bath that had been drawn for him nor the fresh things which had been laid out for his use had been touched.

The waitress, who was also the upstairs girl and more curious than the rest, peeped through the keyhole and brought word that his bed had not been slept in.

His lawyer telephoned at four, and the butler told him, with a twinkle, and the lawyer chuckled and cautiously hung up, as if withdrawing from an eavesdropping. There are thousands and thousands of missing people who never come to port. One step off the path, when everything is right for it, and they are gone like a breath—a consummation devoutly to be wished by many wretched souls, doubtless, but they never seem to achieve it by trying; it is achieved only by accident, the door of the unknown opening and closing and keeping its secret.

Note how fate intervened. If the manservant had not fallen asleep at his empty post he would have gone to the mail box—after Mr. Vlemynck had inspected each and every missive, as he always did to see if they were sealed

properly—and come back to find his master dead or hopelessly involved in dying. They would have telephoned his
physician, who would have said, "Ah, yes, I know all about
it." He did, that physician. On his books he had a dozen
florid old gentlemen like Cornelius Vlemynck, all carrying
around livers they had misused in the tropics. He could
write their death certificates without calling—especially in
the middle of the night. There would have been an élite
funeral and nothing more.

The next day at eleven the medical examiner came out,
turning down his cuffs.

"There is something," he said to a central-office detective
who had dropped in to see what he could pick up. "It will
interest you—cyanide. The dose was a minimum. A slick
case—murder. Too small for a suicide—they take too
much. Before death," he said, getting into one sleeve of his
coat, "we could very easily have confused it with *apoplexie
foudroyante* in some of its forms. After death the effects
are extremely fugacious. But mark the hard luck the murderer plays in. It comes to me! I happen to know! The
mucous membrane is much congested and there's a dark
cherry-colored liquid venous blood. There you are! Thank
me." He got into the other sleeve.

By so narrow a margin did Cornelius Vlemynck, whose
sole ambition was to die at a ripe old age in the house he
was born in, and who died in a gutter, miss potter's field.
A boat leaves the foot of East Twenty-sixth Street every
morning. The next day he would have gone, for no one
would come for him. At home, the servants were answering
the telephone by saying he was out of town. He had been
out of town in the same way before. Except for a little extra
rigidity in his pose, as he lay there waiting for the eternal
anonymity of a pauper's cross, even the medical examiner
would have passed him by.

II

Parr himself, the deputy in charge, who had a trick of smelling out big game without any why or wherefore, got into his things and came uptown when he saw the police slip. The first thing he did was to go through the bag of clothes. There were no labels. Cornelius Vlemynck said to his tailors, "I don't carry around an advertisement for any tradesman. Leave your name off me." Some tailors sew a man's name inside a pocket, where he won't be apt to see it. But Cornelius Vlemynck did not want to be labeled that way, and saw to it that he was not. He had his own laundress, so he had no laundry mark. His shoes were custom-made.

"Ha-ha!" laughed Parr. "Here we are!" Inside the tongue of a shoe was a number, written in ink. Men went from shoemaker to shoemaker until they found the man who fitted the feet of Cornelius Vlemynck. "He was robbed," noted the deputy. "But that was merely incidental. Robbers do not use cyanide. I have an idea," said Parr, "that we are going to resort to the last refuge of a scoundrel—expert testimony—before we are through with this case. Make specific notes and have a good toxicologist check you up."

"The dose was so small it wouldn't have been fatal, except that the old man's arteries were prime for it. If I had taken my day off, as I had planned, this would have been a perfect crime," said the elated medical examiner.

Parr, too, had his moment of elation. Police business is drab at best. It is the same thing over and over again. There is something tragic about the new recruits advancing in waves to retribution. There is something pitifully stereotyped about the cerebral cortex. Thought travels in well-worn grooves; under the same stimuli a million people will do the same thing, with variations *a*, *b* and *c*. And every mother's son of them thinks he is original, especially the crook. The petty sneak who picked Cornelius Vlemynck's pockets when he lay dying, cunningly waited twenty-four, thirty-six hours, and then slipped into a pawnshop remote from the scene of his crime and pledged the watch. One of Parr's men stood there at the end of the show case smoking a cigar, waiting for him—not for this one man in particular, but for his type. There is a certain run of these shops through which petty sneaks come constantly trickling into the hands of the police. Here is one of the bottle necks of petty crime.

There is nothing so drab as police business ninety-nine times out of a hundred. This was the hundredth. The miserable creature who turned up in the right slot with the effects of the dead man—the watch, the keys, the pocketbook—obviously was not the person who had graduated a dose of prussic acid so nicely as to indicate death for Cornelius Vlemynck.

"This should interest you," said Parr to his friend and occasional collaborator, Oliver Armiston, the extinct author. "There is nothing to start from."

It was true—Oliver liked this type of case, with nothing to start from. "Do you recollect that lumberyard in Broadway?" asked he, pausing opposite Number — Fifth Avenue. "There were real-estate operators who would gladly have sent flowers if the owner had kindly consented to pass out."

"This is different," said Parr. "They are using Cornelius for permanent light and air here; they would have paid him to live forever."

They went in. The manservant on the door was at last exercising the functions for which he was intended. Countless people came and went, mostly Parr's scientificos, who went through the place from cellar to garret, as if old Cornelius Vlemynck, when he stepped off, must have left behind him some plasma in which to mold at least a working hypothesis. Experts questioned the servants to the end of their—the servants'—endurance, then went back and covered the same ground again and again. At two o'clock in the morning, when the household was bedraggled with the frightful ordeal of inquiry, a fresh batch of inquisitors started again, back at the beginning.

"He had gone out before and stayed—when? Someone telephoned during the time—who? Be careful! We check you up through Central's records. Don't lie again!"

The lawyer was called in, his physician; men haunted the sawdust aisles at Washington Market where Cornelius, with Martha waddling behind, bought fresh vegetables. They went through his check stubs, letter files, his address book.

"The old man," said Parr, "lived the life of a finicky old maid."

They probed with the eye of suspicion the record of telephone toll calls they found at Central Exchange; they watched, and set the servants to watching the crowds that flocked by the house next day—the murderer would be among them of course. Experts pawed over his investments, looked up the beneficiaries under the will.

"The man on the door was wide awake when the old boy went out," said Parr to Oliver. "He was playing possum."

Parr himself had extracted this information. The questioned ones cling desperately to their little lies. The man had simply been afraid to let his master know that he had been nodding for fear of a scolding, so he had pretended to be sound asleep while the old man passed out. Then the slovenly fellow actually did fall asleep waiting for Mr. Vlemynck to come back. This placed the hour very near one.

"Then he can't swear Vlemynck didn't come back," said Oliver.

"No. But a night watchman saw him go out and he says the old man did not come back. It was exactly one, according to him. Cornelius cut across diagonally, stopped at the mail box in front of the old Rhinelander house, opened it, seemed to reconsider, and let it fall shut and passed on."

"It was too near home," said Armiston.

"Possibly," admitted Parr, nodding. "But where does that get you? It's like a game of chess. In the first ten moves the variants are innumerable. Take your pick."

"Ah, but very few of those variants are sound," protested Oliver. "Actually, the paths a clever chess player would take are very few, and these reduce themselves as the game goes on. A stupid player soon comes to the end of his rope. The game is really not so complex as legend would have it. There was no prussic acid about him at the time he decided to hunt a more remote mail box. That is obvious. We admit he didn't take it himself, or he would have taken more. And no one else had at that time yet administered it to him. He couldn't have gone two steps after taking it. The fumes of the anhydrous acid are so deadly that, in a laboratory, the rules are imperative—an operator is not permitted to be alone when he opens a bottle of it. In its cyanide form it has actually to be dissolved and come into contact with the mucous membrane. But even as cyanide, no man would go off hunting a mail box with a grain of it inside him. Now where are we? First we establish that he left the house at one to mail letters which he decided not to drop in a box too near home. I'd like to see those letters."

"Help yourself," said Parr lightly. "It looks like suicide."

"Exactly—but it isn't!"

"People will go to extravagant lengths, killing themselves,

to escape the stigma of self-destruction," said Parr. "We had a case several days ago of a passenger in an airplane beating his pilot senseless with a wrench. Through some hook or crook the plane landed itself. Otherwise it would have been merely another crash."

"Your cop saw Vlemynck, spoke to him, at——"

"——at 1:25."

"And your bum went through him——"

"——at 1:45. He looked at the watch."

Even the case-hardened deputy had to smile; this was one of the breaks of the game, that miserable sneak thief noting the time, to hang somebody eventually with it."

"He wasn't dead then?" said Oliver.

"No. That bum wouldn't have touched him on a bet."

They regarded each other for a moment in silence. That placed the act within twenty minutes; it was seldom they could box it in so nicely.

"He hadn't taken it when the cop saw him about to drop his letters," pursued Armiston. "Do you notice," he asked, half shutting his eyes, "how the mail-box motif keeps recurring, like a beat note? There is an idea heterodyning us there, Parr, as we talk, and we catch the beat. Do you understand the principle of the heterodyne? Look it up. It's beautiful, mathematically. The waves of one frequency neutralize the waves of another frequency, running alongside, and leave only the excess frequency, to be apprehended and calibrated by our senses. I apprehend the mail box very strongly just now. It beats against my eardrums, so to speak. Let us go on. I'd like to see the inside of that mail box."

"It's been swept out twenty times since then," remarked Parr dryly. He smiled, rubbing his blue chin; he had been shaved only once today—a very unusual occurrence with the deputy.

"Let us take him from the moment the cop saw him about to mail the letters," pursued Oliver. "Sometime in the next twenty minutes he will have been induced to take enough cyanide to render him unconscious and eventually to kill him. He couldn't have gone to any of the rum shops in the neighborhood?"

"He was a teetotaler, I think, and rather fanatic," said Parr. "Suicide!" He shrugged.

"Let's stand on the medical examiner's deduction for the time being," put in Oliver. "He would have taken more. . . . Well, he mails his letters."

"Does he?" said Parr, checking up.

"Let us go back to the moment when he is examining them under the street lamp. Reconstruct that moment."

Oliver moved over to Cornelius Vlemynck's desk, a beautiful ponderous piece of old Flemish carving in which even the wormholes were precious. There was pen, ink and paper, as Cornelius Vlemynck had left it. When a man dies this way the police see to it that everything about him that might suggest a clew is left precisely as it was. His envelope rack stood open, his stationery, with his crest, lay at hand; the very pen was there—indeed, the very ink rusted in the nib; there was the celluloid drum, in its silvery nest, with which he moistened the flaps of the envelopes to seal them. Oliver took out a dozen envelopes, went through the dumb show of sealing them, and went down the hall to the hat tree as an imaginary mail box.

"I read my superscriptions as I hold open the box," he said. "We all do. To err is human. I never mail a letter without a last look. Still, the Dead Letter Office is choked with our mistakes. I examine them. Maybe I have forgotten to put on a street or a number or a town. Maybe I have forgotten to seal one. He drops them in. You say, did he? I say yes. We know he sent out some routine checks and that they arrived. They have been traced to this box, or at least to this neighborhood. See how the mail-box motif continues? You follow?"

"Proceed," said Parr, smiling.

"Very well. He drops dead—or dying. Nothing can save him now."

"You omit a step," said Parr. "You must poison him first."

"Ah! You admit the moment has arrived?" exclaimed Oliver. Parr nodded. Oliver pulled at his single white lock of hair. "Isn't it possible that it has happened before your very eyes?" cried he. "Parr," he exclaimed suddenly, "is that cop still here?"

"Yes."

"Fetch him in."

Parr wrinkled his nose, looking oddly at Oliver. "Lacey!" he called; and the young patrolman who had mistaken Mr. Vlemynck's costume for fancy dress came in.

"I am Mr. Vlemynck," said Oliver, seizing the hatrack. "I am mailing these letters. Have I already mailed some?"

"Yes, sir," responded Lacey, catching the play. "You have just dropped several in as I stop."

"What do I do now?"

"You are examining the others under the light."

"Ah! Am I nearsighted?"

"No, sir—farsighted. You hold them off."

"Good! Do I find something wrong?"

"I—I couldn't say, sir."

The patrolman was looking straight at Oliver. Oliver turned one of the dummy letters in his hand; he discovered it to be unsealed and wetted it with his tongue. He eyed Lacey.

"Wasn't one of the letters unsealed by chance?" he asked.

Lacey hesitated. Then he nodded, a puzzled look on his face. "I think—I think he did close one, sir," he said.

"That's all," said Armiston. Lacey went out, Armiston waiting till the door shut. He went over to the desk and dropped the envelope he had just sealed in front of Parr.

"There you are," he said. He made a wry face. "That dextrin is flavored with peppermint. If it had been flavored with cyanide of potassium, I might have got as far as that areaway—say, ten feet. I don't know. It acts pretty fast."

Parr stared at the envelope a second or two, then up at Oliver. He shook his head. Some of Oliver's deductions had what he called a distinct story-book tang.

"He doesn't use cyanide as a flavor, does he?" he asked, indicating the Vlemynck envelope rack.

"Parr," said Oliver, as he scoured off the tip of his tongue with his handkerchief, "years ago in my youth I conceived the bright idea, in a fiction story, of impregnating a match head with some volatile cyanide salt and offering a light to a man I wanted to kill—in print, you understand. It was necessary, of course, that the victim be a cigarette smoker who inhaled deeply the first puff. It was sound enough—for fiction. It was printed. But it didn't end there. Your illustrious predecessor, Inspector Byrnes, paid me the honor of an invitation to call in person, and he suggested— with a stick in it—that I find some other way of making a living. It seems some crook had tried it—and made it work."

"And?" inquired the deputy silkily.

"At the present moment I find no difficulty in conceiving the brilliant idea of impregnating the dextrin of an envelope flap with enough cyanide to kill a man—if he licked it with a wet tongue."

"He might prefer his own flavor," said Parr. "How would you induce him to change?"

"I'd write him a flattering letter," said Oliver, "asking for his autograph, and I'd inclosed a stamped and addressed envelope. He probably wouldn't bite on the first one. I'd have to repeat—some other request—anything that gave me an excuse to inclose my envelope."

"Morel!" called Parr quietly; and Morel, Parr's shadow, appeared from inside. He was the man through whom the deputy exercised his genius for minutiæ. He would be saturated with this case by now.

"Is it suicide?" demanded Parr.

Morel shook his head. "A man like this old Knickerbocker wouldn't choose that avenue," said Morel, looking around.

"Why not?"

"It's quick—yes," said Morel; "but it crowds too much horror into a single moment." Oliver nodded—time is measured by a succession of impressions; there are instants that stretch to eternity.

"That sounds conclusive," admitted Parr with a smile. "What would you say, Morel, if I told you that Lacey, the cop, saw him take that stuff?"

Morel merely shook his head and waited.

"Listen to this," said the deputy, and nodded to Oliver. Armiston laid down his supposititious case. There was a pause, the three, so used to one another's mental reactions, watching one another narrowly.

"How would you have addressed the return envelope, Morel?" asked Parr, using Morel as a stalking horse.

"If I were the murderer, you mean?"

"Yes."

"Certainly not to myself. I would never be so foolhardy as to attempt to recover it," said Morel.

"Why not? You could disguise it."

"Something might go wrong—anything might go wrong."

"Nothing went wrong," said Parr. He indicated a clutter of evening newspapers. The Vlemynck murder flooded the front page. It was cut to order for the flaming tabloids; it was great news for the regulars. It had all the elements for an indefinite run.

"You'd leave it in existence as evidence, Morel?" pursued the deputy.

"I'd lose it in the Dead Letter Office," said Morel. "It would bury itself like a dud." He nodded at Oliver. "It's clever, sir. There is nothing to trace."

"Unless there were some bracketing shots," said Oliver, using the artilleryman's metaphor.

"Ah!" exclaimed Morel, catching his breath.

"He may have sent a dozen before one took," put in Parr. "Assuming, of course," he said quickly, "that we are on the right track. We are looking for duds that went wrong. That's your job, Morel. See if there is any trash paper around the house—circulars, fancy direct-by-mail sales stuff, begging letters, invitations to join. He must have received tons of that stuff."

It was hopeless, finding waste paper that had been thrown away. But the man-hunter's fame rested on just such quests as this.

"Morel," said Parr.

"Yes, sir."

"These rich houses usually bale or bag their trash and deliver it every so often to a junkman," said Parr. Oliver felt an odd tingling. Needles in haystacks have habits, too, if only one studies them! "Bring me a bag of it," offered Parr, "and I'll buy you a new necktie. Bring me an envelope salted with cyanide," he added grimly, "and I'll give you my gold shield."

"Look for a blue envelope," suggested Oliver casually.

"Why blue?"

"Any opaque color," said Oliver. "The stuff is decomposed by light. If he knew enough to mix it he knew how to take care of it."

It was like a chess gambit. There exist only a few that are sound—you can count them on your fingers, even with a Morphy or a Steinitz to plot them. Some, like the Evans and Rice gambits, will persist for years until some brilliant analyst detects the flaw. Usually it is to be found within the first ten moves. So with murder. But there is no literature of murder, only voluminous notes on mistakes; trial and error is the only technic. Sooner or later your murderer takes a wrong turn; then he is lost. The trash from the Vlemynck ménage was bagged, and collected every Thursday by a bearded little gnome trundling one of those enormour pushcarts; the very picture of him was an Æsop fable in itself. The creature had a loft in Allen Street, where he sorted bond from pulp, spurred on by the wheezy hope of a ragpicker.

Parr took over the dingy loft. The first day his men turned up one envelope—not blue—with enough cyanide in the dextrin of the flap to kill a man. It was a regular stamped envelope of the post-office variety, and so cleverly was the gum substituted that the eye would not detect any trace of what must have been a complicated manipulation. But when the flap was warmed gently, it became slightly tacky to the touch and gave off a distinct odor of bitter almonds. Parr paid mute tribute to Armiston, a nod.

The address was Filson Habern, Number 2 Castor Docks, London, S. W. 1. There was no such place. It was printed; and under the stamp were the usual numerals in diamond type as if to give the date and number of the last printing—the legend ran 8–7–'25–8M. He was a stickler for detail, this fellow with the cyanide.

Genius is the capacity for taking pains. Parr had facili-

ties for infinite patience. In three days his men turned up
three more return envelopes salted with cyanide, all printed
with every semblance of reality; they were all fictitious,
and all directed, through devious routes, to the Dead Letter
Office. They turned up two inclosures. Under date of
March twelfth, one addressed Cornelius Vlemynck as follows:

Excellency: I inclose photograph of what purports to be
a ms. page of the lost Gastein symphony. Knowing your interest
in the subject, and doubt as to the existence in fact of this work,
I take the liberty, as one collector to another, of asking you for
inspection and comment. I inclose stamped addressed envelope
for its return.

It was signed by the fictitious Castor Docks person.
Across the face of it Cornelius Vlemynck had written in a
large bold hand, "Liar," before tipping it into his waste-
paper basket.

The manuscript page of the fabulous symphony was
missing.

The second inclosure they took to be the murder missive
itself. Under date of May nineteenth, it ran:

Sir: May I recall myself to you as the runner-up for the Seven
Pillars, at Christie's? In my chagrin—how we hate each other—
I childishly refused to make note of the serial number. Now,
contrite, might I have it, to complete my records? I inclose card
and return wrapper for your convenience.

The signature was indecipherable. They found none of
the original envelopes, to determine points of origin. But
there was enough stuff here to keep Parr's faculty of voodoo experts busy for days, analyzing inks and watermarks
and type fonts and all the rest of those unconsidered trifles
which hang men by the neck until dead. Oliver arranged
the fictitious names in every conceivable combination, as
if some vestige of the identity that patterned them must

reside within the defiles of choice. He found himself recit-
ing that line from Sir Thomas Browne that Edgar Allan
Poe was so fond of repeating:

What song the Syrens sang, or what name Achilles assumed
when he hid himself among women, although puzzling questions,
are not beyond all conjecture.

III

Does the bird leave a trail through the air, a fish through
the sea? Doubtless. Cornelius Fleming, the murderer, came
out of his furnished apartment in Columbus Avenue on
the twentieth of May and went to the corner newsstand
under the Elevated opposite the car barns.

"I want all the papers tomorrow morning, Ike," he said.
Ike had a surname, but everybody who passed knew him
as Ike the news dealer.

"All the papers? Mr. Fleming," he cried, "what do you
mean—all the papers? The German, Greek, Italian, Svensk,
Armenian, Jewish, Czech——"

"Oh, the English papers," said the young man—"the
World, Times, Herald Tribune, American, and so on—you
know—every morning, for a week."

Ike made no memo; news dealers and laundrymen are
born with some memory system of their own; they never
have to put down names or numbers.

"You go in business, Mr. Fleming?" inquired Ike
politely, with the candid curiosity of his people.

Cornelius drew in his head like a turtle and snapped out
"No!"

"Excuse me, Mr. Fleming. I was only asking," said Ike,
seeing he had offended a customer.

Mr. Fleming stalked off down the street. He was angry
with himself for having made two mistakes. Up to now he
had left no trace of himself that would not eradicate itself

spontaneously, he told himself. No more than a fish, swimming in the sea. He had foreseen everything. But just now he had committed two utterly incomprehensible errors. First, in going to a news dealer who knew him to order his papers. Second, to become frightened, actually to show terror when the news dealer asked him quite naturally—for these people—if he wanted so many papers because he was going into business of some kind. These people are interested in one another. They had so little before coming here; now they have so much—for them—that they are naturally and kindly and curiously interested in what all their neighbors have or are striving to have.

With an intense apprehension, he, Cornelius, prayed whatever gods there be for thieves and murderers that there be nothing in the papers tomorrow morning to point to him.

Ike looked after him from under the angle of the Elevated stairs.

"What is his business, Abie?" he asked of his son.

"I don't know," said Abie. "His finger nails are always black."

Terry the cop, who came on at four o'clock in the morning, paused in front of the lean-to.

"What business makes a man's finger nails black, Terry?" asked Ike.

"His fingers, you mean?" said Terry.

"No, just his finger nails. Isn't that it, Abie?"

"Yes, his finger nails," agreed Abie.

"I was a boy once for Moushkin, the photographer," said Terry. "My finger nails were always brown. Not my fingers —my finger nails. Something they use to make the pictures with." He appraised a skirt passing. "Why?" he asked vaguely.

"One of my customers," explained Ike. "He wants all the papers tomorrow morning, and for a week. I ask him if he goes into business and he gets mad." Ike shrugged his shoulders. "I ask you why he should get mad because I ask him."

"What the devil business is it of yours? He pays for them, don't he?" the Irish in Terry demanded with a chuckle. He moved off rapidly.

As for Ike, he thought no more of his offended customer until the next morning at daybreak, when he climbed three flights of the cold-water walk-up and laid his customer's eight newspapers in a neat pile outside a shabby door that stood at an angle, to save room, in the rear hall. Then he wondered again why such a shabby lodger should buy twenty-four cents' worth of papers every morning for a week. His curiosity flared up again later in the morning when he got time to look at the news headlines.

There was nothing. The gods had answered Cornelius Fleming's prayer; and although the distinguished Cornelius Vlemynck was as dead as he ever would be at the hour the young man with trembling fingers dragged in his pile of papers, there was nothing in print yet about it. A whole day passed. Nothing the next morning either. It looked like another dud.

It was late in the evening of the second day when he went out to buy some food from the pushcarts along the avenue for his supper, when a strong hand gripping his arm sent a chill of terror through him. He was reassured to see the grinning face of Ike the news dealer, who leaned as he walked, like the *Man With the Hoe,* under his great burden of a late evening extra.

"You knew already there was going to be this big murder!" cried Ike, in his big booming voice. "How did you know? Tell me!"

Ike was only chaffing in his playful way. But Cornelius Fleming recoiled.

"Eh?" he gasped, his breath whistling between his teeth.
"I—— What?"

Luckily people had stopped Ike to buy papers and he
was too busy to note the effect of his words on his customer. There came a full.

"Yes, sir," laughed Ike again, "you ordered your papers
beforehand. Tomorrow morning everybody will want
papers and can't get them. You wait and see. It's good business. I like murder. You want a paper now, Mr. Fleming?"

For the first time Cornelius Fleming noticed that when
Ike pronounced his name he gave it a final k, instead of g.
With sudden consternation it occurred to him that Ike's
Mittel-Europa speech always substituted the sonant v for
the surd f of the Western peoples. Vlemynck! "You want
a paper now, Mr. Vlemynck?" invited the neighborly Ike
the news dealer, holding up temptingly outstretched the
green edition of the *Evening World,* across the first page
of which ran the legend in block type: VLEMYNCK
MURDERED!

"No!" snarled Cornelius Fleming, summoning all his
strength to enunciate the word as he turned up his collar
and hurried away.

"Papa," said Abie, later in the night, "Mr. Fleming is
mad with you, I guess, eh? I saw him buy a paper in Sixty-
third Street just now.

"I should worry!" said Ike, laughing. A constant stream
of pennies fell into his big candy jar. Customers made their
own change, and if some left too little, others left too
much. It was good business—murder. Ike knew the feel
of it. It was ten o'clock, but newspaper wagons still rattled
by to a stop. The *Morning American* came out with a
special extra under tomorrow's date. The staid *Evening
Post* replated on the late sports edition. The leather-lunged
squad of newsboys who haunt the hollow side streets in

time of calamity were bellowing their wares. Every time a wagon dumped a fresh bundle for Ike, customers seemed to spring up out of the pavement. Such is the contagion of sensation.

So many people live their lives through the columns of the newspapers, get their only action and adventure there, that the slightest flurry of the unusual in the news sends up the circulation figures. Ike looked at the name "Vlemynck," tried to set it in his mind; but it is doubtful that he attempted actually to pronounce it. If someone had come to him and asked, in words, if he knew the name Vlemynck, the sound would have carried and he would have replied, in wide-eyed alarm:

"Yes! A customer of mine! He came here two days ago and ordered all the papers for a week!"

But no one came to ask. Before morning the name, undergoing the vicissitudes of headlines in the mouths of newsboys, became Lemik, which could be shouted and heard. Lemik! Lemik murder! Poison! Cyanide! Lemik! In another twenty-four hours they were shouting, "Poison Envelope!" That was something the murderer could never have foreseen—his intricate method instantly demolished by the clumsy finger of chance.

Since the Molineux case of more than twenty years ago, there had been nothing to compare with it as to method. Parr called in the reporters; he had determined at once to try this case in the newspapers. There would be nowhere the murderer could flee where headlines would not shriek at him. A big murder in New York becomes a national best seller. In villages, hamlets, around the crackker barrel of country stores, the case would be discussed, intimately dissected. Every pertinent scrap of paper unearthed in that Allen Street loft by Parr's detectives was printed in facsimile. Experts talked in print for syndicate publication on the eccentricities of typewriter type, on which topic it seems that volumes can be written. It gradually evolved that the Gastein Symphony letter of inquiry had been written on a new machine, Series Blank, from Numbers 110,2— — to 115,3— — The Seven Pillars letter had been put out on an old-style machine. Unlike the song that the Syrens sang or the name Achilles used when he hid among women, the solution need not be wholly conjectural in this case. A tabloid newspaper abandoned its cross-word prizes and offered five thousand dollars for either typewriter.

It was not impossible. Five thousand dollars stimulates an enormous amount of genius in the form cf patience. Clerks combed their records, from Maine to California. Dozens of machines of both categories were traced and found and tested. A pawnshop sales store in the Bowery turned up the identical new one among some unredeemed pledges. Samples of typewriting from this machine placed beside the lethal facsimile left no doubt that it was upon this very instrument that the murderer so cunningly composed the letter in the Lemik murder mystery. Extras volleyed through the streets. The machine was put on public view. Throngs, kept in a queue two by two by police, filed by as they would by the bier of a Valentino or a Carranza; and doubtless they got some dread neurotic thrill out of the grisly sight.

It was not beyond all conjecture who made the letter paper on which the missives were written; the date—approximate—of the manufacture of the stamped envelope was ascertainable; the ink of the signatures was subject to qualitative analysis; the printer who printed the superscriptions, with their lying legends, must be in existence —and a reward calculated to stir the cupidity of every printer's devil was offered by a rival tabloid. But no printer was ever found who printed those envelopes. And the inference was that the murderer himself, after he affixed his cruel poison, did his own printing on a hand press.

Parr gave orders to look into the recent sale of hand presses—trace as many as possible. But the type—there is something identifiable about type. It was required of type founders to identify this type, the same font having been used in each instance. Now it so happened that the *t* was slightly upset—walked on its heels, so to speak—and this slight discrepancy, impossible to conjecture for a layman but very simple for a type founder, traced the font to a rejected style from a particular foundry; it had been disposed of to a junkman at scrap prices.

Thus, like the tentacles of the jellyfish, conjecture fed by tiny morsels of certainty slowly reached this way and that into the black night of mystery, delving for the murderer of Cornelius Vlemynck. That is police work—unsung police work.

"Has it occurred to you, Parr," asked Oliver Armiston, "that he, or she, is getting a best-seller kick out of all this? This business of approaching him with heavy tread, through the columns of the press, and scaring him into revealing himself is very good psychology, if it works. As a matter of fact, Parr, you are not approaching. You are merely making a lot of noise—as the old-fashioned Chinese soldiers used to do to scare one another."

Parr reluctantly agreed that this stuff ran thin.

"There isn't much satisfaction in killing an enemy with too much subtlety," went on Oliver. "The enemy wouldn't know anything about it. That's not revenge. When it's too subtle the murdered man has no more idea who killed him than a lamp knows who blew it out. That's what happened in this case. The murderer beats the police—but he cheats himself. What does he do to feed his own egotism? He turns to the newspapers. Parr, look for a man who——"

Parr suddenly held up his hand for silence and turned to a clerk who sat at a police typewriter in a corner. It looked like any other typewriter, but it had this difference: Whatever was written on it, wrote itself automatically on a similar typewriter in every station house throughout the city.

"Take dictation," commanded Parr, and he began: "Instructions, all precincts. All patrolmen on post will inquire of news dealers for customers who have increased their order during the run of the Vlemynck murder case. Get name and address, but avoid comment."

He paused, looking at Oliver, and the operator held his fingers suspended, waiting for more.

"Particularly," said Oliver, as an addendum, "those customers who increased their order several days previous to the first publication of the murder."

Parr nodded. The keys clicked and seventy typewriters, from Jamaica Bay to the Yonkers line, followed it letter by letter. In seventy squad rooms, fifteen thousand patrolmen heard the order read and went forth.

The result before dusk was nearly two thousand names and addresses of customers of thirty thousand news dealers who had suddenly increased their order. These were sifted to three hundred who ordered all morning or all afternoon papers, or both. A detective detail called on them one by one, to mark them off the suspect list.

Terry the cop paused *en passant* in front of the igloo of Ike the news dealer in Columbus Avenue under the Elevated. Pretending to watch the girls go by, he carefully framed his questions.

"How's your friend with the black finger nails, Ike?" he asked.

"The dirty dog, he ran out on me!" cried Ike.

"You mean he didn't pay you?"

"I never saw him again after that first day. I stopped leaving him papers. He wasn't there. Why should I leave papers for nobody," asked Ike logically, "when everybody wants them? I ask you."

"Where does he live?"

"Up over Oberstein's grocery, on the third floor back. He was only paying thirteen dollars a month—and he went off without paying that!"

Terry was watching the girls going by. "What was his name?" he asked.

"Fleming," said Ike distastefully; he articulated distinctly, "Vlemynck." Terry twirled his stick and started off up the avenue to the grocery. In front of it he paused as he was about to go in.

"Go easy," he admonished himself. "Touch nothing. Not so fast, young fellow! This looks good enough to go into plain clothes for."

He went in and satisfied himself with a quick look over the transom on the third floor rear. Then he came out and went to his call box. He told the desk lieutenant he had something and that he wanted to come in to tell the Old Man. Permission was granted; when his relief came Terry went to his station house and told his captain what was in his mind. Terry wanted to talk to Parr himself. His captain thought this over, chewing.

"With what?" he demanded.

"A hunch," said Terry. "This fellow ordered those papers, then was afraid to stay and read them. There's a hand printing press in that room."

An hour later Terry was standing before Parr. Terry was tall and slight and wedge-shaped, as an athlete should be; and he had a pug nose and a high, straight forehead that wrinkled like Gene Tunney's. Parr listened, eying him.

"We've listed two thousand of them," said he dryly at the end.

"But this one ran out when the first extra came," said Terry stoutly. "He was afraid to buy it of Ike, his regular news man, and went around the corner and bought it. He never came back. His name was Fleming. That's American for Vlemynck, isn't it? I'd like to bring him in, sir."

"Go to it," said Parr.

"I'd like some help," said Terry, who was used to sarcasm in high places.

"You might need it," admitted the deputy. "Morel," he called; and Morel came in from an inner room. "There is a rear flat up in Columbus Avenue you'll want to look over," he said. "A fellow named Fleming—Vlemynck—get it?— he dusted the night the first extra came out and never showed up again. This fellow will tell you about it." He nodded at Terry. "Go with him, Terry," he said.

"It's my case, Mr. Commissioner, isn't it?" inquired Terry, wrinkling his nose; he had no intention of being bilked like this.

"You'll have a pro-rata interest therein," admitted the deputy. He liked spunk. "Terry, what would you do if it was your case? How would you bring him in—he gone?" Parr made a wide gesture to indicate the goneness of gone.

Terry said "His finger nails were black, sir."

"Oh, you are holding out some stuff, eh?" muttered Parr.

"He probably was a dark-room operator for some photographer," said Terry. "It's pyro—pyrogallic acid," he went on. "It comes off the fingers, but it sticks to the nails. It stays for weeks sometimes."

Parr took a stogy and examined it carefully. Oliver, in the dark of a corner, cleared his throat audibly.

"I'd make the rounds of photo studios, asking for some

man that's been out of work the last month," said Terry.
"I'd get the list. Then I'd run them down one by one. It
wouldn't be much of a job. Not many operators are out of
work in May and June. Everybody is getting married and
photographed then." He added, as an afterthought, "They
use cyanide in a photograph dark room, sir."

Parr lighted his stogy. "Terry," he said, "have you got
a good suit of clothes that you could take your girl out in?"

"Yes, sir," said Terry.

"Go home and put it on and come back and report to
me," commanded the great Mr. Parr, and he turned his
back on Terry to indicate that the audience was over. When
the door closed on Terry, who went out dumbfounded at
the ways of the mighty, Parr said to his clerk:

"Take dictation—transfer and assignment: Patrolman
John Terry, from Precinct 9A to Detective School. As-
signed temporarily to office special deputy commissioner."

Abie, the bright son of Ike the news dealer, who helped
his father from daylight till school opened and from school-
out till the last extra, had to visit a dozen photographic
studios at the instance of their policeman friend, Terry,
who seemed bent on finding the dirty dog of a customer
who had run off without paying his bill. In each of these
Terry would fetch out a newly hired operator and ask of
Abie, "Is this the fellow that didn't pay your father?" Abie
always said no. But Terry kept on undiscouraged. Then
one day two weeks later at Moushkin's—the very place
where Terry himself used to wear black finger nails as a
boy—Terry brought out a dark-room operator who had
just applied for work and Abie cried:

"That's the fellow! You owe my father money and you
ran off without paying!"

Terry was taking no chances. He produced a pair

of handcuffs and was about to put them on the prisoner,
when the latter, who was really Cornelius Fleming, uttered
a shriek and fell, much as if stricken with *apoplexie foudroyante*. It was not the shock of cyanosis, but of terror.
All the terror which he thought he had finally conquered
when he gained courage enough to come slinking out of
his hiding place and ask for work in his calling again came
back and struck him like the blow of a mighty bludgeon.
When he came to he was securely handcuffed in his dark
room.

"You confess to me," said Terry; "I want a clean case
of this. It is my first."

Probably something of the naïve youth of the police detective who captured him; possibly something of their
common language; or a suggestion of that relief which
comes to the daunted haunted murderer when at last he
finds himself at the rope's end, conspired to open the lips
of Cornelius Fleming. Terry wrote with pen and ink word
for word and made him sign it, shackled.

Parr was uptown when news reached him. He started
down at once. "I suppose," said he in one of his airy moods,
"like the trained physicist searching to isolate the few elements remaining to be discovered, you can predict the
nature of this person we are about to confront."

"Within limits—yes," replied his companion, Oliver
Armistòn. "But it is dangerous. We are apt to become bemused with our own cleverness. His choice of poisons
means nothing. As a photographer, it would naturally suggest itself to him. His manner of employing it, I admit, was
ingenious. But that is a mere detail. As to his character
and station, it might be anything. His habit of thought
would naturally be warped by the burning hate that leads
to murder. We attribute too much erudition to the so-called
upper classes, too little to the lower. He might be a scholar

—one who knew all about the mythical Gastein Symphony of Schubert, which has never been found. Also, he might be eager and able to own the enormously expensive Seven Pillars of Wisdom in its original form. These items suggest the collector, the dilettante. But he also might be merely a very ardent reader of the daily newspapers, intent on gathering every available fact about the distinguished man he planned to kill so as to approach his victim from his blind side. All these details about our rich and great are printed, I may say, often inaccurately for the delectation of the hoi polloi, and are easily accessible to a fellow with an *idée fixe*. For instance, I have seen it stated in print that you shave twice a day and, when you are actively engaged, you change your shoes at least three times in an afternoon."

"And the motive?" pursued the police deputy without batting an eyelash.

"Again, it might be anything," replied Oliver. "The similarity in names suggests collateral lines. The rich Vlemynck, the poor Fleming—one had everything, the other nothing. It takes very little to incite an *idée fixe*."

Arriving at the central office, they went inside. Parr, confronting the prisoner, said, in one of his intensely human moments:

"Well, how do you feel about it now?"

And the prisoner, to everybody's surprise, replied: "I feel the blessed relief of the terrible uncertainty being over."

The signed confession which the prudent Terry had extracted before delivering his prisoner lay on the desk, and Mr. Terry stood by at attention, not entirely unconscious of himself. Parr read the brief lines.

"This is your signature?" he said to the man.

Cornelius Fleming said yes. Parr passed it to Oliver. It

is said that the human brain originates nothing of itself—
merely reacts to external suggestion. This boy's mother,
a gin-slinging bedraggled creature of the back tenements,
had whispered to him, whispered to him, whispered to him.
He had grown up with that whisper in his ears. She would
take him to market to point out the gay old Cornelius Vlemynck, with his cottony bunches of hair and his carnival
attire.

"That's how you got your name," she told him. "He
might at least throw us a crust."

Cornelius Fleming had actually gone to the Fifth Avenue
house and been thrown out—literally thrown out by the
servants, the loyal retainers of that patrician old Knickerbocker. It was then that the *idée fixe* began. He matured
it in detail in his dark room as he worked, while he watched
the images grow into life on the photographic plates in the
developing bath. He thought he foresaw every eventuality
—had eradicated every contingency. His blackened finger
nails, always before his eyes, never entered the pattern
of his thoughts. That his occupational stain would be his
undoing was, to him, beyond all conjecture.

II

THE WEDDING GIFT

THE learned professions are learned in recognizing at a glance the identicals of their calling. Science is the organization of observed facts. A doctor, in the tropics, gets to know all the earmarks of fever and very shortly becomes learned in a narrow groove. Then, there is the magnificent Doctor Blank who does nothing but cut out appendixes; he can do it with his eyes shut, at 5 per cent of his victim's annual income. And the information clerk in the depot waiting-room—people stand in line all day to ask him this or that. But all the questions fall into three or four categories—he doesn't even need to look up from his racing chart to answer them.

People are always doing the same thing, in herds. When they count change for a newspaper at a newsstand they always drop their right glove. My friend Charlie, who has a stand under the L stairs, has a bushel of right-hand gloves to give away—if you happen to be left-handed, which so few of us are. People lose—or find—the same thing, in the same way, at the same place, at the same time, at the same age; just as they get born, sick or buried at a predetermined rate, time, and place. Actuary tables are form charts that are die cast. Of one hundred healthy men at twenty-five years of age, four will be wealthy at sixty-five, one will be very rich, thirty-six will be dead, five will be self-supporting by labor, and fifty-four will be dependent. A business mounting into billions is founded on that table.

At a certain beanery in Forty-second Street three hundred and seventy-nine out of four hundred and fifty customers will choose blueberry pie, instead of apple or lemon, in August. Everybody buys rubbers on the day of the first snow in December. In the forthcoming twelve months automobiles will kill almost as many as we lost in action in the Great War—the actual ratio is about thirty to thirty-five. In twelve thousand years Christmas will fall on the first day of summer—these things are inevitable.

Crooks steal the same thing in the same way, hide it in the same place, and tell the same story to the judge. Of all learned professions, that of felony is the most dependable for the actuary. If one had a mind to give advice to expectant felons, say on graduation day, when they were about to embark on the practice of their profession, the natural thing would be to tell them the pitfalls. But it wouldn't help them. They would all choose the same way to avoid the pitfalls, and merely add another column to the statistics of probability.

"There are oddments and remainders in every category, of course," said Oliver Armiston, "to vary the monotony of human endeavor."

"There are exceptions to every rule," admitted Parr, the police deputy.

"Including the rule of exceptions," said Oliver. "I should think they would get discouraged—the crooks, I mean. It's like bucking a fake faro bank."

"It's like young love," said Parr. "They all think they have found something new that nobody else ever thought of."

"Do any of them get away with it?"

"Love?" said Parr. "No." The old man-hunter chuckled. "Oh, a few of us—but we are the exceptions."

"Some felons, I suspect, retire as successful men," said

Oliver. "You fellows make an awful noise about the ones
you catch. How about the ones that get away? How
many smugglers slip through the fingers of the police? It's
only when an absconding cashier bets on the wrong card
that you discover him. Some of these cashiers must bet on
the right card, and live happy ever after. How about
second-story men? Every little while you pick up one who
has been fooling everybody—even his wife—for years,
making a good thing out of it."

"Yes, every little while we pick them up," agreed Parr
complacently. It was his experience they all went up the
river sooner or later—sometimes he had to wait a little
while.

"What of murder? How many go unsuspected?" asked
Oliver.

"I've had them telephone me," said Parr. "They were
piqued because they weren't suspected or pursued. The
egotism of crime is beyond belief. One thing all murderers
overlook—dead men have habits." Parr shot a swift look
at Oliver. "Let me illustrate," said he. "There are a certain number of drowned people picked up every day. They
don't know it, of course, when they push off, but they are
going to be picked up at certain spots. The tide and current and the harbor traffic take care of that. When we pick
them up outside of those certain few spots, we ask why.
There is always a reason. Usually it is murder. The murderer didn't know that a drowned man has a route, like
a man going home from work. A man going home may
take the long way around occasionally, but not often.
Neither does our dead man. When he does, we ask why."

He picked up his telephone. They were sitting in Armiston's study, the *point d'appui* of many a famous murder
reconnaissance, and this wire went straight into his office.

"What about that Box Inlet drowning, Morel?" the

deputy inquired over the phone, and waited, eying Oliver oddly. He gave heed again, his little eyes beaming. He set down the wire.

"Here we are!" he exclaimed. "Hot off the griddle! We picked up a poor devil that came home the long way around this morning. We asked the usual question. It is a murder!" he said, his teeth snapping shut. "See what a tangled web we weave. . . . In the first place, the body is found on a beach as if it had been washed in by the tide with the wind behind it. The wind wasn't behind the tide last night, or yesterday, or for the past week. So much for that. But there is more. There happens to be a sand bar just offshore, and eddy currents, and nothing is ever washed up at that point. I wonder why this murderer picked that one spot? As if this evidence wasn't enough, there wasn't any salt in the sleeve on the arm that was out of water. The body had never been completely immersed in salt water. Salt is going to take this fellow to the chair."

"Was there water in the lungs?" asked Armiston.

"In the blood in the left side of the heart, yes," said Parr. "That's where we look—not in the lungs."

"He was drowned, then?"

"Yes. But not in salt water!" said Parr. He smiled. "He was drowned in fresh water and carried to the beach. See how these things work out. The percentage is always in favor of the bank." He chuckled. "Every little while they get away, but not for long. The first thing we look at is the left side of the heart. It is filled with blood aerated by the lungs, and if the man was drowned, this blood is diluted. If the blood isn't diluted, the man was dead before being put in the water! Simple enough. If the blood contains too much salt, he was drowned in salt water. If it contains less salt than normal, he was drowned in fresh water. There is no mystery about detecting crime. We get that way—we can't help it." Parr rubbed his chin, his eyes twinkling. This was one of those pat cases, and he loved to display his virtuosity to his friend Armiston, the extinct author of crime thrillers, whom the deputy now came to for help on such mysteries as did not yield to his usually effective nut-cracker methods. "That fellow," went on Parr, "had only five hundred and seventy-eight miles of water front patrolled by our harbor squad to pick from. However, we don't insist that all our murderers be good harbor engineers, especially at a time when they are in a big hurry."

The deputy smiled grimly at the old bronze Buddha toasting his shins by the fire.

"Aren't you a little sanguine?" said Oliver.

"Sanguinary," said Parr. "I'm going to have this fellow by the heels before the week is out."

"You haven't identified your dead man yet."

Parr picked up the phone again.

"Morel," he commanded, "here is a want ad for the *World*, *Times*, and *Telegram*.

"Wanted, for moving-picture work, a left-handed violinist; dark, slight, medium height; should make up well as Hungarian or gypsy; no previous stage experience required. Steady employment for right man."

Parr said to Oliver, "Did you ever see a left-handed violinist?"

Armiston tried to visualize the string choirs of his favorite symphony orchestras, to see if he could find a left-handed player among them. Doubtless there were left-handed violinists—even left-handed violins. But he had never seen one, to remember.

"This fellow was a violinist," said the deputy. "His finger tips show that. But he bowed with the right hand, like anyone else. However, when he took a pen in hand, it was with his left hand. His fingers are ink-spotted where he held the pen; and he used the inside of his right cuff for a pen wiper."

"Even so," remarked Armiston disparagingly; as a rule drownings had little interest for him. This one got nowhere. Parr's solution was still a needle in a haystack.

"Even so," grunted Parr, nodding. "If he is a musician he belongs to a union. If he belongs to a union he goes to East Eighty-sixth Street when he is out of work. Have you never been up there on a sunshiny afternoon? It's quite a sight—art walking the streets for bread and butter. They walk up and down in the block between Second and Third avenues. We keep them moving. Agents prowl among them, recruiting for the big and little orchestras. If they can't pay the union scale they don't say so, out and out. They wipe their fevered brows with three fingers, four fingers—three dollars, four dollars. Tomorrow dozens of poor devils who have been out of work all summer will read my ad, and say 'If I was only left-handed!' They will say: 'So-and-so is left-handed. He ought to know about this.' We'll run down the left-handers. Some of them will be missing. Among the missing will be some we can't account for. Not many. I've got eighteen thousand cops to help me. That's one thing the average murderer doesn't take into account. I can cover a lot of territory, with eighteen thousand cops going from door to door asking questions. It doesn't take brains, it takes shoe leather. We drag in the friends and foes of these few missing left-handed violinists, and take them down to view the corpus delicti. One of them identifies him. There you are! The mystery is 99 per cent solved before the ink is dry on the station-house blotter. . . . How? Because, in this instance, the murderer did not know that drowned men have routes like milkmen. This fellow was off his beat. If we had found him a hundred yards north or south, we wouldn't have gone to the trouble of having a quantitative analysis made of the salt in solution in his left ventricle. What do we find? Not enough salt. There is only one possible conclusion—the man was drowned in fresh water and carried there. Rather clumsy, eh?

"Can't you see this satisfied murderer hovering behind shutters?" went on the deputy. "He reads every paper, every line, fine type and all. He'll find a paragraph: 'Unknown man washed up by the tide at Box Inlet; nothing about him to reveal identity.' He'll chuckle. He has attended to that—he took care there should be nothing. Nothing, Oliver, except the horny finger tips of a journeyman fiddler and a right sleeve used as a pen wiper."

"Maybe the pen wiper was planted to throw off you intelligentsia of the police," said Oliver.

"We will soon settle that," said Parr. "My professors, I believe, can tell a left-handed man by examining his brain. Would you say he wasn't a musician by profession?"

"No," said Oliver grudgingly. "I grant you that."

The telephone rang at Parr's elbow. He took it down and listened.

"What's that?" he demanded sharply; he didn't say it like a man who hadn't heard, but as a man dumbfounded. He commanded, "Come up here!" and hung up.

"We have an identification," he said, staring at Oliver as if he didn't like him.

"As a left-handed violinist, of course," said Oliver.

"No," said Parr. "As Barron Wilkes, the Bull's-Head Bank defaulter."

Oliver caught his breath for a second. Up to this moment the conversation had been merely one of the man hunter's idle little demonstrations of taking rabbits out of a hat with his sleeves rolled up. Now it became something else.

This Barron Wilkes had walked off with the mobile cash of the Bull's-Head Bank. It was a gigantic robbery, executed with such ludicrous ease that the tale of it had overflowed the news columns and found its way into comic strips and vaudeville gags. The Bull's-Head Bank was thief-proof inside and out, by every means that could be suggested by science or suspicion. Every possible danger point was safeguarded—excepting only the man selected to do the safeguarding. That was Barren Wilkes. They were still checking up after him, to find out how much he got away with. He had left a handsome wife behind, but nothing else—not even, marvelous to relate, a fingerprint. He seemed to have cunningly eradicated everything that would be of use in tracking him.

Oliver shook his head.

"No, Parr," he said decidedly. "It's out of drawing."

Parr said nothing.

"Did he ever play a violin?" asked Armiston.

"I doubt it."

"Was he left-handed?"

"Apparently," said Parr, looking up, "he had practiced writing with his left hand recently. We found evidence of that. But he was not left-handed."

There came a rustling in the corridor, and Morel entered. At his heels appeared Pelts, his side partner, from some other point of the compass—probably the backyard fence. This strangely matched pair, Parr's twin shadows, dovetailed their every thought and act; yet they never traveled together, were never seen together except under lock and key, so to speak. The pair stood before their chief—Morel with the easy grace of an elegant cicerone, sure of his patter; and Pelts, always shabby, modestly trying to repress a smile of satisfaction for some deed well done. Parr eyed them sharply, let something of a pause intervene.

"So you have identified him, have you?" he said
smoothly. "How?"

Morel, before replying, looked questioningly at Oliver,
but no hint was forthcoming.

"He turned up a fingerprint, chief," said he, indicating
Pelts.

"So?" said Parr. "Where?"

"There was an old safety-razor blade that had fallen
behind a ledge in the bathroom," explained Morel. Pelts
had taken one last try at the house. It seemed impossible
that a fugitive, no matter how thorough, could get away
and leave no track to be picked up and followed. Pelts had
gone this last time as a window cleaner, union card and all.
Of all the transcendental occupations surreptitiously engaged in by the deputy as opportunity offered, none yielded
better returns than that of window cleaning. It was a privileged calling that enabled a good soft-shoe man, working
inside and out, to do a complete job. Pelts, between wring-
ing out shammies and trips for fresh water, had probed in
unseen places for just such a find as he had turned up.
When he produced the razor blade downtown, Lemaire,
the finger print professor—who had been searching his files
hopelessly for a left-handed fiddler—pounced on it like a
cat—printed in rust on the tarnished metal wafer were the
whorls and apices of somebody's thumb. It was what he
was looking for—it was the thumb-print of the man with
the deficiency of salt in the left ventricle. There could be
no doubt of it.

A pause followed the telling of this tale. Pelts produced
the telltale blade, unwrapped it, and laid it before his chief.

"Oddments and remainders," thought Oliver. He was
watching the group—Parr and his two interlocking shadows. They said nothing in words. But they were in perfect
accord. Whatever illusions the pair may have fetched with

them into this room a moment ago, they put aside all pretense now. Before Oliver's very eyes there had occurred one of those swift dramatic transitions for which the Greeks coined the word *peripeteia*—the about-face. Greatly pleased with his strategy, Parr turned to Armiston.

"Do you get it, Oliver?" he asked, beaming.

"You mean he planted the razor blade for you to find?"

Parr raised a quizzical eyebrow.

"We were expected to find it—and we did," he said. "We seem to have done everything he expected of us, so far."

"But wait a minute!" interposed Armiston. "Do you realize where it takes you—do you follow through to the inevitable conclusion?"

There was a little hush in the room, and the man hunter's teeth showed in a grim smile.

"That he planted the body? Why, certainly," replied Parr. "For us to find. Well, we found it. He is very clever. But I still maintain he is not a very good harbor engineer."

"Does it look like him, Morel?" asked Oliver.

"Reasonably so, yes. Ordinarily I should say there would be no question. There are discrepancies in drowned bodies we make allowance for. I should say the fingerprint would clinch it for the insurance people," said Morel.

"Oh, there was life insurance too?"

"One hundred thousand dollars!" said Parr.

"In whose favor?"

"Hers," said Parr.

At this point there came another pause, the four men turning the idea over and over in their minds.

"The difficulties seem insurmountable," said Armiston, speaking out and capping his own thoughts. "Yet, successfully accomplished, it presents a pretty picture for any defaulter to contemplate—to be comfortably dead and buried. That's what he expects you to do, Parr—bury him."

"That's what we will do," said Parr.

"To enjoy the use of an independent fortune," went on Oliver, thinking aloud, "one must remove the fear of pursuit. That is what he has done. Even those inveterate surety-company sleuths wouldn't continue to pursue a dead man."

"That brings up a point, sir," put in Morel. "What am I to do about the surety and insurance people? Their sleuths are beginning to horn in. Am I to invite them in on the ground floor?"

Parr knitted his brows. He shook his head.

"No," he said, "we won't interfere with their line of reasoning. Why clutter up their logic? They are pretty high class, and I should hesitate to intrude on their inveterateness."

The eerie question that had been at the back of Oliver's head from the beginning now came out.

"Where did he get his dead man, Parr?" he asked. "Not in Eighty-sixth Street. That is too near home. He couldn't risk a hue and cry."

Parr had picked up his telephone again and was talking in low tones with his *scientificos*—gentlemen of the police who work with test tube and miscroscope.

"Anything in the ears?" he was asking.

The answer came startlingly distinct, audible to all.

"Portland cement, sir, in the cerumen."

"Put me on my desk," commanded the deputy; and in a moment he was telling his secretary: "Brewer, we'll have to go farther north than Eighty-sixth Street. Forget those ads. Get up a list of towns east of the Mississippi with Portland-cement plants—preferably those without precipitators. There is cement dust in the earwax. Wire the police of those towns for a missing fiddler, left-handed preferred."

He set down the instrument and turned to Oliver. "One more break in favor of the bank," he said grimly. "I wonder how many expectant murderers consider earwax as hanging evidence! . . . Morel, I don't want to do anything he doesn't expect us to do. Be very careful how you seem to fall in with everything he wants. Go up and get her and take her down there. Let her identify him. Don't prod her. Don't make her look too close. It's hard on a woman, you know."

"She will probably bear up," put in Oliver.

" 'Bear up' is hardly the phrase," said Parr, with a smile. "She seemed to have been bearing down on him. She was an expensive piece of bric-a-brac to have around. There were some things she wanted that he couldn't afford to buy for her when he was building up his good reputation. But she got them, one way or another. I think there must have been a third party. He was away from home a good deal. Wilkes seems to have been something of an authority on thief-proofing, and he was loaned to various banks about the country as a consulting engineer." He turned to Morel. "Look up this business of the third party, Morel," he said. "Pelts, put Terry and his partner, Clancy, on the house. If she spots either of them, I put the two back in harness. If she gets clear, I break them!"

II

The defaulter's wife, whom, it seemed, he left behind with much the same care as he did that fingerprint, sat at her piano, musing over the keys. It was a fifteen-foot interior, one of those narrow-waisted private houses that are still to be found holding out in some side streets, waiting for the block to come down. Everything in this room was cut to size, including the abandoned wife, who was petite.

A maid appeared at the curtained doorway.

"Yes, Mary?" said Nora Wilkes, without looking up.

The servant explained that one of the surveyors working in the street asked permission to go through the house to the roof. The story was that the owner of this precious parcel had applied for still one more mortgage, and that the trust company—hopeful, suspicious creature that it was—was searching the title with transit and tape, to surprise an overlooked half inch.

"Tell him to fetch the policeman," said the mistress. "If the policeman says he is all right he may come in."

The girl withdrew, and in a moment there came the murmur of voices at the basement areaway and the closing of a door. A winged chair at the one street window now moved, revolving as if on a turn-table, and presented to view a good-looking young man, slight and dark, who could have made up well as a gypsy or Hungarian.

"I haven't seen her before," he said. "Where did she come from?" He stressed the "her" significantly. The woman at the piano lifted a silken shoulder in a barely perceptible shrug.

"From the usual agency," she said, with a sigh of weariness. "Must I suspect even that dull clod?"

"No. Leave that to me," said the young man idly, and he turned to the window again.

He had possession of his hat, his stick, and his gloves, as if this were a formal afternoon call which presently would terminate with the mutual interchange of those meaningless Chinese courtesies reserved for such occasions.

For minutes on end the pair now paid each other the compliment of silence, not of speech. It was an intensely intimate silence. It was like that scene toward the end of the Henry James story—if you still read your Henry James —in which the American wife looks for a revealing sec-

ond on her husband and Madame Merle, seated in deep
thought before the fire. It was not what they were doing
but what they were not doing that lent the implications
to the situation. When our good-looking man just now came
up the steps and rang the bell the policeman on post, polish-
ing an apple at the vegetable stand opposite, said to the
green grocer: "That's the feller. He used to come a good
deal. Now he has begun again."

Three months had elapsed since the Bull's-Head Bank
episode, and it had long since ceased to be news. The
woman's consistent attitude throughout had seemed less
one of outraged grief than of mute indignation. It gave the
public, that takes its tinge of prejudice from the tabloids,
no clew.

The young man at the window, while the woman mused
over the keys, was watching the green grocer. This was a
fashionable block, but, like all our fashionable blocks, it
had its hovel, usually given over to some low trade. There
was an awning in front, over a bank of greens from every
clime; the entire business transpired out on the sidewalk,
and for this reason it afforded an ideal lookout, if the
Wilkes home was still under espionage, as undoubtedly—
the young man thought—it was.

"Why do you sigh?" he asked, looking around the wing
of his chair. She shook her head. She was unaware that she
had sighed.

"Time passes quickly for me," he said. "I suppose it
seems interminable to you."

"I'm tired of being poor," she said; she modulated a
chord through a richer resonance, running in a suggestion
of melody with the left hand. He arose and picked up a
little straight-backed chair and carried it over to sit down
beside her. He studied her for a moment in silence.

"Continue playing while we talk," he said under his

breath. And as she struck into a bolder theme he asked, "Is it getting on your nerves?"

Her hands half paused, but she did not reply. He continued: "You recollect we anticipated it all, foresaw these long becalmed intervals. The hardest thing in life is not to lay out the difficult course, but to stick to it in all weather. We cut no corners!" he added decisively.

"That constant watch," she murmured, closing her eyes and throwing back her head, like a player enthralled by some celestial harmonies. "It still goes on."

"Naturally," he replied. "They are not fools."

There came a babble of voices from the basement court. The policeman on post had obligingly vouched for the targetman; and the young surveyor, who came tramping up the stairs, heavily burdened, paused at the drawing-room door and said, with a flash of white teeth, in a soft drawl:

"Please, ma'am, can I leave my case here by the do', where I can pick it up when I go out?"

She nodded assent. He mounted the stairs, and they listened till the sound of his footsteps died away.

"Do you recollect that good-looking gentleman who took me downtown the first day, to make the—the identification?" she asked through the prelude she was playing. "I thought I saw him in the street yesterday morning." She raised troubled eyes to his gaze.

"You did," he replied, nodding. "At ten o'clock. He stopped and bought some things at the grocer's stand. He has stopped there three times in the last four days. Don't look startled. Continue playing. I have thought it best to move into the neighborhood, where I could watch them while they watched you. I have a room down the block. Oh, never fear. I'm getting to be a genius at disguise. Look at me!" She turned obediently to him, her gaze flinching a trifle at the moment of contact, like that of a woman who felt her tenderness thrust back. "Do you recognize in these features a single lineament of your la——"

"Hush! Hush!" she entreated; she was in a panic at the moment. He smiled, but she had dashed into a mazurka. There was a red spot in either cheek.

"I do it before their very eyes," he said. "I can walk into a hallway and come out somebody else—like poor Chevalier! That's the moment to change—at the very instant they lose sight of me. At that instant my image is so deeply printed on their retina that they can see nothing else. I confess I think myself rather clever, and find it very amusing," he said, with a little bow to his own image in the mirror.

"Is he really a policeman? He doesn't look like one," she murmured as she bowed over a slow phrase.

"This fellow Morel, you mean? Yes, indeed! Very special. They only use him for fancy stuff. They never use him among crooks. He is utterly unknown to the criminal world. He and his partner, Pelts." Her startled eyes sought his again.

"There are two?" she breathed incredibly.

"Pelts, the other, is a little fellow," he explained. "He looks like a tramp, usually walks on the cuff of his trousers. He glues his nose to a show window like a man starving to death. You'd think he was eating the things inside. Actually he is looking at your reflection in the glass. Oh, I know them!" he said with a short laugh. "I could write a full monograph that would be a best-seller in the trade. I spotted them," he added, with a peculiarly unpleasant emphasis, "before I stepped out, so I would know what to look for when the time came."

"I had begun to hope," she said absently; "things went so well at first."

"That's part of their game," he put in.

"Then I saw that man again yesterday," she went on, her tones wavering a little. "If we have t-to undergo that surveillance again I'm not—sure I can—stand it. It's having to sit still that's hard. They let us alone once. Why do they come again?"

He shook his head.

"They never let us alone," he said. "The screw is always turning—constant pressure. That's Parr! Just now he's— clumsy; letting us detect his espionage. That's another turn of the screw!" His eyes momentarily glinted. "He tries that and watches for the reaction."

"Oh! What are we expected to do?"

"Run away!" he answered flatly. "The guilty flee when no man pursueth. How he would chuckle if we took to the tall timber! It's anything to surprise us into some inadvertence. He knows nothing. He merely suspects. That's Parr—he persuades everybody to give up the case as solved with a funeral. Then, when nobody is looking, he comes sneaking back and watches and waits! I've seen him do it in a dozen big cases—play 'possum." He shot a quick glance at her. "That's what he is doing now. Just sit tight."

He arose and stretched his legs. He moved casually about the long narrow room; the sonorous chords, melting from key to key, rose on the air with a louder song. He managed to push aside the hangings and looked up the stair well. He could hear the man climbing about on the roof; from below came the clatter of dishes in the butler's pantry. In thrusting aside the portière he uncovered the surveyor's instrument case. He bent down and touched it with the back of his hand. It was slightly warm. He knelt down, put his ear to it. Something was moving in its interior with a barely audible whir. It was a listening device with some sort of amplifier. He went back and resumed his chair beside her.

"Play just a little louder while we talk," he said close to her ear. She burst into a brilliant cadenza; soon she dropped back into moody chords with heavy bass. He nodded approval, smiling. They were in a soundproof chamber so far as any eavesdropping was concerned.

"We should feel complimented by all this attention," he said sardonically. Her fingers slipped from the keys.

"I tell you," she murmured almost inaudibly, "I can't go much farther."

He lifted her hand lightly and laid it back on the keys.

"They count on that," he said quietly. "They expect you to break, sooner or later." He eyed her sharply.

"But they know nothing!" she muttered, improvising as she spoke. "Why endow them with a superlative intuition?"

"You need to steel yourself," he counseled. "They have already been out West, looking me up. They have found— just what we planned they should find—that I am a harum-scarum young fellow, a devil among women, and so on. I haven't been home much, in the last five years, but there are plenty of reputable men in town who would identify me as Rising. I am Rising. Who else could I be? That rather puzzles them—Parr, I mean." He gave a sardonic smile to the mirror. "Sit tight!" he cautioned darkly. "They'll be playing their last card before long."

"What is that?" she gasped, her hands flying to her throat.

"They'll give you a chance to betray me," he said with a suddenly hardened gaze.

"Never," she breathed.

"Don't be too easy with your 'never' and 'forever,'" he said. "In an ultimate emergency——"

"Do you deliberately torture me?" she moaned. She kept on playing, nevertheless.

"No. I am preparing you for any contingency. You say you are tired of being poor. Well, so am I. And we won't be poor much longer. But I want you to know what you have to go through. I say don't be too free with your 'never' and 'forever.' What you might do in the security of your own drawing-room is very different from what you might do under other conditions. What if I had left you for another woman?"

"But you wouldn't!" The hands crashed into a sudden dissonance.

"No, I wouldn't. They have skillful ways of making it appear that I would—to seem actually to show me to you in the arms of another. They count on jealousy, not on love. What would you do? Would you squeal? Would you say, 'No, he isn't dead and buried! There he stands!' Would you do that?"

She said, in a low tone of utter despondency: "If I saw you with another woman in your arms, yes."

He arose to go. He indulged in a little gesture, sardonically egotistical. He had carried his point, no matter how terrible.

"No one, without being forever on guard, is a match for the police," he said. He was drawing on a glove. "Be armed! You are not going to see me for some time," he went on easily. "I think it well not to seem too assiduous. I won't be far away. If anything goes wrong or seems to impend I will be the first to know it."

"Sometimes, if I could merely see you—just to be sure that you are all right! Anything might happen," she whispered breathlessly, terrified at the thought of his leaving her again for no one knew how long.

"That's fair," he conceded. He seemed to weigh a confidence. "I will confess something to you," he said. "I have to be near at hand, where I can keep watch. At the same time I have to be inconspicuous. The safest place to hide," he went on, with his odd smile at his own image in the mirror, "is in the very arms of the police. I am a taxi driver!" he explained, and at her sudden look of amazement his fingers pressed her arm warningly. "The police are my patron saints! They license me; they affix my portrait to my ticket; they vouch for me to my patrons; my permit is signed by the commissioner himself." The smile deepened. "I arranged it months ago, before—before I became famous."

A little shiver ran through her. Sometimes she wondered about him; he was like one fascinated, possessed.

"I cruise, nights," he was saying. "Early in the evening I park at the Lexington Avenue corner. You pass that way usually. I think it improbable that you would recognize me. It would be too dangerous to give you a sign. Whatever happens, never approach!"

He moved toward the door, and she hurried after him.

"If I could only take you in my——" she began convulsively.

"Hush!" he commanded under his breath, with a terrible look. He pointed to the eavesdropping box. Standing over it, he bent over her hand, saying with elaborate courtesy:

"You are behaving so magnificently in what to most of us, I am afraid, would prove an intolerable situation! You are dominating the circumstances with such calm and courage that any help we have to offer would seem superfluous."

The young targetman was coming down the stairs, holding his staff like a petard. As he surprised this little scene he picked up his instrument case and, with a word of thanks, went out. The afternoon caller followed immediately on his heels.

III

"It's odd, how values change," said the happy bride-groom as he wrapped the carriage rugs about her. "I mean, when put to the actual test. Things on paper look shock-proof. You can allow, so you think, the proper plus-and-minus tolerance for every eventuality. But only by actual trial—under field conditions, as an engineer would say—can you detect the weak point."

He settled back comfortably in the broad carriage. They were driving along a narrow road that skirted a precipice at the foot of which boiled a soapy stream. Snow peaks looked down on them. On a little foot-bridge crossing the chasm an old pink sow and her little ones gazed up at them with humorous snouts.

"Actually, the most difficult thing we had to resist was each other," he said, laughing.

"And to endure time!" she replied, nodding.

"There were moments, I admit, when I was on the point of letting my Spartan resolve go to pot," he said. "There was always the temptation to yield to the sense of security, which every instinct told me could very well be false. I think probably we attributed to our friend Parr a little more genius than he actually does possess."

She laid her fingers lightly on his lips. That name, all reference to that personage, was prohibited now.

"You thought me hard and cold," he went on. He laughed. "It was only sheer fortitude that carried me through. I never knew I possessed that stoical quality."

He was watching her closely as he spoke. The thought came to him, as he studied the shades of understanding that came and went in her sensitive face, that she was not the beautiful woman she had been, never would be again.

"I thought it best to go to Kandersteg by carriage," he

explained. "To get away from all those people at the hotel.
We can make connections with the express there."

They were at a little watering place at the end of the
railroad in the Kander valley, where the lesser mountain
climbers go. He had found her there by chance—or so, at
least, it seemed to her tourist friends, with whom she had
become intimate during these last few months at the hotel.
They all knew her unhappy history, and the chance coming
of this handsome young American, Rising—who had been
her boyhood sweetheart—promised a real romance. It was
with some difficulty, only after he had enlisted the help
of some of her new traveling friends, that he had finally
prevailed on her. The wedding had taken place at the little
English church in the village. There was no occasion for
word of it to be cabled home as news now, as this valley
was so remote from news centers. The event would pass
unnoticed. Later, when his business took him back, there
would be the disagreeable rehashing of her history in the
newspapers, but time would minimize that too.

"I've taken a villa at Como," he said. "Fortunately, there
will be some people from home there, and that will make
it easier for you."

"Everything is easy now," she sighed. She nestled close.
"You don't know what the wait has cost, especially these
last few months, when nothing—nothing happened!" That
surveillance had been finally lifted so gradually that she
never could be quite sure it was gone.

They had a half-hour wait for the express connection.
The depot functionary, with a very natural suspicion of all
Americans, consulted their tickets and summoned a brass-
bound superior, who summoned others; and they all
marched pompously with them to the train and threw open
the door of their compartment with jackknife bows. Force
of habit caused the bridegroom to examine the interior

before entering. It held only two passengers, one an official
of some sort—to judge by his gold braid—and the other a
traveling American—from his shoes—who was reading an
ancient New York paper.

At sound of their entrance the American looked up. It
was Morel. The door shut behind them and the train
moved. Wilkes, with a sudden rush of blood to the temples
that seemed to bring him to the very verge of a stroke,
was aware that a little group of depot attendants—who
probably knew what it all was about—were running alongside, peering in. But the accelerating speed of the train
soon left them behind. The official with the gold lace rose
and took some papers from a pocket. He bowed, first to
madame, then to monsieur. He said, in an English tinged
with French, German and Italian:

"M'sieu', madame, it is my painful duty to inform you
that you are under arrest. This gentleman, as I see you
recognize, is M'sieu' Morel of the New York police. Before
the proper authorities he is prepared to make the necessary
representations looking to your extradition on the charge
of murder. I am Ferrand of the Swiss police."

There was a ghastly silence. Morel looked up from his
paper as if he were a mere outsider. The bridal pair stood
frozen.

"My name is Rising, inspector," said the bridegroom,
clearing his throat and speaking with great effort. He
pressed the arm of the woman, who gave no sign beyond a
waxy pallor. "This is my wife," he said. "We have just
been married."

"That is correct," said the inspector, reading from his
documents. "The name is Thomas Rising, alias Barron
Wilkes. You are charged with the murder of one Samuel
Herden, a musician, of Gary, Indiana."

It was evident the man was not prepared to withstand

the impact of that identification. It was the name of the
man found on the sand of Box Inlet with a deficiency of
salt in his left ventricle. He trembled violently. He put out
a hand to support himself. The woman shrank against him,
staring wide-eyed.

"I never heard of him—this—what is the name—Mer-
den—Herden? I've—I've never been to Gary, Indiana."
His words came wildly; he made an effort to get a hold of
himself again. "We are on our way to Como; there are
people there who can identify me from—from childhood.
. . . Who is this Barron——"

Morel looked up from his reading.

"It's no use, Wilkes," he said quietly, in a not unfriendly
tone. "Better not try to say anything just now."

Morel resumed his paper. The trapped pair sank down,
fell back against the cushions, their fingers interlaced. The
train sped on, faster and faster. From time to time the
woman closed her eyes and put back her head, a habitual
gesture with her. The dignitary of police turned the crisp
leaves of the *dossier* he held, going back to reread a line
or a page occasionally. Concluding his perusal, he folded
the *dossier* into a flat package, snapped a rubber band on
it and put it away. He turned and looked curiously at the
pair in the corner. His moody eyes passed from them and,
traveling about the compartment, finally lit on Morel, and
he moved over beside him. Speaking with the careful intonation of one used in the delivery of those Chinese courtesies of speech that serve so well for any occasion, he said:

"M'sieu', permit me to felicitate you, and through you
your distinguished colleagues, on the successful termination
of one of the most remarkable and difficult cases in my
knowledge. You are a young people, burdened with prob-
lems of police in the solution of which our experience and
our archives, going back for centuries, can suggest no help.

Accept, I beg, this expression of my admiration for what you have succeeded so brilliantly in accomplishing, as most heartfelt and sincere."

Morel, something of a Chinaman himself on occasions, laid aside his paper and cogitated for a moment before replying.

"I am afraid," he said, "you do us the honor to exaggerate a little in your praise of our cleverness. We, in our country, are only beginning where you over here left off a hundred years ago. Our methods are crude, compared with your finished masterpieces. In the matter of this identification of the drowned man, which, after all, is the crux of the case, we merely applied your time-tested theories. The horny finger tips indicated the dead man's calling; the residuum in the ear wax revealed his habitat."

"I thank you, m'sieu', for myself and my colleagues," said the functionary. He rubbed his chin through his beard. "Yet your dead man has lain buried under another man's name for a year," he interposed.

"Yes," agreed the American. "Fortunately for our purpose, he was one of those obscure, unknown persons with no one to mourn him. In fact, except for a poor widow who inquired because he owed her room rent, we might have, even then, failed to identify him."

The functionary hovered over a phrase.

"Pardon me, m'sieu'," he said. "You say 'fortunately for your purpose.' What was your purpose, if I may ask? As I read your so admirable *dossier*, the mystery of the murder was solved completely on the very day the body was found. Within three days you had identified the dead man. Why did you wait one year—until, in fact, this very day, m'sieu'—to make the arrest?"

Morel, before replying, examined the pair in the corner. They were oblivious to everything.

"She was equally guilty," he said, close to the police official's ear. "But we could not prove it to a jury! We had no choice but to wait until she had completed her part by accepting the insurance money and marrying him again. When she did that, we stood ready—with the bracelets for a wedding gift."

"Ah!" gasped the Swiss explosively, touching his wrist significantly. *"À mettre les menottes!"*

The train, with a warning scream, suddenly plunged into the gloom of a tunnel. At the next stop they would change to the northbound express for Bern.

III

THE JAPANESE PARASOL

OLIVER ARMISTON had been playing solitaire for three days with a bushel of newspaper clippings. They appertained to the practice of murder and the various degrees thereof. There were hundreds of them, thoughtless murders for the most part, but nevertheless a sizable proportion of thoughtful ones. It was these latter over which the shadow chaser paused, weighing and considering as he built them up into neat little stacks, like a game of Canfield. His original notion had been to write a monograph on the tools of the craft, on the broad assumption that a carpenter's idea of lethal weapons differs from that of a bacteriologist; and that only a blacksmith would be occupationally stupid enough to tack a horseshoe on a maul and use it as a bludgeon.

Given a thousand or a million instances, it was pleasant to note how the little ball of chance was tied to the apron strings of probability. In fact, given race, climate, creed, and trade or calling, chance did not enter in at all, or to a degree that was practically negligible. Taken by and large, the deliberate murderer used the tool in which he was most skilled. The more clever he was, the more sure he was to fall into this error. Murderers, theorized Oliver, pulling at his single white lock of hair, do not begin to be subtle until they cease to be clever.

This thesis was developing beautifully, like all solitaire games, with a little help from the manipulator. But toward the end of the second day Oliver—if an informed outsider might have watched him—would have been observed to turn away more and more frequently from his fascinating problem to stare at his street window. At two in the morning, with the atmosphere rank with the empyreumatic odor of the yards of stogies he had been consuming, and the fire all but dead on the hearth, he paused in the act of going to bed to lift the blind and peer out into the street, hollow with night. An expanse of brownstone opposite, without a single light to suggest wakefulness, greeted his eye. He yawned, recollected his couch and departed.

At six in the morning he was back at his desk again, the prey of an idea that had been simmering slowly overnight —on the back of the stove, so to speak. His game was on the desk, but he didn't see it, although his eyes were on it.

At seven the door opened softly, and the housekeeper looked at him fixedly and conveyed to him by lip movement the portentous information that Mr. Parr was calling. At seven! This was splendid.

The famous man hunter, special deputy in charge of the detective bureau, affected his friend Oliver Armiston from varied approaches. In the first place, and principally, he was wont to come here to consult his medicine when his usually efficacious nutcracker methods of solving crime did not work.

Oliver was an extinct fiction writer, teller of tall tales, who preserved through the years he had been out to grass a singular facility for whiplash endings. He had written last acts to the frozen plots Parr brought him, with occasional startling results. Then there were other occasions when the famous man hunter would come here in much the same frame of mind as a methodical cat that will now and then make it a point to squat by a mousehole of good repute. But never before at seven in the morning.

The deputy, as usual, deposited himself in his favorite elbow chair, that fitted him like an old shoe, with the single movement of a tired dog. He was freshly shaved, as usual, and his expansive jowls presented that live-boiled look that comes from the habit of taking a hot towel in lieu of a night's sleep. He selected the least disreputable of the stogies, and while he applied a light with a single magic twist of the wrist he eyed Oliver's game, of which he had some inkling. He shook his head gloomily.

"Murder isn't a system," he said, staring stonily at old Buddha squatting in the chimney corner, "it's an accident." He scratched an ear, scowling ferociously. "Things are a little slow," he complained. "I disappeared mysteriously from the Century at midnight and mailed myself back to town by airplane." He smirked at Oliver. "My pets simply won't do their stuff when they think I am watching them, Oliver. Could you put me up for a couple of days?"

Splendid! There was no telling what high-class pet was in the immediate focus. Parr wasn't exactly a *provocateur*, but he occasionally played possum to revive confidence among shy crooks.

They smoked for some time, each paying the other the flattering tribute of being alone with his own thoughts. After a time Oliver swung his chair to the window. He went over and stood against the jamb, looking out. "Parr," he said abruptly, "I want to look inside that house."

"What house?"

"The one with the dirty windows."

Parr was examining the ash of his stogy abstractedly. His great head turned slowly on the pivot of his bull neck. "You? Yourself? In person?" he asked.

Oliver pondered. "I think maybe you'd better do it for me," he concluded.

"All right," said Parr, with the air of a parent temporizing with an unreasonable child. Then with a maddening indifference he closed his eyes and went to sleep—wherever that is. His stern jaw rested on his creaking shirt front. His hands were folded like an old lady's dozing over her knitting. His stogy continued to smoke itself.

Old Buddha, in his corner, appeared to be cocking an ear, intent on the portentous pool of silence. The clocks thudded, one little one hurrying along with a faster trot now and then, as if to catch up. There was a fog on the river, emphasized by the dismal wails of tug, ship and ferry, which seemed to move up to the very doorstep; now and again a ship's bell would clank hysterically; and at precise periods the old grandfather of all the foghorns, staked out on Governors Island flats, bellowed like a pensive bull.

Oliver had returned to his game, but without zest. A thousand murders, like a thousand beautiful women, become mere abstractions against the immediate contiguity of one. The minutes dragged on. It was too early yet for those houses opposite to wake up, except for the drawing of occasional window curtains in the basements, or the clink of a casual milk bottle or early ash can. This block, one of the few still reserved for private houses in the old residential Fifties, did not begin to get up until after the rush hour, and then it took at least two hours to the task.

Number 56, opposite, with the dirty windows, belonged to the old Dilk estate—one of the ancient landed families of the island. The original Dilks had scratched a living out of corn on these arid acres, never dreaming of the wealth that lay for their descendants in lazy fallow. Old Cadmus Dilk had been buried from there a year ago—an ironic event wept over by a single mourner, an irregular female who had eased his last palsied years. The family had thereupon locked up the house, sealed it with its contents and its tainted memories, and left it to wither and decay. There are plenty of such mansions in this neighborhood abandoned with even less excuse.

Shortly before eight o'clock a street sweeper, in a uniform that had probably been white enough for the last parade of his clan, trundled his rattling barrow into view and unlimbered his tools to murder sleep. In an instant he was sedulously scraping, scraping the velvety asphalt, already buffed to a high polish by automobile tires. Reams of letters have been written to the *Times* by indignant taxpayers in protest against this process that shrieks along the edge of a nerve and drags one from the deepest dreams. Still it goes on.

In front of the coalhole of Number 56 the street sweeper came to a stop and went around in front of his scoop and stirred his catch with a stick. He picked up some treasure and hid it in a pocket. A clever street sweeper will get more than his wages out of a good block, mused Oliver, watching him from his window. The fellow resumed scraping, an artist at setting teeth on edge and getting the most out of it. Armiston was vaguely disturbed by something oddly familiar in the outline, but White Wings had propelled himself out of the angle of view before Oliver could analyze it.

The street was empty again. Some more basement windows opened their eyes and yawned torpidly. The fog was lifting slightly—the spires of the cathedral, over the housetops, were smokily attaching themselves to flying buttresses. Then, quite casually, the coalhole cover in front of Number 56 lifted itself—or was lifted—with a dull pung that caused the window to shudder convulsively, as if to free itself from its mortal frame. The coalhole cover returned to earth with a clatter after its ineffectual attempt at flight. A mushroom of jet-black smoke emerged from the coalhole, like the plume at the muzzle of a great gun as it recoils. The mushroom arose; it uncurled itself with dignified calm; it divided itself into billows that somehow, without any visible means of support, seemed to pile themselves up and up and up. The house was afire.

Nothing happened. That is the way with a fire. It doesn't break out. It simply emerges and looks around. Oliver arrested himself in the act of springing up—someone ought to pull the box at the corner.

Someone was pulling the box at the corner. There came the sound of tinkling glass and of a languid bell unwinding itself. Then came the street sweeper, galloping like a maniac, and screaming at the top of his lungs, *"Fuoco! Fuoco!"* He danced up and down in front of the vomiting coalhole, brandishing his stick to conjure the terrible genii to return to their bottle.

Then, with no time out for intermission, a long low wail, like a panther burying its head and howling in a cavern, rose on the air, a weird unearthly yell that expanded in volume until it shook the panes. A volley of musketry uncovered itself at the head of the street. It was punctured with dull vicious thuds—hand grenades! It was only the fire truck arriving from the outer void with its trailing demons; then steamers, hose wagons, water towers, patrols and the busy little red flivver of the commanding general. It seemed impossible that any agreement among the fiends could have settled on any single moment in eternity on which to erect such a pandemonium of howls, shrieks, bangs and clangors. Noise is quite as important at a fire as in a Chinese battle, and for exactly the same reason.

Curtains ran up, windows flung open, terror-stricken faces peered forth. Basement entries suddenly vomited forth inhabitants, each soul in some magical way snatching and bearing off with him at this last moment some darling treasure, as a soul will snatch for its darling sin at the Day of Judgment. Axes and sledges were ringing and crashing against the basement doors of Number 56. The breach opened, and through the opening squirmed those helmeted pirates as if to the loot. The teakettle steamer, that had come to anchor by the fire plug below Oliver's window, suddenly began to sing in a violently vibratory voice. Hose lines swelled and wriggled like snakes come to life. The pillar of black smoke dancing on tiptoe above the coal-hole, casually changed its hue to a dirty white. Then, quite as casually, it was gone. The fire was out.

The elongated fire truck extricated itself from its narrow quarters in this little side street, going home and taking all its noise with it. The commanding general was off to a fussy clatter of bells and whistles. The steamer suspired quietly; the spring lines that held it fast to the fire plug were cast off and the monstrosity drifted away down the street with a fluidity of motion amazing in its bulk. In five minutes there was nothing left but a squad of patrols folding unused tarpaulins and the crew of a hose truck taking in their slack. All disappeared.

On the basement steps sat a little group of police, fire-men and some other plenipotentiaries of such occasions, taking down and exchanging notes on the pedigree of this affair. They too drifted off, leaving behind as sole pos-sessor of the scene a handsome fire laddie, who lifted the basement blinds and sat down in Number 56 to study his morning racing forms. He—and his relief—would stand guard in this house for twenty-four hours. That is the penalty for indulging in the luxury of a fire.

Now the street sweeper who had stood by and freely offered advice and assistance throughout the run of the piece, loaded his instruments of torture on the barrow, and prepared to depart. As a preliminary he filled and lighted his pipe. Something in his aspect as he drew the first puff and gazed soulfully at Oliver's window caused the author to stir uneasily. Parr seemed not to have moved.

It was Pelts. It wasn't a street sweeper at all. It was Parr's prize possession. Pelts was a shabby little fellow who, on occasion, could look like anybody—excepting only a policeman. When he was a barber he cut hair with the best of them; when he was a snowbird he sniffed something that looked like coke; when he was a street sweeper he was nothing else. Pelts moved off the scene.

Oliver smiled wanly. Then fresh suspicion smote him. He took up his field glasses and focused them on the fireman guard in the basement window. Morel! Not a doubt of it. These two men, Morel as handsome as a prince, and Pelts as shabby as a beggar, were the great man hunter's attending spirits. It was said Parr never strolled abroad without having one ahead and the other behind. Not much escaped those three pairs of eyes.

So this was the explanation of Parr's early morning call, this tale of his having been up all night and wanting a place to hide out in. This was Parr's private, personally conducted conflagration, staged with all the accessories and facilities to which the versatile man hunter had access. And it had been set off merely for the purpose of installing his handsome pet, Morel, inside, with eight hours to look around in and no questions asked. Then there would be two reliefs of eight hours each, to drain any additional milk from the coconut. Very neat.

Parr stirred, opened his eyes; he seemed surprised to discover himself out of bed, as chair sleepers will.

"With your kind permission, I think I will retire," said he, fixing a dull malevolent eye on Oliver.

"You have it," said Oliver, not to be outdone. "Try the third-story front. You will admire the view." He summoned Mrs. Albaugh, the housekeeper, who took charge.

Passing out, Parr paused by the radio, an elaborate super with ornamental loop. He sat down and turned it on.

"What's the matter with this thing?" he asked sleepily.

"Nothing," said Oliver.

"What? Isn't there anything wrong with it?" demanded Parr.

"Absolutely nothing."

Parr chuckled as he turned it off and arose. "My friends brag about their radio sets like new babies; but half the time they go dumb when I come to see them do their tricks." Parr patted a yawn. "I'll play with it later, Oliver," he said, departing.

II

The first evening papers came in at eleven. Since Oliver had gone up for his thesis on the technology of murder, he had been getting all editions of all city papers. This was to check, in a small measure at least, the activities of his clipping bureau, with which he had put in a blanket order for murder at so much per thousand.

But this morning he did not look for murder. He was interested in the technology of spontaneous combustion. Undoubtedly that was spontaneous combustion, with the assistance of the street-cleaning department. The *Sun* stated prominently on the first page, head of the column, Exploding Coal Dust Pries Open Dilk House.

Just what constitutes news? The records of the fire department would show that fifty other alarms had aroused quite as much din within the same hour. Yet of them all, the bagful of smoke that had so spontaneously issued from the Dilk coalhole was the only one worthy of space in the early newspapers. Apparently the simple bulletin had inspired every city editor in Park Row to the same decision—"We'll take a column and a half on that."

It was fitting that it should be so. All over town newspaper readers skipped over expensive cables of monarchies falling; of the British Empire trembling before a coal shovel; of untold telegraph dots and dashes that went to make up a page of testimony of the Wet drive in Congress; of the pleasant details, with picture layout, of the screen tryouts of the Atlantic City beauty parade; a learned analysis by a prominent clergyman on Why the Beautiful are Dumb; fashions, sports, schools, churches —these things were not news this morning.

The man on the street, taking his cue from the make-up expert, with a magnificent disregard for ordinary values, as he hung suspended from a Subway strap, folded his paper with one-armed dexterity, wrinkled his brows and muttered, "I'd forgotten about that house." Women marketing for dinner, thriftily stealing headlines as they passed news stands, paused, bought papers, read; and each and every one asked herself the same question: "What do you suppose is inside?"

That especial leather-lunged squad of newsboys that knows news when it sees it burst bellowing into the canyons of the side streets with hollow yodeling cries of "Extra! Fire! Dilk house in flames! Oho!"

Circulation experts in Park Row, studying knees of curves plotted on graph papers, looked up casually with the instructions, "Tell them to give us fifty thousand more on Number Two." City editors called up veterans, tried old war horses, and said, "You can get in there, if anyone can. Go to it!"

An inquiry arose simultaneously in a dozen sanctums as to the present whereabouts of young Barry Dilk, that miscast youth in the scheme of life who could always be counted on for a scare head, no matter what he was doing. Cables under the sea and telegraphs over the land began to whisper the inquiry to chosen sentinels stationed at live spots on the surface of the earth. The electric curiosity also began to ask the question: "How is that marriage getting along? Is she still living with her count?"

At Aiken a flowery-dressed young man accosted a charming widow emerging from her limousine at the golf links, and she cried in sullen rage, "How dare you address me, you impudent upstart!"

He replied, bowing, "Madam, I am only a reporter, with no social status requiring me to be presented. I am to inform you that there was a fire in your New York house this morning."

"Good! I hope it burned down."

"Could you tell us where your son Barry is, Mrs. Dilk?"

She looked him through and through, and informed him icily that she was without information.

Passers-by stopped and gazed curiously at the house. Before noon a sizable crowd had collected. The house presented the same front it had yesterday, a week ago, a year ago, fifty years ago—except for the fact of a shattered basement door and a smudge about the coalhole. But the Dilks were one of those unfortunate families doomed to publicity; and when the public forgot them occasionally, as even a great war will simmer down for the seasons, the obsession only flared up again at the slightest excuse. Had it not been for that clever street sweeper and his spontaneous combustion, Number 56 might conceivably have continued to stew quietly in its own juices for a decade, or even until some wrecker came along to tear it down and properly capitalize its precious fallow with a skyscraper, to the further engorgement of the fabulously rich widow, her daughter the countess, and poor miscast Barry.

Shortly before three Parr came downstairs and Mrs. Albaugh brought him his coffee. He merely tasted it and turned to the radio. He thoughtfully aimed the loop, as if it had been a rudder, at Number 56 and tuned in a capricious lady mixing a lemon meringue at about 316 meters for the benefit of that vast unseen audience that concocts tibits for fastidious husbands by such ethereal methods. Oliver had firmly determined to show no curiosity. He could match Parr's reticence with his own. The man hunter took out his watch and attended sharply as the second hand slowly traveled to the precise hour of three. The silvery voice of the culinary coquette was abruptly marred by the mush of some telegraph station, a spark that seemed to have lost its logarithmic decrement.

"You've got some interference in there," said. Oliver testily. He prided himself on the razor-edge selectivity of his super—it could cut out anything.

"Yes; I wish she'd shut up," growled Parr. He held up a finger for silence, and began making marks with a pencil. The mush ceased abruptly. Parr folded his paper and shut the thing off. He handed the paper to Armiston to read. He grabbed his hat and coat, calling over his shoulder "Come along!" and made abruptly for the door.

Before he had taken six steps across the pavement, with Oliver hard on his heels, he was recognized by the hounds of the press, and pounced on. Parr looked them over grimly. They were all there, the regulars of this sort of thing; some nose as sharp as his own informed these creatures when to pause suddenly in their eternal stirring-up of the dust of human affairs, to concentrate on a single mote in the beam, insignificant to the untrained eye.

"Ah, Monte," said the deputy, nodding to a grizzled old-timer, "you can smell a corpse a mile."

"Is there a corpse, chief?" cried Monte, growing young in a breath. Parr nodded.

"Yes," he said. With his instinct for headlines that made him beloved by the trade, he said, "There are some bones buried in the cellar in a lead box that's been soldered up. Tin foot—looks like young Barry."

As if he had produced a TNT bomb with sizzling fuse, the close-pressed circle about him broke; and on the instant those lay observers who were gathered in knots up and down the block holding senseless vigil on the old house were astonished to see these dozen men racing madly away from the scene. They were bound for telephones, the devil take the hindmost. As the winged words impinged on waiting ears thundering presses ceased, were stripped of leaden cylinders of Wall Street closing prices. A machine operator, smoking a calm pipe, picked out the letters on a keyboard; and an intelligent type-casting machine produced by magic great blocks of trimmed and polished type which, when strung together, made the legend that ran straight across the eight columns of a page: Accidental Fire Discloses Murdered Body of Barry Dilk in Abandoned Home. That was all.

The rest of the page was filled with the history of this unfortunate young man who had been handed uncounted millions in his youth with the same disregard as a baby is given a box of matches to play with—and had been further dowered with the mind of a moron that ceased expanding at the age of ten. Everything he had ever done was duly set down. Over the swift course of his hectic years the newspaper clippings of his escapades and exploits had been filed away for just such an occasion. Presses rumbled forward. The wretched youth, who should never have been born, touched a lofty climax in circulation figures by dying.

Morel, as handsome as a probationary fire laddie fresh from the training gym, wore his unusual uniform with a saunter. He opened the basement gate for Parr and Armiston and locked it hard and fast after them.

"Did it come through all right, chief?" he asked eagerly.

"Fine!" said Parr, beaming, "Once a telegrapher, never anything else!" He paused at the kitchen table and took up the innocent-looking little electric buzzer, by means of which, at an agreed zero hour, Morel had telegraphed his report wirelessly to that waiting sensitive radio receiver across the street. Parr had never used this trick before, and was as pleased as a child.

III

The records of the protective agency—for land left to fatten on fallow in this expensive neighborhood requires an intricate burglar alarm—showed that the house had been opened on request of representatives of the family three times during the year. It was quite an intricate process, getting through a burglar-alarm mesh, and the record was explicit. Old Cadmus Dilk was buried from there in October; the dates of reëntry thereafter were December third, February thirteenth, and April seventh. This was November eighteenth.

"So much for your infallible burglar alarm," commented the Comte de Sorges, holding up his hands. "It was in May that he came out of the hospital with a silver plate tacked in his skull. He got tangled up with a polo mallet, you may remember." He picked up a newspaper that recounted the episodes in the career of poor Barry, who in his nursery days already had twenty millions to play with. "Here it is—ah! The twenty-fourth of May. He went abroad the next week, as I recollect. I can get that date exact—it was on the *Paris*."

"With his bodyguard?" asked Oliver.

"Always." The comte nodded, and looked keenly at Parr and Armiston. They were sitting in Armiston's study. "The poor devil never had a chance, from the day he was born," said the comte. "His mother was obsessed with the idea he would be kidnaped. He used to crawl out through a hole in the fence when he was a kid. She was always changing the army of nurses and guards. He ran away and went fishing with a stick of dynamite when he was twelve —blew off his right foot. And even with that tin foot he would try to stick on a horse and play polo!"

"When did he come back from abroad?" asked Parr.

"We didn't know he had come back until we got the papers in Washington last night. That may sound odd to you," added De Sorges.

"That is six months. You didn't make inquiries during that time?" asked Parr.

"No, we took particular care not to."

"We?" said Parr. "Who?"

"His mother," said De Sorges. "His escapades had become very distast—painful, to her. I think she prayed he might die. She refuses to come here now. This past six months has been the only peace she has known. I honestly believe she hasn't a tear left to shed."

"Yet she kept his guards, didn't she?" asked Parr.

"No, not of recent years. It was he who employed them. He never would fight unless he was drunk—and then he couldn't. He always had his huskies handy. Pick them up and you'll find out when he came back." The comte added after a slight pause: "Find the electrician who soldered that lead box and you'll have the man you are looking for?"

"Why an electrician?" asked Oliver.

"It would take an electrician to walk through that

burglar-alarm mesh without tripping it," replied De Sorges. "Or," he added, "turn up the man who touched off the fire."

"That was spontaneous combustion," said Parr. "It's not unusual in coal dust."

"But there was no coal dust there," said De Sorges. "There hasn't been an ounce of coal in that house for years. The old man used electricity for heat. It was one of his eccentricities. No, that house was fired to destroy it and everything in it."

A musing silence fell on the group. Mrs. Albaugh came in in the midst of it with some fresh newspapers and a fat envelope from the clipping bureau—more murder. Going on, she examined the stranger with ill-concealed curiosity. She had brought in the card—Comte Alène Marie Louis de Sorges—and had been hovering outside the door.

De Sorges was not the usual comic-opera or Sunday-newspaper type of count. There was nothing in his accent to betray his lineage. It was a careful English, but he paraded the localisms and colloquialisms like a native. He was of that easily assimilable type, his attire quite as inconspicuous and in as good taste as his speech. To look at him now, lounging easily in his chair, an athletic trainer would say that he would strip well.

To see him with his wife, Barry's elder sister, the contrast was amusing. He was entirely democratic in his attitude toward the world, while the comtesse assumed all the airs of Continental arrogance—that was her adaptation of *noblesse oblige*. As the male representative of the family, the comte had motored on from Washington during the night to place himself at the disposal of the department. He was well known to the public as an amateur sportsman and athlete, an avocation he pursued with dignity and distinction. For a number of years he had held several swimming championships; he fenced and played tennis among the foremost few. He did not play golf—that was a young man's game, he said, and it came in when he was too old to learn. He was thirty-eight.

He dabbled in science. Recently he had presented a paper before the Engineering Societies on The Decay Effect of the Oscillating Current and its Application to the Pendleton Theory, whatever that may be. Coming into the Dilk family when it was running to weeds, it was the general opinion—even of the ironic newspaper-reading public—that he fully accounted for himself to the world.

The door opened and Mrs. Albaugh announced with *empressement* that the comtesse was calling on long distance.

"Better take her in here," said Oliver quickly, and he led the way to the little writing room in the rear. Returning, he closed the door behind him and resumed his chair. Parr raised his eyes and regarded Oliver with that curious fixed stare that was so much a habit with him. When the comte returned Oliver was playing solitaire with his clippings.

"How is she taking it?" asked Parr.

The comte hesitated. He had a curious look of distaste. "You know, I have been brought up in a family where death, in whatever guise, has invariably meant something stupendous," he said. "Here," he said oddly, looking from one to the other, "it is nothing. Except for the outrageous manner of taking off, perhaps a desirable elimination. After all, I suppose, we can hardly blame them. As you say in your language, a dead sorrow is better than a living one." He made a motion as if to brush his own words aside. "It is something we must finish decently, that is all," he added.

"You went to considerable trouble to save him from drowning, off Point Carmel last winter, didn't you?" said Parr.

The holder of a hundred championship swimming medals passed this off with a shrug—to him it was child's play, where to another it would have been heroism. He did save Barry's life. De Sorges turned in his chair, glanced about the room like an alert dog trying to scent out something. A soft sputter, a sharp snap came from one corner. He stared. "Is your radio turned on?" he asked.

Oliver was idly snapping on and off his desk lamp. "Yes," began Oliver. "Yes—that is—yes; I am ageing some tubes." As he turned the lamp on again, simultaneously from the far corner came a loud click.

Parr laughed. "Ageing your grandmother," he chuckled. "We don't have to be mysterious, Oliver." He turned to the comte. "I get reports from my office by code," he explained to him. "It's handy because they can catch me any place I happen to be where there is a receiver. I'm leaving that open on the chance something will turn up."

This pleased the technical mind of the noble scientist. He went over to the corner looking for the loud-speaker whence the sounds came. He found none until his eye lit on a huge Japanese parasol that clung to the wall like a circular butterfly, as an interior decoration. This was Oliver's cone, a four-foot affair. The comte was delighted.

"Why would any idiot go to the trouble or incur the danger of breaking into that house and burying the lead box in the cellar?" demanded Oliver. "There are so many simpler ways of disposing of it."

"But once done," said De Sorges, resuming his chair, "you must admit it is very effective. The sea does give up its dead. The cadaver doesn't burn very well. It's quite a problem to hide a thing like that and have it stay hid.

That old house wouldn't be opened for say twenty years.
Then what? Nothing. I think it was a masterly stroke,
and that you have to deal with a very clever fellow."

"That is speculative, very questionable," objected Oliver.
"That house might be wrecked in a week."

"Not at all," said De Sorges. "Study the history of the
Dilk holdings. They are not for sale. They are not im-
proved. Several of them stand boarded up. Meantime the
land under them is doubling in value every six or eight
years. Let the other fellow do the improving. Hang on—
twenty, thirty, forty years—then skim the cream. That is
the history of the Dilk fortune. That house was as safe
as a tomb."

"Then why try to burn it down?" demanded Oliver.

"I think he lost his head there," said De Sorges. His
eyes narrowed. "That's where you will burn him," he said.
"That's something he did yesterday morning. The rest
of the clews are old and mildewed."

"Would you have done it that way?" broke in Parr.

"Burned it down, you mean?"

"No. Buried it in the cellar."

"No."

"Yet you think it effective," said Parr.

"For someone else, not for me." De Sorges smiled
slightly. "You overlook the fact that I—or rather my wife,
which is the same thing—would profit to the extent of
some, oh, say thirty millions by Barry's death. We would
have had to produce evidence of his death to collect. Why
hide it away?"

"Only seven years," said Parr. "Then you could have
had him declared dead. Meantime your estate would go
on doubling every six or eight years. It would be very
good interest for your patience."

A curious look of disgust spread over the comte's face.

"I think it might seem too long a time for me, under the circumstances," he said.

Armiston, toying again with his little reading lamp, accidentally turned it on and off, and the Japanese parasol snapped angrily in response. Then, quite abruptly, the parasol emitted a rapid succession of snaps, dots. Someone was calling, a telegrapher somewhere was fanning his key. It chattered "di, di, di, di, di, di, di, di, di——"

Parr held up a finger.

"Just a moment," he cautioned. He stepped over to the radio receiver; he lifted the lid and touched some tender spot inside with a finger tip. He tapped it twice, then once. The parasol in response chirruped in a birdlike voice, "Di, di—di."

"Are you sending?" cried De Sorges, infatuated.

Parr smiled, pleased himself with his little show. "I'm telling him to go ahead," he said. "That's about the extent of my fist these days. I can read though. One never forgets that. It's like swimming."

"But does that receiver radiate enough for you to get a message out of here—to actually transmit?"

"They all do," said Parr comfortably. "Very handy little domestic utensils, if you know how——" He held up his pencil for silence.

The Japanese parasol, speaking in rough gutturals, the voice of an archaic spark with no logarithmic decrement, began: "Di, di, dah, di—di, di—di, dah, di—di, di, di—dah——"

Parr's pencil moved, forming letters in that telltale chirography of the old-time operator who learned his trade before the days of the typewriter. A tense stillness prevailed in the room. Once, when the thing paused, the comte breathed to Oliver, "Can you read it?"

"No. Can you?"

"No. Tremendously clever, eh?"

The spark came leaping out of the parasol again. Parr wrote: "First June. Did not sail. Name on passenger list. Two previous attempts."

The thing ceased to utter, like a mechanical doll run down. Parr crumpled the paper and tossed it aside. His eyes traveled from Armiston to De Sorges and remained fixed there in sightless reverie. Few men could withstand the fixed gaze of the man hunter for long. De Sorges shifted uneasily. Finally Parr roused himself. He turned to Oliver.

"This affair should clear up quickly now," he said absently. He turned and stared at the magic parasol. "Did it ever occur to you that a murderer does not begin to be subtle until he ceases to be clever?" he asked. Oliver looked up as if he had heard this somewhere before. "He uses the tools he is surest of," said Parr. "That's where he falls down. That's where this one is falling down badly."

"If you will permit me, I think you are rather sanguine," said De Sorges. "It seems to me much more involved than you appreciate. These things don't solve themselves."

"You don't know the man I've got working on this job," replied Parr. He smiled grimly. "He's probably sitting on the murderer's doorstep now, waiting for him to come home." Parr suddenly leaned forward and tapped De Sorges on the knee, the while he held him with his famous glare. "Murder," said Parr, rolling the word on the end of his tongue, "is not an accident. It is a system. He can't escape his own scheming—that is, if he is clever. If he is stupid he has a pretty good chance of going scot-free. It is the clever man who loses his sense of proportion. He overlooks trifles. For instance, in this case, the time of day."

"Do you know, within three months, when this crime was committed?" said the comte, who was not impressed.

"The murderer entered Number 56 at 10:13 A.M. on the first day of June," said Parr. "He came out at 11:12."

Even Oliver turned to stare. The comte was staring at Parr with that curious unflinching gaze of a man looking at the sun, a rare accomplishment.

"I'm afraid I don't follow," said De Sorges, after what seemed an interminable second, with an air of apologetic doubt. "Poor Barry sailed on the *Paris* on the third of June."

"Oh, it was the third?" said Parr.

"I recollect very well now—it was the third," said De Sorges. "It is a date easily verified. In any event it was after the first."

"Did you see him off, De Sorges?" asked Parr.

"No."

"Did any of the family?"

"I think not."

"Then of your own knowledge you can't swear he did sail," said Parr.

"The passenger list will show," replied De Sorges.

Oliver was again snapping his light on and off. The Japanese parasol snapped angrily. The comte turned on Oliver with some irritation. "You will pardon me, I am sure," he said, excusing his gesture. "My nerves are on edge. This isn't a particularly pleasant——"

The parasol came to life abruptly with a long flutter of dots.

"Here is something now!" exclaimed Parr, and he went over to the receiver and tapped out his go-ahead signal on that tender spot. Parr looked at the clock, took up his pencil, paused, waiting. That guttural spark coming out of the void began again with its dots and dashes—di, di, dah——

It was slow sending, about ten words to the minute.

Parr's pencil moved, forming each letter perfectly. He had the old trick of his train-dispatcher days of never lifting the pencil from the paper; and he had the manner of one utterly oblivious of the purport of the letters he ran into words, and of the words he ran into trailing phrases. Oliver was leaning back in his chair in the dark of his corner. He made no movement, not a sound came from him. De Sorges had turned, and in a frozen attitude was staring at the parasol.

Parr wrote: "First, January, with boat; second, May, with mallet. First prevented by rescue stop catboat appearing inopportunely from behind inlet. Lighthouse keeper telescope witnessed beginning. Stand by. Coming." The thing ceased to click.

There was a long silence the while they waited. The three men, who seemed hardly to be drawing breath in their rigid attention, stared at the parasol. De Sorges made the first move. It was a simple enough gesture, taking his watch out of a vest pocket, but the eyes of the two men instinctively followed the hand. De Sorges studied the watch for a moment.

He said in a level voice, "I promised to call my wife at this hour. She is naturally anxious." He arose, bowed to Oliver. "With your permission," he said. It was Parr who nodded assent.

The comte's eye lingered almost imperceptibly on his hat and stick, but he made his way to the door without them. His nervous tension betrayed itself as his hand fell on the door knob. He drew open the door swiftly—and stepped back. Two people, in the act of entering, blocked his exit. One was little Pelts, the street sweeper of yesterday morning, now his own shabby self. He had a woman in tow—an over-dressed dowdy thing who had been weeping through her make-up. At sight of the comte she threw up her hands and shrieked and made to flee, but Pelts held her fast. De Sorges was glaring at her.

"Ah, the irregular female!" exclaimed Parr, who still held his chair. It was the sorceress who had beguiled the last hours of the disreputable old Cadmus Dilk. Since that key had been turned against her she had come back to haunt this block day after day, the scene of her brief taste of luxury and magnificence.

The handsome Morel, no longer a fireman, appeared suddenly from nowhere and pushed his way into the center of the group. He glanced at Parr for instructions.

"Better put on the bracelets, Morel," said Parr. Morel never took his eyes from the woman, whose very features seemed to fade beneath the mask of terror. His distaste for this cruel act, the clap of doom to every prisoner, showed in his face. He fumbled at his side pocket for the bracelets. He made a single gesture, and the things clinked metallically on the wrists of Comte Alène Marie Louis de Sorges. The woman, the irregular female, fumbling helplessly at her throat, fell in a heap.

De Sorges, with mutterings of imbecile rage, raised his hands as if to rend the manacles apart with his enormous strength. Then the sudden sense of the depth of the degradation these shiny wristlets symbolized came over him. His hands fell, his face set. He looked down on the woman who was opening her eyes.

"So it was you!" he snarled.

There was no need of an accuser now, of the man who had finally succeeded in blotting out poor Barry after two bungling attempts. That first fluke, when he had all but succeeded in drowning the drunken boy, he had cleverly converted into an act of heroism when those fishermen so inopportunely came on the scene. The press of two continents had lauded him for that act. Then, in May, the same damnable luck that pursued him had deflected his polo mallet by the shade of a hair. And now this woman —and the fire! The woman, crawling behind Pelts, was muttering, "I saw you! I saw you! Thank God, I saw you!"

"So you do read the code?" came the drawling voice of Parr. The comte said nothing. "Take him away," ordered Parr. The door shut on the unpleasant spectacle. There was some commotion outside, of the wagon arriving. Morel ran back at the last minute.

"Did it come through all right, chief?" he asked eagerly.

"Fine!" said Parr, beaming. "Once a telegrapher, never anything else."

It had been Morel, concealed in a room across the hall, who had tapped off the code messages which the Japanese parasol had enunciated with such deadly effect. Oliver himself had written those messages earlier in the morning in preparation for this test, and had given the cues for their sending with the clicks from his innocent electric light.

"His nerve broke," said Oliver as Morel withdrew, "when you gave him the hour and the day he moved the box in. Did you notice his hands grip the chair arms?" Parr nodded, his eyes gleaming. "Weren't you taking a long chance, Parr?"

"Not at all," responded the man hunter. "The recording instrument of the burglar-alarm system showed a slight disturbance on the time chart for that day. They sent a man around; but he found nothing. I happened to notice it in going over the charts. I thought I'd like to have a look inside that house. That's why we touched off that spontaneous combustion yesterday morning."

He selected a stogy, making a wry face over it. "Speaking of long shots," he said, striking a light, "you seem to have potted a bird on the wing yourself."

Oliver picked up two newspaper clippings. They were not stamped and dated by his clipping bureau. They were from his private collection. One recorded the heroic rescue from drowning of Barry Dilk by Comte de Sorges, the international champion. The other related the episode of the polo mallet, an accident during practice.

"He might have got away with it once," said he. "But not twice. It was simple enough. Occupational tools of murder. That boat was scuttled too far offshore for anyone but a great swimmer to get back. And a polo mallet." He turned and looked out of the window. "And the house." He shook his head. "He couldn't resist that house!"

"How about the lighthouse keeper and his telescope?" asked Parr, with a grim smile.

Oliver admitted that was pure fiction, a final touch in the process of applying the third degree via the Japanese parasol.

IV

THE DEAD END

AUNT IVY, trudging home in the cool of the July evening, paused as was her wont at the top of the steep pitch of the red-shop hill. Not for breath, however; it was freely admitted in her family, which had built the Stone House in the days of the second redcoat war, that the hill itself "wasn't nothing." The old woman's pause was for retrospect. She never passed this spot without stopping to remember the unforgettable night of her wedding feast, when Leander Cotton, fetching her home as a bride to the Stone House she brought him as a dower, had prudently got down at the foot of the hill to screw fresh calks in the plates of his horse's shoes before risking so precious a burden on the glare ice of that perilous ascent.

She trudged on to the second rise, where the road forked. A worn path edged with a faint wheel track led to the Stone House; the other track was a forgotten road that stumbled on, up and around the shoulder of the Mountain, as far as the resolute ruin of the old Seymour place, where it gave up the ghost.

She was crawling through the fence to take the short cut across the overgrown night pasture, when she suddenly shrank down, her heart skipping a beat. A man in khaki breeches and putties sat on the wash bench by the kitchen door. Duke, the old dog, deaf and half blind, and the house cat idled on the bench beside him; and two adventurous little pigs had crawled through the fence to do the honors in the absence of their mistress. With his stick the man was drawing in the clean gravel of the dooryard, instructing the small porkers in their A B C's. Chickens were strutting about with the dandified air they assume at mealtime. Cossy, the old cow, had come up from the brush on the edge of the woods, where she had been hiding from flies all afternoon, and stood crowding the bars, gazing on the domestic group.

Aunt Ivy wore the gray she had put on after that black night years gone by when blunt neighbors had brought her word that her husband had backed his cart off the bridge when the river was in flood, and father, son and plunging team had been swept off into the swift oblivion of swirling ice floes. Now, stepping back into the alders, she was instantly lost to sight, like an animal. She retraced her steps and presently came on the Stone House again, this time through the sugar bush, reconnoitering from the cover of the dilapidated old sap arch.

The man was large and raw-boned, and about the age of her son. But it was not her son. Young Leander had the imprint of a horse's hoof on his forehead.

The watcher held her breath, listening. Nothing happened. Only familiar sounds came to her ear—the cathedral whisperings of the tall tree tops; the echo of cowbells telling of herds coming home; the musical murmur of the river. Finally, her caution satisfied, she climbed down and discovered herself to her creatures at the gate. At sight of her, pæans of Chinese flattery rose from the assembled multitude. The man, hat in hand, said his name was De Groot, Peter de Groot, smiling down on her puritanly prim little figure with a question in his eyes whether the name itself meant anything to her. His eyes were too far apart and his ears set too far back on his head. He was explaining that he would like to buy the place—if it was for sale.

She shook her head. It didn't belong to her; it belonged to
her son. He might come home any time.

"I suppose you have heard that I am expecting my son
home almost any time now, haven't you?" she asked, looking up at him quickly with so clear an understanding in her
eyes that he averted his gaze; and he answered awkwardly
that he believed he had been told something to that effect.

Aunt Ivy knew just how much he had been told; she
knew that any stranger who tarried in the village long
enough for the gossips to get his ear would be told the fantastic story of Aunt Ivy Cotton, who had been bravely
coming and going for years now, with increasing faith that
her son was not dead, had not been drowned with his father
on that tragic night, but would some day come back to her.
They would tell how she kept his room ready for him, the
kitchen bedroom, the cozy room of the Stone House; how
she would set out his shaving water of a Sunday morning
in the same pewter mug his father and her father had used
before him; how she would change his clothes in the bureau
drawers with the seasons; and how, on cold mornings, she
would warm his boots by the kitchen fire. Most of the tale
was true, except the manner of telling. She knew how they
smiled at her doting foolishness; she was not deceived.

The old woman moved across the yard in silence, the
clamorous flocks swirling about her feet. When all her
creatures were busy over their supper she let herself in and
straightway began preparations for her own evening meal.
She touched a match to the made fire in the stove, and
while she filled the shining kettle at the spring, lazy cottony coils of smoke rose like dancers on poised toes from
the stove lids and filled the air with the delicious fragrance
of fresh kindling.

The man De Groot leaned in the doorway, his head bent
a little because of his great height, which she had not noted

outside. He watched her, fascinated; his gaze ranged over
her shoulder as she moved about the stove, through an open
door into the bright room beyond, the room the village said
she kept for her son's homecoming. When she went out
to milk he followed her and watched in silence the white
ribbons of milk that flowed at her touch, and the creamy
foam that rose in the bucket. Inside again, she skimmed
off the froth with a single dexterous turn of a saucer and
invited the old dog and cat to share this meditative meal
of bubbles. De Groot rocked absently in an old chair, to
the tick-tock of the clock.

"Aunt Ivy," he burst out abruptly, "I want to adopt
you for my mother! I've never had a mother—that is,
that I can remember, and——"

"Fiddlesticks!" she sniffed. "Who ever heard such talk!"
Busy as a bee, she did not pause, but, passing him, she
shot a triumphant look at him and cried out: "I know who
you are now! You are one of the surveyors down at the
hotel."

He nodded; he was the chief of the party. Every few
years a surveying squad would appear from nowhere and
without a by-your-leave draw a circle of doom above the
heads of the village on the hillsides; evenings on the hotel
porch they would astonish the natives with wild tales of a
reservoir two hundred feet deep with the village lying
water-logged at the bottom and tenanted only by fish.
Nothing ever came of these visitations; and the village
had finally come to regard its suspended doom with a
languid serenity.

For the past week such a surveying party had been running out flood lines on the opposite hillside. Aunt Ivy
behind her curtains mornings had watched for the helio-
graphic glint of the sun on their transits, vaguely she had
speculated how soon they would cross to this side of the

valley; even, she had thought, with a tightening of the heart, they might now be scrutinizing her with the all-seeing eye of their telescopes, taking stock of her, eaves, pane, lintel and sill. De Groot was one of these.

"I have been watching you evenings, climbing that hill," he said.

She darted one of her quick looks at him. She said with a queer smile, "You needn't to waste your sympathy on that hill. It ain't nothing."

"Gravity overcomes traction on that first pitch," he said, in the lingo of his craft. "There isn't an automobile made that could climb it. And yet you climb it every day, Aunt Ivy."

"I expect that's because I ain't never heard about gravity and traction," she retorted with a sly twinkle.

"The water will come up to that hitching post in your dooryard, Aunt Ivy," he ran on, letting his eye search the vista of the open door again. "I'll come in a boat. I will have to live around here for some time. This will all be water when I get through."

She nodded over her stirring at the stove.

"I expect that won't be in our time," she said dryly.

"I'm serious about adopting you, Aunt Ivy. I'm going to settle right down in this kitchen." He looked around, tasting the flavor of it again. "I never saw a woman I'd rather have for a mother. And I never saw a room I'd rather live in. And there's my valley sitting right out in the dooryard. I'd make it well worth your while."

"Thanks! I've got all I want—and more too!" The touch of asperity was present in her tones. Yet she must smile again at the absurdity.

"Couldn't I be your son, Aunt Ivy?"

"But I have a son!" she cried, turning on him. "A big, fine, strapping fellow—as big as you!"

The men of her family had always been big men, and she had such a woman's contempt for lesser creatures. Now, as on sudden inspiration, she went to her son's room and brought back his picture. It was that of a healthy young giant growing up in the image of his father. Leander Cotton, the father, was of a different breed from these people of the valley, who had originally been whalers come home from the seas to bury their anchors here, as the saying goes. How he ever happened to be born here was a mystery. He belonged outside in the big world; all through his life he always talked big of going out; but he never did go, until the river took him that night. But the boy—the mother knew, felt in her heart, he was out there, taking his rightful place among men, a friend to the four corners of the world.

She stood behind De Groot looking down on the picture with a fine pride.

"If you have been everywhere I expect sometime you have seen my Leander," she said, the tinder of hope alight in her eyes.

Then to De Groot's surprise, she drew out a chair for him at the table; and he sat down, bowing his head under her simple blessing.

"You've probably forgotten, if you did know him," said Aunt Ivy, pouring the tea. "Leander would never stay long in one place."

De Groot picked up the picture again and studied it.

"If he only had the imprint of a horse's hoof on his forehead," he said slowly, "I'd swear—sometime—somewhere—— There was a chap—kicked by a horse! He'd carry that mark to the grave."

His eyes fastened upon her in an effort at remembrance. Aunt Ivy, halting her teapot, responded to his scrutiny with a sudden smile.

"It was Louis, the black colt," she said brightly. She filled his cup and passed it to him. The old clock seemed to clang through a tense silence, while each held the other's eyes. "It was three months after that picture was taken," she said, without haste or emotion. "His father wanted he should break the colt for the haying." Her eyes strayed momentarily. "They all said I'd lose him." She shook her head with a wistful smile. "But I knew I'd never lose him! He was so big—and strong! He could handle any of them in the village. How they hated him for his strength!" She turned to the supper again. "Won't you try my pickles? They are called the best in the valley."

De Groot roused himself with a start. He accepted the offering mechanically. He ate in silence, his eyes continually straying to the picture at his elbow. Aunt Ivy chattered like a magpie.

Afterwards, when she got up and began clearing the table, he took down a dish towel, and while she was pouring the steaming water into the dishpan he found his tongue.

"I've never known anybody named Cotton," he said. "It is an unusual name I couldn't forget."

There could be no doubt about the identity.

"But he wouldn't know his name was Cotton," she said quickly. "You see, strangers pulled him out of the river, half dead." She spoke of something real rather than fanciful. "Poor Leander didn't know who he was—couldn't remember. It happens that way, you know. That's why he hasn't come back home. Some day he will remember. Then he will come."

Her skilled hands moved ceaselessly. Seated by the table under the lamplight, she opened a stocking bag gathered with a gay red ribbon, and unrolled Leander's socks, stretching heel and toe to the light with one hand inside, looking in vain for a hole to darn.

"There was that dealer in curios in San José," murmured De Groot, his eyes roaming the rag rug as he leaned forward with elbows on his knees. "He had a native wife—they sold pottery—they said it was dug up from Toltec graves; and they had a collection of little gold gods, about the size of my little finger—virgin gold, as yellow as a pumpkin!"

When he paused, musing, she covertly watched him, waiting for his words to flow again, as if he talked in his sleep.

"It was in a side street—near the umbrella tree with the fence around it—not more than a pistol shot from the savanna. There was something about him that——" He checked himself.

"That what?" she urged gently.

"I think not!" he said, as if shaking off some disagreeable idea. "That chap's name was Safford—or Stafford—I am sure it was the scar of some greaser's machete."

She stirred uneasily, but said nothing. De Groot rose and paced off the maple boards of the floor to the entrance of Leander's room; he was looking in, but his eyes seemed to be focused on infinity.

"No, that wasn't the chap," he continued, turning. "That fellow had a father living. I remember distinctly, because it struck me so curious that he always spoke of his father as if he were an elder brother. Your son's father isn't alive, is he?" he demanded abruptly, halting in front of her.

She shook her head.

"No," she said with slow deliberation. "He is dead. You know the old saying," she added, folding her work—

" 'Ghosts can't cross rivers.' " She had accepted the fact of her husband's death. She had put up a headstone for him in the graveyard, because she had never had any difficulty in conceiving death for him.

It was going on to nine o'clock; she told him he must go.

"Come in and sit tomorrow evening," Aunt Ivy said as she stood in the doorway with him.

Her spare arms folded in her apron, she watched him away into the night; she could follow him across the pasture by the occasional flash of his pocket torch.

Inside, she filled the box behind the stove from the woodhouse off the kitchen, a cheerful cricket greeting her as she pushed open the door and let in the lamplight among the neatly stacked rows of stovewood. The last time she passed out the door clicked behind her. The old dog clawed at the door once or twice and whined, then sat down, nose to the crack, to wait.

II

A pair of Devon stags moved up the steep pitch of the red-shop hill with the casual air of the impossible. At their head, inching up the incline backward and addressing them in the stentorian tones of Demosthenes, as he cracked a large bullwhip over their heads, moved Jason Selfridge, Aunt Ivy's nephew, who though he had a degree in technology was home this summer for the haying. Behind trailed a stone boat laden with a pair of tackle blocks, a coil of rope and a log chain, lashed fast. And still farther behind, trailing in the dust, climbed a tattered little red-eyed old man, helping himself up with a crowbar fashioned from some remote wagon axle. This latter was Gran'ther Noah Seymour, the last of an illustrious line.

At the top of the rise where the worn path turned off to the Stone House, the cattle continued on up and around the shoulder of the Mountain; and when the stone boat at last attained an angle of repose, and floated along like a dinghy in a calm wake, Jason suggested that gran'ther get on and ride. The old gentleman ignored the insult; when he was so feeble he couldn't follow a pair of cattle he wouldn't bother anyone any more, not even the cattle, but would fold his hands and lay himself out.

It was Gran'ther Noah's thoughts on the approaching hereafter that had inaugurated this expedition. This morning, grinding his adz in the mists of dawn, it had occurred to him it was high time he should go fetch the headstone under which, he had determined long ago, he could sleep peacefully through eternity. He had therefore solicited the aid of Jason and his pair of cattle to get the stepstone of his father's house. Since only bats and owls now tenanted the old Seymour place, and only ghosts crossed the threshold, Jason readily consented to lend a hand in the sentimental journey.

When they finally turned in at the Seymour homestead there was nothing left of the once-busy thoroughfare but a memory that burned in the old man's eyes as he gazed up at this stubborn relic of the past grandeur of his line. Jason turned the stags loose to graze, noting uncertain paths, probably of deer, stamped in the rank grass of the dooryard. The old man was sitting on the stepstone.

"I've cracked butternuts on it," he said. "I've skinned bullheads on it! I set here nights, looking at the stars, thinking and listening!" He took a villainous-looking toadstabber and whetted its edge on the smoothed granite that had known so many feet. "And now I want to lie under it when I die!" announced gran'ther, knocking out his pipe and going to work.

It was a task of judgment and precision. The old man fetched water from the spring, and flowed it over the great blue stone, watching, fascinated, as the beautiful grain deciphered itself. After deep study he struck a chalk line, turning to the sightless windows with so rapt a look over the nice problem he was weighing that Jason's gaze involuntarily followed his, as if he expected to see the ghost of some old Seymour communing with his ancient companion. The old man began to chip the stone with tiny drills.

"This here corner, Jason," he said—"there ain't a flaw in it." He looked keenly at the youth. "Now I'm going to show you something they didn't learn you at college!"

He was drilling holes two inches apart along the chalk line. It was a slow process, an example of that archaic patience that had built these stone walls, cleared these meadows and pastures, so much labor gone to seed.

The shadows shortened into noon; thick heat came down and left them gasping under the July sky. When Jason would have helped with the drilling gran'ther waved him aside. A fence post, yes; but his headstone, no! It was a lost art—or at least an art that would cease and determine with him, the old man's manner seemed to imply. Jason balanced his hat over his eyes and stretched out under the old apple tree, listening to the ceaseless strumming of the July day. He eyed the vacant windows through convenient holes in his headgear. He lazily traced out the lost path to the spring; he had a vision of an ancient velvety lane with its hundred cattle straggling up to the bars.

He watched gran'ther, who, now the drilling was done, put steel wedges in the holes, cocking an ear as he tapped them gently with a little hammer. He was tuning them. This done to his satisfaction he lighted his pipe again and visited with himself, holding one ragged knee in his bony hands. A long time later he tapped the wedges again. Then he took a walk, hands clasped behind like a leisurely church warden stepping piously among revered relics. Again and again he returned to the stone, listening, rapt. Finally it whispered to him the message he so patiently had awaited. It was something like the sound of a mouse scratching under the floor. Gran'ther's eyes listened in triumph. Under his breath he summoned Jason. A tiny hair line was creeping stealthily from drill hole to drill hole. As they watched, spellbound, the stepstone suddenly gave up its struggle and parted, one half—which was to weight gran'ther down in eternity—turning lazily over and showing a fracture cleaved four-square.

"They didn't learn you that in college, I expect!" said the old man complacently. Jason was fain to admire.

The rest was common mechanics. While gran'ther draped a loop of the log chain over one corner of his stone, and set the crowbar—fed with a nice amount of bait— at the other, Jason snubbed the tackle blocks to an old stump, and hooked the falls to the oxbow, the stags now being summoned back to toil. At a word and a crack of the whip, the stags put their shoulders against the creaking bows; and the severed headstone moved with slow dignity upon the stone boat. Dusk was settling in the vale of evening when they deposited the raw stone on blocks by the populous Seymour plot in the drear God's acre of Beech Plain. On the morrow gran'ther would come with gads and chisels to carve in homely script a fitting epitaph. It is good to carve one's own ave, to sleep among one's own people, and under so beloved a stone!

Jason plodded on home. He mooned over the milking. Those tracks were not deer tracks; it was the absence of all deer signs that was significant. That spring, it must have been cleaned out about six weeks ago; the fresh crop of cress would prove that; a crop that had been fed on by someone—not deer or cattle, because they don't eat cress. Who had chopped wood and been so careful to pick up every chip? That piece of hemlock bark hiding in the grass showed the slice of a sharp ax. And the kitchen window closed with a whole sash, in place of the empty one Jason had thrown stones at, as a boy. Gran'ther had done a heap of walking around—it was all as plain as print—the old man must have seen.

Jason moved, still mooning, down to the village, where from his accustomed perch on the post-office porch he listened with flattering solemnity to the tall talk of this latest party of surveyors who were to tenant the village with eels and other deep-swimming fishes. Now and then when a pause seemed to call for a demonstration, Jason would interject an astonishment mark or a query. When he spoke it was in the patois and with the nasal drawl of his native hills, not in the precise English of his mother's supper table or his senior thesis.

About nine, at the approach of a familiar wheel creak, he got down. Orlo Sage, the constable and factotum of law, drove by, in the dark, and Jason hopped a ride, settling himself luxuriously beside Orlo on the bags of feed draped as cushions over the wagon bolster. The journey home was pursued in communing silence.

When Jason got down at his gate Orlo drew rein and said, "Them fellow ain't surveyors."

Jason yawned, and said nothing.

"They're looking for something," muttered Orlo.

The two friends chewed in silence for a full minute over this portentous utterance; then Orlo clucked to his team and moved off, creaking.

Jason's dog came down to the gate and was sent back, disconsolate. The ledge that buttressed the high plain loomed immense, invulnerable, in the dark. But there was a path, a ladderlike scramble known only to the foxes in desperate flight, to Jason's hound dog Nip, and to Jason himself. From the top of the ledge he could come on the Seymour place by way of the old lane. It would be an outsider, of course. Only one wholly ignorant of the local signs and omens would pick the old place as a refuge. Solitude is to be found only among the multitude; not up here where there was treachery in every bent twig, every broken leaf. Telltale signs were everywhere. No; it was none of the village people or their kind; a fugitive from somewhere outside, stumbling blindly into this dead end; some poor wight deluded into a sense of security had picked the likeliest spot on earth, to stand discovered in the blinding light of rustic curiosity.

Wet to the skin with the heavy dew that dripped from the matted grass of the lane, Jason edged forward slowly and painfully. These surveyors—who were not surveying! It was a clever ruse for spying. No questions would be asked. A surveyor, to the rustic mind, is a mysterious animal at best. Jason had seen that something was wrong, from the beginning. Their talk on the porch, evenings, didn't hold water; neither would the weird bench lines they were drawing out on the hillsides. The better part of De Groot's crew didn't know a rod from a link, a chain from a transit. Afternoons, from the thicket on his side of the valley, the young technologist had studied them through field glasses. For the most part the men idled in the shade of the woods; now and then, through their powerful telescopes, they would sweep the valley, with cross hairs pausing, fixed on road, meadow or summit.

At first Jason had thought the Stone House was under scrutiny—but what would there be in the comings and goings of Aunt Ivy to occupy the attentions of such an outfit? Now that the Seymour place had come into the

picture, events began to dovetail. With the trail hot, he
almost wished he had brought Orlo Sage along.

He was worming his way along the wall of the woodhouse when the unmistakable tones of Aunt Ivy Cotton
broke on his ear from the pitch dark of the old kitchen.

She was crooning in soft accents, "It seems to me you
might tell your own mother."

Jason held his breath to still his thumping heart, which
threatened to burst his ribs.

After an interminable pause Aunt Ivy continued coax-
ingly: "There isn't anything you have ever done that you
couldn't tell your mother."

There was a pitiful yearning in her voice, all the more
poignant coming out of the inscrutable night. A board
creaked; there was a sudden scurry of rats; a startled
movement of alarm in the kitchen was succeeded by smoth-
ering silence.

"Who is that? Who is there?" demanded Aunt Ivy
sharply. She was in the doorway, not three feet from where
Jason lay. He cowered down, feeling suddenly sick, for he
loved the old woman as he loved his own mother. She
fronted the unknown danger, brave as a lion.

"Come out of that!" she cried, her voice tense. "You
skulking rascal!"

Not even an echo answered her. Jason lay still as death.

"I'll come and fetch you!" said the determined old
woman.

She struck a match and lit a candle, which she held high
over her head, moving it hither and yon and shading her
eyes as she searched the obscurity. The candle shed a vague
circle of light as yellow as a sun dog; its feeble beams
seemed only to make the night more black. But she was
advancing. In another moment she must stumble over him.
Jason shamefacedly arose, and revealed himself.

"It's me—Jason, Aunt Ivy," he mumbled. He had a swift impression of her deadly white face and big startled eyes. "You ain't see or heard of my belled heifer—have you, Aunt Ivy?" he asked, hang-dog. "She broke through the fence. I heared something over here, so I come to see."

Jason's lie trailed off into miserable silence under her piercing gaze. Some night murmur caused her to turn her head, to his infinite relief. When she looked at him again Jason had his ready smile. She beckoned him into the kitchen, and when he paused inside she held the candle to light his eyes in their tour of inspection. As he had feared, the room was empty. He would almost have wished to find anybody, anything here, rather than this eerie emptiness. There was some food set out on a board on the sink, and a milking stool stood empty at the feast. Jason would have put his arm about her, but she gently deterred him.

"You know him, don't you, Jason?" she begged eagerly; she shot a keen look at him. "He hasn't changed at all!" Aunt Ivy waved a hand towards her phantom son, smiling her wistful smile. "It's Jason, Leander," she said, addressing the invisible guest. "Don't you remember Jason? The chubby little fellow—why, he used to carry your bats for you! What?" Aunt Ivy cupped a hand to one ear, listening to a phantom voice. "Now, now! You mustn't fret!" she said quickly. Over her shoulder she gave Jason a knowing nod. "He's timid," she whispered to Jason. Then drawing Jason gently to the dilapidated entryway she said softly, "You go out! Wait for me by the gate? I'll be along directly."

Stunned, Jason took up his wait by the gate. This, then, was the end of the search—Aunt Ivy finding her lost Leander, beyond the border line! Through all these years cheated in her faith, now at last a God-given delusion had come to comfort her! Here was the human taint—Aunt

Ivy preparing the hearth for her beloved ghost. It was minutes later that she crept up on Jason in the dark, her groping hands finding him before, in his preoccupation, he heard her steps. It gave him a shock; his nerves were on edge.

"I can't make him eat," Aunt Ivy said sadly. "I fetched him some goodies tonight too. It worries him to have folks about."

These two, who could see in the dark, so well did they know the ways that marked the plain, moved on in silence. Aunt Ivy clung to Jason's arm. There was not another word of the phantom. But when a hello came suddenly out of the near night she cowered against him.

It was gran'ther, his stalwart tones materializing from nowhere.

"Hello! Jason! Hello! Hello!"

Aunt Ivy's sinewy grip on Jason's arm relaxed; she pushed him from her, and he understood he was to go on alone.

"Hello!" voiced Jason to the night, striding forward.

"She's in with Orlo's cattle, Jason!" gasped the dissociated voice.

He meant the lost heifer! There was art here. Jason had to admire, even as the unwelcome truth flashed over him that the wily old man had seen everything, heard all. Gran'ther came floundering out of the thicket.

"Where's your lantern?" demanded he querulously.

"It went out," responded Jason, taking the cue.

They moved on without a word.

"Won't you come in and visit?" invited gran'ther at his own gate.

This was epochal; old Noah was never known to have company. They sat in the dark, for gran'ther never struck a light till he went to bed; then the lamp burned all night. They discussed their cattle, the hay weather, the new highway coming down the valley; but no syllable gave reference to the scene they had just shared up above. At length, during a protracted yawning pause, gran'ther lit a match and methodically scraped the wick of his oil lamp before lighting it. He motioned to Jason to go out; and when he had set the lamp that was to stand guard at the bedside the old man joined him.

All along Jason had known that they were to go back together; but as gran'ther beckoned him he felt the gooseflesh creep. There were still some formalities to be gone through to satisfy Noah. His own extravagance in leaving his lamp burning over his empty bed was to advertise to the world at large that he had retired. Jason must do likewise. Jason must climb to his own attic and leave a lighted lamp for ten minutes in his window; then he must blow it out and quietly creep out again. Thus without prejudice to their adventure they paid homage, each to his habit, for the benefit of anyone who might be overcurious.

III

The low-hanging clouds lifted for a moment and disclosed the kitchen L in the milky obscurity of the moon. A shadow detached itself from the indefinite doorway and, like some tarrying ghost surprised by a cockcrow and making haste slowly, gradually dissolved itself into the deeper obscurity of the interior. The light was tricky. A second shadow, as if from a wind-tossed branch of a tree, moved across the rusty old clapboards in the fantastic outlines of a huge gorilla, swinging with long flail-like arms from window ledge to window ledge, and to door frame. Cloud wreaths torn by upper currents of wind scurried across the misty face of the moon; then suddenly the moon was gone, and in the place of the eerie half light there was the impenetrable black.

On the instant the dazzling circle of an electric torch appeared full-blown on the wall of the interior. Framed in its light, livid, was the face of a human being—a man caught in a sudden movement of alarm. He had turned his head to look back over his shoulder. An unlit cigarette hung loosely from his lip. The flash held him as rigid as if there were a hidden dagger in its beam that pinned him to the wall. In its revealing glare the imprint of a horse's hoof burned red on his forehead.

"Hold it! Hold it!" drawled an easy voice from the doorway. There was a low chuckle, then a self-satisfied "Aha!" and the lazy tones said: "Jocko, my boy, I always knew that horseshoe would bring you luck!"

The eyes of the other shifted furtively, then held firm again. The hands were clasped before him, not in prayer but around a match he had been about to strike when the flashlight uncovered his image.

"Not so ghostly," chuckled the man with the torch. "I always wondered where you got your cunning. I know now! That mother of yours could deceive the Almighty!"

It was De Groot. He came on softly, one hand aiming the torch, the other swinging at his knee, with something in it.

"We could use her in our business, Jocko," he was saying in a conversational tone. "It's a crime to let native talent like that go to seed. It's a gift. She strung me for a week. But tonight—well, here I am. And you don't seem a bit glad to see me, Jocko!"

Now he was standing over Leander Cotton, gently adjuring him to "Hold it! Hold it!" meaning the unlit match in that attitude of prayer, the while his skilled hands patted Leander for hidden weapons. The search evidently bore fruit, from his low whistle of mock surprise. The circle of light that had danced through the brief scene now took its abrupt departure. De Groot reached out in the dark, hooked up the milking stool on the end of a toe, and drew it over to sit on. As he sank down on it he was playing with a knife, which he jabbed methodically into the floor.

"I suspect Aunt Ivy's told you all about me," mused the suave De Groot. "And at that," he added in a comic aside, "she seems to take to me. I honestly believe if I had a clear field I could adopt her—like I did Mother McNab in Nevada City!"

The darkness was sepulchral. De Groot might have been alone soliloquizing.

"She thinks you are a good boy!" he rambled on. "She's expecting you home almost any time now. By the front door, of course." He chuckled. "It would have been a crime to disturb the dear old lady. I didn't tell her, for instance, that there are a couple of yellow-bellies hiding out down below the village, awaiting a word from me to come in and call on you. I might have told her that they were the brothers of your departed native wife, laboring under a delusion, like herself, that you were bound to show up here almost any time now. Jocko, if you will cry over your little white home in the hills and your sainted mother every time you take a drink, you can't blame us for following you in!"

There was a long pause, during which De Groot played a tattoo on the maple floor with the point of his knife, and whistled softy some dolorous air.

"So you brought Mike and Pedro with you," said Leander quietly.

"No. Not so bad as that," De Groot replied airily. "I saw them headed this way and I decided their instinct was

better than my reason. So I trailed along. I thought I'd
hang around and see the fun." The rogue laughed harshly.
"I had my own little account to settle. If they would be
good enough to settle it for me it would save me the trouble
of soiling my hands."

Softly, without heat or emotion, Leander Cotton delivered a flow of vile invective.

"I didn't kill her, Charlie," he said blandly. "I don't
know why. But I didn't. She just up and died—con-
veniently."

"Well," drawled De Groot, "Mike and Pedro seem to
have a divine revelation to the contrary. Anyway, it's too
late to change the minds of your beloved brothers-in-law
now. They have taken oaths on their machetes. You know
how it is with that breed. The romance of life doesn't begin
until something turns up that calls for revenge. I never
went into their psychology, but I wouldn't be surprised,
Jocko, if deep down in their hearts they are actually grateful to you."

"We seem to be having a nice quiet chat," said Leander
dryly.

"Oh, yes; why should we quarrel—now?"

"You've thrown in with the yellow men—against the
whites—as usual?"

"Well, I had." De Groot drove the knife into the floor
savagely. "Up to nine o'clock tonight I was standing by,
waiting for nature to take its own course." The heavy
breathing of the two men was the sole indication of the
tension in the dark. "Then who should come in on the late
stage," muttered De Groot, "but our old friends, Meeks
and Devore!"

"The dicks!" A guttural curse escaped Leander.

"The dicks. Man may die—but the dicks go on forever!"
There was a long pause.

"That alters the situation a little, doesn't it, Charlie?" There was a note, almost of jubilation, in Leander's tone.

"I ought to cut your throat here in the dark!"

De Groot stabbed again viciously at the floor. Leander laughed softly.

"You haven't the nerve. That's a job you always hire for, Charlie!" he sneered. Heavy silence settled down again.

"One thing is sure, Charlie—if I go back to Guatemala City, you go with me. And you'll sit there, board and found, until even the rats and fleas lose their appetite for you."

De Groot rose suddenly, as if goaded to desperation.

"If they had held off for another twenty-four hours——" he snarled. He broke off suddenly. "Now I've got to take you with me," he muttered. "If that old witch hadn't played me for such a fool your hide would be drying in the sun now."

"Yes, Charlie, you've got to take me with you," said Leander. He rose, yawning and laughing. He threw an arm carelessly about De Groot's shoulders. "I'm your little mascot now, eh, Charlie? We're rats in the same trap, Charlie!"

De Groot broke away from him.

"We're not through yet!" he cried. "You damned squealer! Yes, I've got to take you with me." He turned away abruptly to the door. "The car is in the schoolhouse barn. I'll wait for you below the mill."

"No, you don't!" cried Leander. "We go together!"

"Stand off! I've got the artillery," cried De Groot menacingly. Leander laughed easily.

"You don't know the hill roads," he grunted. "Without me they would have you before sunup!"

De Groot seemed to hang fire over the decision for a moment. Then the pair crept off together in the dark.

Orlo Sage opened his eyes like an animal, and lay listening in the dark. He was trying to determine what had roused him from sleep, when there broke on the stillness of the dawn two quick shots. He sprang out of bed listening. Through five seconds there was silence; then, two more shots, slow and deliberate. He sprang to the window, thrust out his head. Everything was quiet. Up on the Mountain, high behind the Stone House, the dawn had shot its first phosphorescent streamers. He got into his clothes, every movement so stealthy his keen attention was not disturbed by the slightest rustle. He slipped out through the open window and moved down the road. His body was bent forward, every sense was alert. He started and held his breath at what seemed the squeak of an animal. He stood rooted in his tracks, his ear bent, waiting.

Then it came—the telltale sound he expected. It was a hollow rumble. Every minute of the waking day, if one stopped to listen for it here in the valley, one's ears could catch that dull rumble like distant thunder. Now in the night before dawn it was vital. It was an automobile rolling over the loose planks of the sawmill bridge. He waited for the flutter of the motor, but there was not a sound. The constable put two and two together. Everything must have been in readiness. The car had waited on the incline. They could start it with a gentle push downhill, move off without a sound.

Whose car was it? That puzzled him. None of the cars that belonged in the valley, nor either of the two the surveyors used. He could have identified them with his keen ears a mile off by the beat of their motors.

Motionless, he continued to listen. A second rumbling sound of thunder should have come from the passage of the red bridge below. There was none. It was a plain trail to the still-hunter. The car had not gone down on the main road that led out of the valley to the south. There was only one possible turn. Up Beech Plain Hill! He dashed madly back to the house. He seized the telephone receiver and pumped it patiently. Finally he got a response out of the dead of night.

"Thirteen, sister! Ring! Ring! Ring! Ring it! Sit on it! It's murder! Keep at it! I hold the wire!"

The town constable arranged himself comfortably, and now without irritation waited, a smile on his face. There might be a dead man lying out there in the dawn, not a hundred yards from the house. Undoubtedly. There was a grim finality about those last two shots, as if they had been put in, not because they were needed but for some ironic good measure. Some blundering fool was priding himself on the neatness of his plan, and he had taken the one road in the neighborhood where escape was utterly impossible. The Beech Plain road was a one-horse driving track. It led towards Tyringham, where it encountered the state highway. There were no turn-offs for five miles, except here and there a log road that no automobile made could negotiate. If he was a judge—and he was a good one—that car was a heavy one—an engine that ran like silk—probably a long body that wanted all outdoors to turn in—it would go far in the bogs of a wood road! Whatever it was, it was weaving a trail behind as plain as a hangman's rope.

Occasionally Orlo would speak to the night operator and hearten her. Stephen Whitman lived in the only house on the plain that boasted a telephone. Whitman had cut his own poles and strung his own wire for the boom, a fact on which the complacent Orlo now mused with satisfaction. Suddenly he cocked an ear, put his mouth to the transmitter.

"Hello, Steve! Listen! Let me do the talking! Car coming! Stop it! Say, Steve, is that stack of ties still decorating your dooryard? Good! You might accidentally drop a couple of them across the wheel track—then lay back and wait—with your gun! Ain't you skeered about it?" He chuckled.

He waited for no response. He hung up and finished his dressing without haste. He took down his holster and strapped it on, as became his office, and calling into the next room "Oh, Minnie! I'm going out," he stepped outside.

Down by the schoolhouse he came on a shadowy group that broke up as he approached and ran toward him. Jason and gran'ther, Horace Benson, Homer Twining, Angus Weeks—these and a dozen others were there, coming in like crows from the valley and hills.

"They made a clean get-away!" bellowed Benson. "They must have taken to the timber. Nobody heard them go out."

"Didn't they?" drawled Orlo contentedly. "What did they leave behind?"

The dead man lay in the old shed. The face had been completely shot away. A dozen lanterns illuminated the ghastly find. A babble of voices demanded "Who is it? Who is it?" De Groot came running up. He had drawn his breeches on, over his pajamas, and hadn't taken time to put on his putties, with which the village had always associated him. He stared down at the body, his lips curling back as with instinctive disgust at the horrible sight. He turned his fierce eyes on the circle of faces that looked up questioningly to him, and he, too, asked, "Who is it?"

"We don't know. Isn't it one of your men?" asked Orlo.

De Groot stooped over and pawed at the clothing as if trying to find identity in some patch or shred. But he shook his head; it was none of his crew. Indeed, as he spoke, his four men ran up with excited questions.

"Probably thrown out of some car passing through," said De Groot. "Did anyone hear a car go by?"

Apparently no one had. This seemed the obvious explanation. They brought horse blankets and a stretcher, and the party moved off slowly down the hill to the village, gaining numbers as it progressed. Jason, straggling behind, asked Aaron Beddes, the stagedriver, who the two passengers were he brought up on the late trip last night. Beddes said he had come alone on the last trip. No strangers had arrived during the day. No Meeks, no Devore! Jason found himself looking into the watery eye of old gran'ther. They moved on in silence. The stretcher stopped beside the post office, and the village clustered about it like a swarm of bees on a bent limb. The sun was just showing above the Stone House high up on the Mountain when Stephen Whitman telephoned Orlo.

"Got 'em," reported the dependable Stephen laconically.

"What do they look like?"

"Not so much," mused Stephen.

The car had been running without lights and had broken its wishbone against the nest of railroad ties the forehanded Whitman had planted in the wheel track. The two passengers had dismounted through the windshield, and there had been little for Whitman to do but pick up the badly shaken pair like meal bags and deposit them safe and sound behind lock and key in his strong woodhouse.

"They are yellow men—greasers," muttered Orlo to Jason as he hung up the wire. A gentle pressure of Jason's fingers on his arm shut him up, wondering. Jason looked for De Groot, but the big surveyor had gone in to dress; he was taking the early stage to run in to the city for the day.

"Anyway, it's none of our funeral," commented Jason. "I'd turn the body over to the county. Let them worry over it. We can't identify it."

A meeting of the elders had already come to this conclusion. The responsibility of an anonymous crime did not rest on the shoulders of the village. Aunt Ivy, punctual to the minute on her day's work, was coming down the red-shop hill, bucket on arm, when at eight o'clock the little truck moved off towards Barrington with its burden starkly apparent under horse blankets. Orlo would follow later and pick up the two prisoners.

Jason took Orlo's arm, and together they strolled through the hotel to De Groot's room.

"Let me do the talking," Jason whispered as they were about to enter. De Groot was shaving at a mirror; his things were scattered around and a suitcase lay open on the bed. Jason and Orlo took chairs with an assumption of easy privilege.

"Well, what do you make of it?" asked De Groot casually.

It was Jason who answered him.

"Rabbit drive," said he curtly. "I know who the rabbit is," he added. He dropped the name like a bombshell: "Leander Cotton!"

De Groot's head pivoted on his bull neck, the features frozen in a moment of swift intensity.

Orlo half rose, but fell back.

"Leander Cotton?" said Orlo. "Why, Leander's been dead for ten years—drowned with his father."

"No," said Jason. "He hasn't. Maybe for ten minutes or so. But not for ten years." He fixed all his attention on Orlo, while De Groot in the mirror kept watch of both faces. "Orlo," said Jason, "Leander Cotton has been hiding out at the old Seymour place for the last six weeks." His pose was perfect. "Aunt Ivy's been feeding him—carrying him his food after midnight, every night," continued Jason with the air of saying nothing extraordinary. "Aunt Ivy wasn't as crazy as we all thought her, you see, Orlo."

"But where did he come from?" cried Orlo, all at sea.

"I dunno," mused Jason. "I expect Guatemala—or some place like that." His eye wandered to the looking-glass. De Groot had stopped shaving. He was mopping his face with a towel.

"But what was he hiding from?" persisted Orlo, who had forgotten De Groot.

"Retribution, I guess," said Jason slowly. "An all-round bad egg! 'Spect he didn't have no other place to hide, so he come up here, wished himself on poor Aunt Ivy."

Orlo rose in disgust.

"Rot!" he exclaimed. "I don't believe it!"

"It's true, Orlo," protested Jason mildly. He turned his calm gaze on the mirror again and met the eyes of De Groot. In a sneering drawl he added, "It is true, isn't it—Charlie?"

The mimicry of the accents of the sneering Leander was a bit of pure realism. A snarl as of an animal escaped De Groot.

"Don't pull your knife!" cried Jason, tense in his chair. "You haven't the nerve to use it, anyway. That's a job you always hire for!"

In a single step De Groot was at the door. There was nothing between him and freedom. And then, quietly gran'ther stepped out of the shadow and halted him in his tracks. It was only a feeble little old man shaking with palsy, but something in his eye, and something held in one hand in a ragged pocket as he advanced, made De Groot retreat before him, backing into the room step by step.

"Well, I'm damned!" swore Orlo, coming to his senses at last; he slipped an arm through De Groot's two elbows, pinioning him, and quickly went through him for weapons.

"Hush!" cautioned Jason. Through the open window he could see a group of women, Aunt Ivy among them, whispering, heads together. "Shut that window! Lock the door!"

De Groot slumped into a chair.

"We've got Pedro and Miguel!" said Jason.

De Groot burst out passionately: "It was their vendetta—not mine! He killed their sister! They followed him up here! My hands are clean!"

"You planted them up here! You drove him into their ambush like a rabbit!" snarled Jason. "What did he ever do to you——"

The question was never finished. There came excited cries for Orlo from outside. Someone ran along the hall and pounded at the door.

"Orlo! Orlo! Whitman is telephoning!"

"Well? Well?" demanded Orlo, thrusting his head out.

"The two greasers tried to kill themselves in the woodshed. Slashed their own wrists. He wants you—and the doctor—quick!"

Orlo stepped outside. "Find Doc Cudworth," he commanded. "I'm busy now. I'll be along directly." And he returned.

He encountered a changed De Groot. The big surveyor had risen to his feet. Something of his braggart assurance had returned. A nasty grin was on his face, his eyes shone with an unholy light.

"I knew it! I knew it!" he was crying exultantly. "I knew you couldn't hold them alive! Their revenge is too sacred to them! They wouldn't answer to your damned law!" He turned to Jason. "What have you got on me now?" he cried. "Out of my way!"

He strode forward menacingly. It was quite like the old De Groot. But Jason stood his ground and De Groot paused, eye to eye.

"What have we got on you now?" drawled Jason.

"Meeks, and Devore!" he cried point-blank. "Oh, you are going back to Guatemala, Charlie. And you are going to sit there—and sit there—till even the rats and fleas lose their appetite for you!"

For the second time the astonished Orlo saw the gigantic De Groot crumple before a word from Jason.

"I don't get this at all," he said crustily.

"Meeks and Devore are dicks," said Jason. "This miserable skunk drove Leander into ambush this morning with the tale that the dicks were on his heels." He faced De Groot again. "They are on your heels, Charlie! I've wired New York for them!"

"No—no," murmured De Groot. "Anything—I'll do anything——"

"Stand trial for procuring the murder of Leander Cotton?" demanded Jason huskily. And he answered the question himself:

"No, you will not! Outside of this room Leander Cotton died ten years ago! We don't want him identified as a cutthroat pal of yours. Aunt Ivy has had enough on her poor old shoulders. She will never know if I can help it."

Half an hour later Orlo and Jason, with gran'ther standing by for an emergency, spirited the limp De Groot out of a back door into a closed car and took him to town. That evening two elated detectives, Meeks and Devore, with De Groot manacled between them, put him aboard the New York train, en route to Guatemala. Yes, they wanted him, a little more than usual. He and his side partner, one Horseshoe Jack, had knifed one of their fellow operatives who had been sent into Guatemala to bring the pair to the States on extradition for forgery. Had Jason and Orlo by any chance seen such a man—with a horseshoe on his forehead? No? Well, the two rogues had probably parted company—

there was a story that they had quarreled over some woman.

Gran'ther Seymour lingered over his carving, through the hot days of July, on into August. Attaining perfection, he must yet improve it. The legend complete, all save that final grim numeral, that must be carved by other hands than his, the old man must add a spray of laurel, and he labored over the outlines lovingly. Sitting there among the silent graves of his people, he wore the sod smooth under his heavy shoes, chipping and blowing and squinting and smiling. Jason used to stop on his way by, and visit with the old man in silence. Aunt Ivy, bucket on arm, coming home from the day's work, discovered him late one afternoon, and sat with him, resting, until the light was too far gone to work. It had long been said that Aunt Ivy and Noah should have married in their youth.

Again and again she paused to rest by gran'ther and his endless task. Occasionally he would spell his old eyes, and sit with one knee coddled in his clasped hands.

Aunt Ivy said that the time was now at hand when she must prepare a stone for herself, and would gran'ther carve it for her, with a sprig of laurel over the inscription, just like his? And she would like a stone for her son, too, one like his father's. Leander was dead. Gran'ther nodded in sympathy over this news, just as always he had smiled and patted Aunt Ivy on the hand when she told him that she was expecting Leander almost any time now.

So once more the cavalcade of oxen straining at the bows, the stone boat with its gear, Jason at the head with crackling whip, and old gran'ther fetching up behind with the crowbar, toiled up the hill, over to the homestead. Once more they chalked off a chosen square in the ample stepstone and drilled and wedged with the nicety of an art that was about to die in the person of its last votary. Before the snow flew that winter Aunt Ivy had gone to rest, and gran'ther, with Jason for silent company, carved the grim numeral on her headstone. Leander's stone bore no other inscription than his name in Roman letters.

V

THE MAGICIAN

SHORTLY before midnight, when all the lights on the hillsides were out, except Aunt Ivy's high up on the mountain, a flivver mistook the turn at the bridge and rolled into Jason's yard on his new stone driveway. Its loose-jointed rattle ceased abruptly as it hit the good going; and the driver gave the beast its head, thinking, no doubt, in a sleep-muddled way, that he had run into luck after miles of ruts and bog holes. The car spurted at a lively pace past the dark house looming in the night, past the chicken coop, awakening a few witless biddies to uneasy clucking. Then suddenly it came to a stuttering stop, like a sleepwalker who awakes to find himself on the brink of a chasm. Jason had run out of road-building material at the barnyard bar-way; and here his road disappeared, like a sunken river, under green sod clipped to a velvety smoothness by the dry cows, which had the habit of hanging around in mournful silence outside the barn night and morning while their fresh sisters were having their udders emptied inside.

Old Shep, the cow dog, lurking in the shadows, was the only one to see what was going on. This thing had happened before and would happen again. The fellow would back out, with some murky soliloquizing, and pick up the lost thread of the public highway. But, instead, this particular fellow got down to reconnoiter. He ascertained beyond a doubt that his headlights were in the act of kissing a substantial bar of soft maple, peeled. He crawled through

the barricade, squirting a little flashlight ahead. He moved
forward on the springy turf. He paused and looked aloft.
It was a clear night. Andromeda, the chained lady of the
heavens, was wheeling overhead in the dusty sky, poising
for her nose dive into the west. A larch stirred; a poplar
fluttered; a group of timid hemlocks huddled close together
on the river bank. Near by in the dark there was a horse
picking grass; the creature paused, probably to inspect the
newcomer, and then resumed with utter indifference. There
were subdued giggles—ah! water playing among little
stones. Some one, or thing, was sneezing at regular intervals under the bank, like a hayfever addict—probably a
hydraulic ram, dutifully punching thimblefuls of water up
an unseen hill.

The driver reached back through the bars and shut off
his spark; and the grateful engine, closing its headlight
eyes dreamily, subsided with a death rattle, giving up the
ghost. Having nothing on his mind, the fellow draped himself on the bars and whistled *sotto voce* a mournful air.

Then he seemed to suspect that he might not be unobserved, for he spoke in a low, enticing tone: "Come out
here, fellow!"

He clucked his tongue against his teeth and snapped a
finger. And poor Shep, creature of impulse that he was,
came trotting out of his hiding place, a little ashamed of
himself for being taken in by so simple a trick, but, still,
wagging his feathered tail.

"I knew you were there!" chuckled the driver. "Even
if you didn't bark. Dogs don't bark at me." His fingers
were exploring Shep's head. "I don't know why—neither
do they!"

Shep stood up and planted his forepaws on the man's
shoulders; and he nestled against him while the fellow dexterously scratched his right ear. Now old Doll, the emeri-

tus driving mare, with a crease in her back, and sides fat enough to rub shafts, came over and joined them. She placed herself alongside, and with a languorous droop on all quarters she assumed the attitude of true love, asking nothing, expecting nothing, only propinquity. The man filled his pipe and began to smoke.

"I'll stop for the night, if it's all right," said he. "This is the best bunch of pals I've seen for a long time!" He hummed dolorously, some song of a cave man before the world got so crowded; meantime he intelligently pursued an imaginary flea under the shell of Shep's right ear.

Now abruptly Shep lifted his head and cocked an ear, his body rigid. He dropped on all fours noiselessly and pressed against the man's legs, listening. The stranger turned. He saw nothing at first. Then he caught the light of a lantern; its beams came dancing to him over the shallows of the river. Then another lantern; a third; then a fourth. The lanterns came on slowly. They came abreast, four men, wading slowly upstream, examining the bottom foot by foot by the light of their lanterns.

"Spearing eels!" muttered the watcher. Shep stirred impatiently as if to enjoin silence. There was a crash as a steel spear descended.

"D'you get 'em?" rumbled a disembodied lantern. Unintelligible mumblings bubbled in the thick dark. Then a curse, audible and awful in the stillness. The water seemed suddenly to boil up from the bed of the river.

"Blank gast him! He got away! There—— Damn him, where is he?" An interval of silence. The lanterns clustered together, as of men searching. "Must have weighed seven pound!" wailed a lantern. "Twisted it right out of my two hands!" Finally, "Come on!" commanded a voice. "You can find it tomorrow. I got an extra spear, only it's got one tine gone."

Shep growled, a mere whisper deep in his throat.

"Someone you don't cotton to?" asked his new friend.

No answer.

The lanterns spaced themselves across the river bed again, began to move; they disappeared behind the island.

The flivver tramp got out a sleeping bag from the pantry end of his car and, guided by Shep, looked for a soft place to sleep. There was a velvety knoll by the cove where the cattle drank, and he spread out his bag and crawled in, Shep settling down beside him. Shortly Doll heaved alongside; and after thinking it over for some time she laboriously lay down and drooped her head dejectedly, to dream of the prehistoric days when she had five toes to each foot. Andromeda began her dive into the west with ladylike decorum. Soon the smoky pigeons of the Pleiades came flying over the rim of Pray's Hill, fleeing before Orion, the mighty hunter with glittering sword at his belt. Morning began to paint the looming sky line. Somewhere a flivver rattled and popped; the loose planks of the bridge rumbled; the lid of the mail box in front of Jason's gate clanked—it was Babe, the mail-stage driver, on her early trip to town. This was Shep's alarm clock. He rose and made the rounds of the fortifications. Finding everything trig, he made for the house just as the chickens were hopping down from their perches with squeaky wings and silly laughter. In the bedroom Shep surveyed the cherubic countenance of his beloved master for a single moment, then deftly touched it on the nose with his own cold muzzle. Jason fought off imaginary flies. It took several applications before he swung out of bed, tousled and blear-eyed. He mumbled, by rote: "Time for the cows, Sheppie!"

Shep was off like a shot. He raced up the lane by the sap house, through the short cut to the night pasture. Except for a slight demonstration against a chipmunk on a rock,

Shep had an eye single to business. He perched himself on a big boulder, with red tongue lolling. The herd saw him after pretending not to; they filed slowly past him to be counted; he took up his station behind the last swinging tail. Rosa, the leader, paused at sight of the sleeping bag by the cove, but Shep started her again—that fellow was all right! The milkers wheeled into the barn and nosed their heads into the ties and looked expectant. A dry heifer dared to enter, but Shep sent her about her business—he had his orders! He nipped Clytie on a tender hock with a remark that plainly said, "That ain't your place, you old fool, and you know it!" and the shameless Clytie backed out and put herself where she belonged. When all was correct Shep went back to the sleeping bag, which had now awakened and was starting an alcohol stove for breakfast. While the water was boiling he shaved, against a mirror on a gatepost.

Jason, a nest of buckets on one arm and rubbing the sleep out of his eyes, paused, astonished at sight of the flivver. He moved on to the cove.

"Hello!" said the stranger, eying his chin critically in the mirror.

"Who let you in?" demanded Jason, with early morning crustiness.

The man grinned. He indicated Shep, who wagged his tail.

"This fellow said it would be all right," he said. "Have a cup of coffee?" he invited. He dropped a slice of bacon into a sizzling little creeper; the odor smote Jason's nostrils with a blow that famished him. Jason set down his buckets and himself and drew his feet up under him comfortably. The man wasn't a bum; his clothes were too good, and he was clean, and he had a good square head, well barbered. Jason watched him get breakfast, fascinated. He had never been so hungry before in his life. When the cook passed him a wooden pie plate, decorated with an egg, sunny side smiling up at the morning, nestling in a neat ruff of curly crisp bacon, it was worthy of the black art. Jason grinned his delight. Well, Shep was completely sold—that was a good sign. Shep drew a hot dog—too hot; Shep worried it in the grass like a mouse, and then sat down and barked at it.

"My name is Roddy," said the cook.

"Mine's Jason."

"Nice little river you've got here!"

Jason admitted as much over the rim of his coffee.

"Much fall?"

"Six hundred feet in six miles!"

"How much water?"

"A hundred and fifty second-feet!"

"What! And you are farming for a living?" This man understood many things besides bacon and coffee.

"It's a long story," said Jason; and wiping his mouth on the back of his hand he arose and picked up his buckets.

Roddy cleared up his dishes; in five minutes all signs of the feast were erased. He came into the barn, singing softly to himself, Shep now completely his slave, alongside; he paused, listening to the pleasant voices of the byre—the cows nosing their millet and munching it luxuriously as they stretched their necks; the soft tinkle of the ties; the padded patter of their little feet as they moved about; and above it all, the rhythmic flow of milk in the foaming pail.

Jason watched him around the rump of old Rosa. Roddy picked up a pail and moved down the line. He selected a creature to his liking, drew up his stool, and sat down, pail resting on his shin bones. Jason chuckled to himself. He listened, pretending not to notice anything that was going on. There were some few preliminaries on the part of the volunteer hand, and then zim, zim, zim—streams of milk suddenly pelted the bucket bottom; its timbre changed to a deeper zoom, zoom; then to a zud, zud, as the foam rose. Jason half turned on his stool.

"How do you like her?" he asked.

"A bit snug," said the milker, his head against Flora's flank.

"Snug?" Jason roared with laughter. "Snug?" he cried, delighted, getting up with his filled bucket. "Tight, I call her. Why, man, there isn't one chore boy in ten that can wet the bottom of a bucket with her!" He picked up a fresh bucket and moved over a step. "Do you want a job?" he asked.

Roddy considered this, changing quarters.

"I might stick around for a day or two," he said. He was finishing Flora, with one last two-handed pull on each quarter. No need to strip her—Flora was a hundred-dollar cow this morning.

"What's your line?" asked Jason casually.

"Well, I do a little jit hopping in summer," said the other.

This was too cryptic for Jason, and he gave himself to his chore. Roddy started the black heifer with a fresh pail. Shep was torn between two loves. Usually he moved from cow to cow with Jason, keeping his eye on everything in his province the while; now he squatted between the two, eying them impartially. The milk flowed in singing streams and the air picked up the perfume of it. Jason found himself on his mettle.

A shadow darkened the doorway. It was Orlo Sage.

" 'Lo, Orlo!"

" 'Lo!" said Orlo. He had been up since two. He leaned against the door post, lazily attentive to the scene. He surveyed Roddy as he came out for another bucket, nodding to him as if he had known him all his life; and Roddy, not to be outdone, said laconically " 'Lo!"

"You got a new man, Jason?" asked Orlo.

"Yep."

"Where'd he come from?"

"Dunno."

"Who is he?"

"Dunno. He can make a cow talk!"

Tommy, the black barn cat, appeared and gently pricked Jason's knee as a reminder. Jason directed a strong stream of milk down the red gullet. Tommy held up one paw, seeming to say "That's right, hold it!" Orlo yawned. He caught Jason's eye and moved away, and Jason got up and followed him, wondering. Orlo stopped by the tin lizzie at the barway and examined it carefully, especially the tires.

He and Jason talked in low tones. Jason returned to the chore and found it finished.

"Want me to turn the cows out?" asked Roddy.

Shep stepped up at the magic word "cows"—this was his cue. Bringing in the cows and taking them out were the high spots of the day for him.

"Sit down a bit—we want to visit," said Jason; and the three sat down in the doorway.

General Konchakoff, the premier rooster of the flock, iridescent in the morning light and strutting like a dandy, stepped up to inspect the gathering. The great bird permitted Roddy to pick it up without a flutter. He carefully set it down on its feet on the floor and pressed its head forward until its beak almost touched a crack. Then he released it gently. To the amazement of Orlo and Jason, the bird remained motionless, as if frozen in this posture, staring fascinated at the crack. Ten seconds passed.

"Gosh!" ejaculated Orlo. "What do you call that—hypnotism?"

"Some folks do, but it isn't," laughed Roddy. With a

sleight-of-hand movement he captured Admiral Tom
Thumb, the game cock, who was craning its neck at the
spectacle. Roddy passed Tom Thumb to Orlo. "Try it," he
said. "It's simple enough."

Doubting, Orlo tried it. The game cock stood petrified,
staring cross-eyed at its crack, like the gaudy General
Konchakoff.

"Well, I'll be squitched!" muttered Orlo.

Roddy brushed the two birds aside, and they rushed off
with wild cries as if they had just been released from the
clutches of their personal devil.

"Nothing queer about it," said Roddy. "Lead a woman
up to a new hat in a show window, and she does the same
thing."

He was lighting his pipe, and drawing the first puffs he
turned to Shep and resumed his quest for the imaginary
flea.

There was a pause. Jason was leaning forward, staring
absently at a straw he was tearing to bits between his
fingers. Orlo was filling his pipe slowly.

"What time did you get in last night?" he asked, as he
tamped the tobacco deliberately.

"About midnight. I mistook the road here at the gate or
I would have been over the state line this morning, instead
of sitting here letting the milk get cold."

"Were you aiming to get over the state line last night?"
asked Orlo.

Jason's fingers mechanically ceased their activity.

"I calculated to. I thought I'd run through to Winsted
before I'd call it a day." Roddy's eyes met Orlo's squarely.
"But I met Shep." Shep thumped his tail. "We seemed to
hit it off pretty well—and here we are."

"Which way did you come?"

Roddy turned and pointed up the valley.

"I ran into a detour above here—just below Ellis," he said. "Awful! Rocks—windfalls—mud! Look at my car!"

"I've looked at it," said Orlo. He glanced up quickly. "That detour has been abandoned. They let us through on the state job three weeks ago. Was it dark?" he asked. There was a snap to the words.

"In the woods, yes," said Roddy. "But the sky was bright enough. It was a fine clear night."

"Did you happen to notice an old log bridge near the outlet of the reservoir?"

Roddy nodded. He turned and waited.

"You stopped there, didn't you?" pursued the questioner.

"How do you know?" There was no challenge in the tone, curiosity perhaps. Jason shifted uneasily.

"I saw your wheel marks," said Orlo. "Did you get out?"

"Yes, I got down," said Roddy. "You probably saw my foot prints, too, didn't you?" he asked. "I walked over to the bridge."

"And onto it?"

Jason might have been General Konchakoff, for his rigidity.

"Yes."

"What for?"

Roddy stared at him for a moment, a strange far-away look creeping into his eyes.

"There was something on the other end of that bridge," he said, dragging his words out. "I couldn't just make it out. It was alive, because I saw it move. I thought it might be deer. But it wasn't. I stopped and watched for—well, say five minutes. The light was very deceptive—the woods stand in so close." He paused. "I got down and went over to it. It was a team of cattle, Devons," Roddy said, eying Orlo again. "They were yoked. Hitched to a stone boat.

There was a crowbar, and a sledge—and some log chains—
and—and a cant hook on the boat." He ticked off the items
slowly on his finger tips. Orlo nodded, his heavy brows
meeting above his eyes in a frown. "The cattle had been
there a long time," went on Roddy's even voice. "They
were lying down." Jason shot a look at Orlo. "I thought
it damnably odd—that hour of the night," went on Roddy,
still possessed with the weirdness of that picture. "There
wasn't a house I remembered within a mile. I let out a
yell! Nobody answered. Finally I came away. I've been
worrying about it all night," he said. "I was going back
there this morning."

"Did you look in the water?" asked Orlo.

"Yes."

"Did you see anything?"

Roddy shook his head.

"No," he said. "It was too dark. Inky, down under there.
I only had a little flashlight." He had the air of a man
without nerves waiting for a thunderclap. "Should I have
seen something?" he asked slowly.

Orlo took one knee in his clasped hands; he pulled several puffs at his pipe before answering. Jason seemed to
be holding his breath, to have forgotten to breathe.

"There was a dead man down there," said Orlo. "His
feet were sticking out of the water. His head was wedged
tight between two stones." He pressed his two powerful
hands against his head to illustrate his meaning.

"Under water?"

"Yes."

"Curious," said Roddy. "I dreamed there was a man in
the water. That's why I was going back. I suppose a dozen
people have passed by this time, though."

"Ordinarily, no," said Orlo. "That detour got so bad that
the state people let us through on the new construction.

But the sign is still up—that's what sent you wrong. About the only one that used it was Johnny Boag." He was watching Roddy as he pronounced this name; but the name seemed to mean nothing to the man who faced him. "Ed Peters went up there last night after supper to get an old tube from the sawmill," he said, "and he saw the cattle on the bridge then. He knew Johnny had been repairing his dam, and he didn't think anything queer about it. Johnny is the dead man," he explained, eying Roddy again. Roddy nodded. "Ed and his brothers were eeling last night," went on Orlo. "They got up there about one o'clock—just after you came through, according to your tell. The cattle were still there. They found Johnny in the water. It looked as if the cattle had pushed him off the bridge—fighting flies or something. And he had fallen head first and been pinned between those two rocks. There wan't enough water to drown a cat. It was them rocks that held him. Must have been stunned."

Orlo paused and smoked absently. An observer would have detected no tension in the group—Roddy listening quietly; Jason resting his elbows on his knees, idly tearing at the straw again; and Orlo, for the moment, intent on a crazy kingfisher under the river bank.

"The Peters boys looked around with their lanterns," resumed Orlo. "They found your heel tracks on the bridge." There was a barely perceptible tightening of the action. "Rubber heels," said Orlo; "with cups in them." He looked down at Roddy's shoes. "Then they began to wonder if it was an accident. They came down and roused me up."

He stopped abruptly.

"You are the sheriff?" said Roddy, half question, half statement of fact.

"The constable—yes."

"You trailed me here by my wheel tracks?"

"Yes."

"Good work!"

"Rot!" exclaimed Jason, springing to his feet; he was completely sold on Roddy—more so now than he had been over the bacon and eggs, or even snug Flora. "This man didn't have any more to do with it than——"

"It isn't rot!" exclaimed Roddy. "It's nice work! Sit down, Jason," he commanded; and he drew Jason down again. "Johnny Boag either jumped or was thrown over that rail."

"He didn't jump," said Orlo quietly.

"All right—then he was thrown. I was there just before the body was found. You've got my heel tracks and my wheel tracks to show for it. That's not rot, Jason, by a long shot."

"It was the cattle!" cried Jason. "Johnny was always filled up to the neck with cider. He was a rotten sort, anyway. He put a charge of birdshot into Shep once!"

"No. It wasn't the cattle," said Roddy. "It couldn't have been. That rail wasn't broken—he couldn't have fallen through."

Orlo turned slowly, his mouth falling open.

"It wasn't broken?" he repeated, almost in a whisper. "Are you sure?"

"Absolutely. I worked my way along it. I was holding on, because I was afraid of the cattle getting up and pinching me against it. A team of cattle is pretty clumsy getting up, yoked."

"It was broken when I got there," said Orlo. He lowered his voice again instinctively. "It had been smashed with a sledge!" he said.

There was a long tense silence. It was Jason who broke it. He cried again impetuously, "I tell you, Orlo, this man had nothing to do with it! Johnny was selling apple-jack —dealing with all sorts of thugs. He had a lot of cash around all the time."

"Wait a minute, son," interposed Roddy. "This thing is pretty. Let's keep cool. Let's eliminate without prejudice. Thanks for clearing me without a trial," he said with a queer smile at Orlo, "but just remember that confidence is the stock in trade of crooks. Don't bank on confidence." He turned sharply to Orlo.

"You aren't so sure that I didn't throw Johnny over that rail—and then smash the rail—to put it on the cattle—are you?"

"No. You didn't do it," said Orlo. "Johnny weighed a hundred and eighty."

"You don't believe I can throw a hundred-and-eighty-pound man over my head?" Roddy's question was casual.

"No," replied the verbally thrifty Orlo.

"Well, let's separate the milk, so we can go up there," suggested Roddy. "Your hogs are getting querulous, Jason," he said.

He got up and started the separator. The opening whine of the gears fetched a peal of thanksgiving from the porcine group crowding about the skim milk trough. They turned out the cattle; and Shep, first counting them and getting them into line, started off to the back pasture. The last pail of milk had gone through the skimming when Shep came bounding back. He reported in person to Roddy.

"You know when I thought Orlo had come for you," confessed Jason, "it was Shep who told me Orlo was on the wrong track. I don't know how he happened to let you in last night!"

Roddy laughed.

"Now you are talking about something entirely different," he said. "The best one-man dog I ever knew belonged to a cut-throat. Don't bank too much on Shep's snap judgment." Shep looked conscious. "He doesn't answer for me to the world—he answers for me to himself." His hand fell softly on the upturned head.

Orlo was looking out the barn door. There was the sound of a flivver coming to a stop in the dooryard, with a sudden snort.

"Ed Peters and his brothers," said Orlo. He smiled. "I guess they think I need help handling you, Roddy."

There were three of them, of a size, six-foot men, with blond curls and round thick necks that bulged under their collar bands. They halted to look over Roddy's flivver at the barway.

One of them seeing Orlo regarding them said quickly "Come on," to his brothers, and they started, with a sense of haste to get away from something that their curiosity impelled them to examine.

"Which one is Ed?" asked Roddy.

"The one with the blue shirt," said Jason. "Wait—watch this! It'll be good!"

What "this" was, was immediately to transpire. Jason's black Tom, the barn cat, was dancing across the velvety turf, shadow-boxing a bit of thistledown floating on the light air. The man in the blue shirt stopped short in his tracks, his eyes on the cat. A sudden fear distorted his unshaven features.

"Scat! Scat!" he cried, his voice husky with terror. He dashed at the creature, kicking at it viciously; but the nimble Tom bounded away like a streak.

"He hates black cats," explained Jason, chuckling. "I guess he was marked for them—leastwise he'd sooner take a licking than have one cross his path."

The three stalwart brothers came on. At sight of Roddy

they stiffened perceptibly. They went to Orlo, who had seated himself in the doorway again.

"I see you got him," said Ed in a low tone to Orlo, while his brothers bestowed glassy stares on the stranger. "Want any help?"

Orlo shook his head.

There was an awkward pause; and Jason, to bridge it over, said, indicating Roddy, "This is my new hard man," by way of introduction, and using the local "hard" for "hired." "He blew in this morning looking for a job, and I tried him out on that trick cow you sold me last spring, Ed. He's all right!" exclaimed Jason, and he patted Roddy on the back. "Roddy, shake hands with Ed, Jim and Joe Peters. They are the biggest men in town. There ain't five pounds to give and take among them. These are the three that found Johnny Boag up the river last night."

Roddy offered his hand, and Ed was the first to take it. The big fellow put his great strength into the grip and stared malignantly down on the smaller man. He didn't release his viselike hold.

"You came down the river road last night," said Ed darkly, his fierce eyes gleaming under his ragged brows.

"Don't damage that hand—that's a good milking hand," laughed Jason, and he reached between the two men and broke their grip. "Ed tries that grip on every stranger," he said. "He thinks he can lick any man he can crunch."

The two combatants of the grip didn't take their eyes from each other. So intense was their gaze that it seemed momentarily they would spring at each other's throats.

"Yes," said Roddy. "I was up the river last night, Ed. About midnight." They continued to stare at each other.

"Ed!" cautioned Orlo in a low tone; and Ed, with a sneer, turned away.

Roddy turned to the second brother. For an instant they

stood as if galvanized; then their right hands gripped each other with a movement as swift as a snake's thrust. A straining of biceps, then Jim, his face wrinkled with pain, went down on his knees. Roddy released him.

"I can lick you," laughed Roddy.

"You got the jump on me!" cried Jim in a rage. "Try it again."

Roddy shook his head and went on to the third brother. Joe turned away and spat contemptuously as he put his own horny right hand into a pocket.

"You're mighty fresh for a man that's left his tracks all over the town!" Ed was bursting out, turning fiercely on Roddy, when Orlo's quiet voice again interposed "Ed!" and Ed subsided, sitting down by Orlo, but with dark looks at Roddy.

They all ranged themselves in the broad doorway. Another awkward silence, and this time Jason made no attempt to ease the tension.

Ed leaned toward Orlo and asked out of the corner of his mouth, "You going to take him to Barrington, Orlo?"

Orlo nodded assent.

"Want I should come along?"

Orlo shook his head.

"I don't reckon I need any help handling him," he said modestly.

There was silence again. Jim, the second brother, broke it this time; as usual with these people when something important impends, he felt it necessary to make talk on trivialities.

"Jim Benson says Scotty O'Brien sold his place," he said.

"Go on!" said Orlo, with stark disbelief.

"Yep. City people," said Jim.

"No?" insisted Orlo.

"Yep. He had 'em out yesterday; he gave 'em a meal in his kitchen."

"Give city folks a meal! In his kitchen!" Orlo guffawed. "Why, I wouldn't eat there myself!"

The three brothers and Orlo and Jason fell excitedly to discussing the unthinkable occurrence, as if it were much more important than the fact that they had a murder on their hands with the three brothers standing by to help take the suspect to Barrington.

General Konchakoff, the Rhode Island rooster, came strutting across the grass and paused within a few paces of the multitude, his head cocked on one side. The general, too, was politely incredulous. He took one step forward— two—three; cocked his head on the other side. Roddy, with a movement of one arm that had neither haste nor delay, reached out and took up the general. The bird made no protest. Roddy set it firmly on its feet on the floor and gently bent its head forward till its beak almost touched the crack. Then he gently released the general. As he drew away his hands this time he made smooth little passes in the air, as if he were propelling some mystic force from his finger tips to overpower the bird. The general stared, squatting, at the crack.

"Sleep! Sleep!" whispered Roddy softly; and still projecting his psychic force through the tips of his fingers at the stricken bird, he rose in his tracks without a rustle. The entire assemblage did likewise. The brothers were staring, wild-eyed. Jason and Orlo looked at each other curiously but made no sign that they had seen this trick before. The two younger Peters boys backed away, open-mouthed with awe at this legerdemain. Ed held his ground for the moment, but beads of sweat showed on his forehead. This was witchcraft! This was worse than a black cat. He lifted one ponderous foot slowly to take the first step to put a more comfortable distance between himself and the magician. He stared from the man to the rigid bird.

Roddy turned suddenly on him, looked him hard in the eye.

"Don't move! I want you, Ed," he said in a low enticing tone. And he thrust his head forward, staring fixedly into the spellbound eyes of Ed Peters; and he made gentle passes through the air.

"Sleep! Sleep!" commanded Roddy. "You are going to tell us all about it, Ed!"

Orlo looked from one to the other in amazement. With a scream choked in his throat, half terror, half rage, Ed plunged forward. He was as quick as a cat, for all his bulk. He seemed to cover the ten feet that separated him from Roddy with a single bound. Just what happened then it would have taken a slow-motion camera to analyze. Jason had the astounding spectacle shot before his eyes of the gigantic Ed, two hundred pounds of bone and sinew, suddenly launching himself in a flat dive through the air over Roddy's head, to fall with a splintering crash ten feet behind the amateur magician, while Roddy seemed to have turned a back somersault under the human projectile, landing lightly on his feet at the precise moment that Ed hit the partition and smashed it. Ed made one feeble gesture and lay still. And strangest of all, the bemused rooster still stared at its crack. It was hard to tell which sight struck the more terror to the hearts of the two younger brothers— that of the rigid cockerel or that of their Herculean brother hurled over the head of this soft-looking stranger. Roddy snapped his fingers at the rooster and sent it scurrying away with protesting squawks. He motioned to the two brothers.

"Come in here," he ordered; and they came, trembling. "Take care of him; he's broken his collar bone," he said, pointing at the groaning Ed. He turned to Orlo and Jason and asked, in a low tone, "Are they likely to be heeled—armed?" He slapped his hip.

Orlo shook his head. Still dumfounded, he was questioning Roddy with his eyes. Jim and Joe had drawn Ed to a sitting posture now, and were trying to ease him, though it was plain he was badly hurt.

"Ed?" muttered Orlo to Roddy—and the one syllable sufficed to convey the startled question.

"It looks like it. We'll see," said Roddy softly. "Give them time to think it over." He drew the two men outside.

"What was that trick? What did you do? I didn't see you do anything," sputtered the admiring Jason. "Ed went through the air as if he had hold of a sawmill belt."

"That's the barrel turn," said Roddy.

"It must have taken a lot of practice," cried Jason.

"That's the first time I ever tried it," confessed Roddy. He laughed. "I saw a Jap do it on the stage once. He simply pulled the other man over on top of him, and rolled like a barrel, feet in his belly. The bigger the man and the faster he comes the farther he'd dive. I always thought I'd like to try it. This is the first chance I've ever had." He laughed again. "It isn't exactly a trick you want to practice on a friend—unless you want to brain him. Better telephone for a doctor, Orlo. Or, you go."

Jason looked back over his shoulder.

"Can you handle those three?" he asked Orlo.

"He don't need me, I reckon," smiled Orlo, with grim humor. He turned to Roddy. "I don't make head or tail of this business," he said.

When Jason came back the brothers were bathing Ed's face with cold water from the pump. Ed was opening and closing his eyes in a torment of pain and fear. He had just seen more of heaven and hell than was comprehended in his philosophy. Roddy was advancing. He had that damned black cat in his arms, coddling it. He sat down in front of Ed on a milking stool. He laid the black cat on an outstretched arm, made a few hocus-pocus passes over it, and the cat lay motionless on its perilous perch.

"Look at me—all three of you!" suddenly commanded Roddy. And they looked at him, wide-eyed. Orlo and Jason stood behind Roddy. Roddy stroked the cat and took it comfortably in his lap.

"That eel only weighed six pound and a half, Ed," he said in a droning voice. The three brothers twitched, as one man; an expression of blank stupidity fell like a shadow across the three faces. "I found your spear, Ed," Roddy's rhythmic tones pursued.

Ed's lids closed slowly over his staring eyes; with an effort he lifted them again, to meet the steady gaze not only of Roddy but of the black cat too. The black cat seemed to have now discovered its enemy, for it arched its back and spat.

"It's a lie!" A stream of foul oaths burst from Ed. He tried to rise, but fell back with a moan.

"Oh, you didn't lose your spear, then, when you were passing the island?" said Roddy. The glowing eyes of Ed shifted momentarily. Roddy leaned forward. "Look at me!" he said quietly. "Is it a lie that four men went up the river, and only three came back?" he asked in the same quiet tone.

Here the two younger brothers ended the scene with a crash. Hurling horrible curses on the head of the helpless Ed and calling the wrath of the devil down upon him, as if he were the cause of their destruction, they broke for freedom. So formidable was their onslaught, so sudden and ferocious that for the moment it carried the three watching men off their feet. But the two desperadoes were finally downed and thrown, badly mauled, beside Ed.

Then the floodgates opened. The brothers were damning each other. No need to question now. It all came out, through blurring expletives. Johnny Boag had bilked them—he had held out on them—they were all in it together, the rum business. He had squealed on them—he was in on the game-club raid! And sitting there, under the bridge, their eel spears dangling in the shallow water, he had laughed at them, dared them.

The picture was vivid—it was simple enough to see it all. The cattle, a happy chance—so it had seemed to them. Ed, always the foremost, had struck. Then the momentary terror, the crafty planning. Johnny had started to work on his dam late in the afternoon, but had gone down the river on some secret errand and forgotten all about the patient yoked beasts standing there. When the quarrel came, with its tragic ending, the solution of the dead body was ready at hand. It was not until they had jammed the body down between the stones and smashed the rail that they came on Roddy's footprints. To their dulled brains this seemed even a better alibi—and Ed, the only level-headed one among them, went for Orlo to discover the telltale heel marks.

The doctor came.

"I don't get this at all," said Jason. "What is this about the spear?"

"They lost a spear going by here last night, the four of them," said Roddy. "An eel twisted it out of their hands. They let it go, promising each other that they would find it downstream, today. I took a chance and said I found it. They thought I had seen the whole thing then. That broke their back. It was simple enough."

"Say, what do you do for a living?" demanded Jason.

"Me? Why, I teach school winters," said Roddy.

Jason gave him one long look. He thrust his hands into his pockets and wandered off in a dazed sort of way. He came on General Konchakoff, who paused, with uplifted toe, and cocking his head on one side regarded him with an air of polite incredulity.

"I know just how you feel about it, old man," said Jason. "I feel the same way myself. I feel as if—as if I had been through a barrel turn!"

VI

A START IN LIFE

THE man who was to be known as Nate was examining through the bleared leaden panes of the kitchen window, with the delight of fresh discovery, the frost shadows that still lay on the grass where the sun had not yet struck. The broken gable of the old wing, the peak of the barn where the hay beam stuck out like a finger of doom, the round-shouldered cock of a stack and even the gaunt maples, all cast these rime wraiths that fearfully withdrew into themselves, melted away as the sun crept forward in its vast enveloping movement.

The kettle was steaming on the stove, the fire crackled, and the open ash door showed a grinning row of fiery teeth. An iron pot, simmering, gave forth a faint fragrance of savories. A man in a checkered apron tied above his middle, giving him an odd matronly look, was washing dishes at the sink. This man was to be spoken of and to as Jake. In the next room, the public room of the old days when this place was a tavern, four men, dressed *pour le sport,* as we say this winter, were yawning and stretching luxuriously about an open fire. It was the after-breakfast rite of the tobacco pipe. The huge person in the Windsor chair, with a fat face as guileless as a child's, had acquired the label of Sam for all purposes of the rendezvous— a name many sizes too small for him. His companions, seated, reading from right to left were, first, the dapper little fellow with the large head and torpedo beard and the spindle-shank calves—Horace. He wasn't a man of tweeds at all; he should have been habited in black to match the ribbon of his eyeglasses, with which he constantly gesticulated; second, a very bald man obviously Scotch in a complete glossy-eyed way—Scotty; and the last, a plump squat person who suggested a weakness for facial massage—Frank. Standing at the window, shaving before a handy mirror with cross-eyed intensity, was Pink.

The precise little man with the spindle shanks cast a look of admiration. He was filling his pipe—by Sandhill, London.

He said: "That is blatant stoicism—shaving in ice water."

The elephantine Sam craned in an effort to behold the stoic, and turned himself to the fire again, feeling of his own stubble.

"Why, damn it!" he muttered lazily, "Pink hasn't enough beard to dull the back of a razor."

Outside in the kitchen, the dishes tinkled, clinked and rattled pleasantly.

"Glassware and silver first," cautioned the dishwasher, dipping his hands gingerly into the red-hot suds. "Isn't that what your mother told you, Nate?"

Nate picked up a tumbler; he dried it with one whisk of his cup towel, polished it with a second and held it up to the light for lint; he set it in its row on a shelf decorated with scalloped white oilcloth, turned and reached for another one.

"Funny how it all comes back," he said. He had a curious trick of lifting his head and closing his eyes when he began to speak; then he would open his eyes again and stare at the man he was addressing. When he looked at you, you saw he was much younger than the first impression had led you to believe. He was the baby of this rendezvous.

"I was chopping wood this morning, Mister—ah—Jake," he corrected himself hastily.

"Chopping?" inquired the dishwasher.

"Splitting," substituted the helper with a smile. "It was a beech chunk. It fell open like a book!" He had a moment of pleasant egotism. He nodded toward the open door. "Birke—that is, Sam—Sam said, 'Damn it! Let me do that!'" He imitated the baby voice of the big man perfectly. "He took one swing—an awful wallop." He shook his head, laughing silently. "All he got was a dull thud. Sam said, 'Damn it, how'd you do it?' I didn't know. I give you my word, I didn't know. I tried it again. My fingers remembered the minute they gripped the ax helve. There was that final twist, like cutting a tennis ball. I'd learned it as a boy." He polished off another tumbler and held it up. "Fitzsimmons used that same twist of the wrist in his punches. He could knock out a man and his whole family with a six-inch hook." He passed an arm slowly through the air, illustrating.

"You were in that game, weren't you?" asked the dishwasher.

"Yes. I was welter champion."

"Why did you get out of it?"

"Pretty rough game," said Nate, shaking his head.

"Any rougher than this?" inquired the dishwasher. He dried his red hands on his apron and refilled his pipe. His companion did not answer the question, if indeed it was a question.

Instead he said "This is a good towel, Jake."

Jake drew a few puffs, tenderly nursing a spark.

"Our Illyria Division turns out a centrifugal dryer for the East Coast Chain," he said, turning to his dish pan. "It's all right for the hotels. But it isn't what grandmother used to use. It's hard to improve on linen. Better take a

fresh towel, hadn't you?" He reached up and took down
a towel from a rack. "Hello, some fool ironed this towel!"

"Why shouldn't some fool iron a towel?" inquired his
helper.

"No reason at all," agreed Jake. "But it wasn't done in
our family." He turned a momentary look, piercing in its
intensity, on his companion. "When my mother was a girl,"
he said, "she worked out in a Swede family. They made
her iron the dish towels. It came to be a sort of symbol
of useless drudgery to her, and she never let our dish
towels be ironed."

"Your mother worked out?" repeated Nate in a color-
less tone. He stared at his companion's bent back. That
would be worth a page in a Sunday newspaper.

"Yes. Why not?"

"I thought you were of the blood royal."

"No. I've been through the mill."

"You are New England," stated Nate.

"No. Illinois, Center prairie. Hub-deep in mud. Our
barn was thatched, and our house wasn't sealed. Grand in
winter! This was when I was a boy."

Nate was plainly puzzled.

"I thought this was your ancestral place," he said oddly.

"No."

"But you own it."

"Oh, yes." He turned out the dish pan and wrung out
the cloth with a double twist. "You New Englanders have
something on us," he said. "I don't know just what it is.
I bought this place to find out. I never have found out,"
he added with a queer smile. "Everybody calls me Jake
up here. They think I'm a carpenter in New York. I
shingled the barn. Quite a roof," he said proudly, nodding
at the window, bright with morning. "Forty squares."

He brushed off the top of the stove with a turkey wing;

peered into the pot of simmering meat stock that perfumed the air so deliciously; he swept up a thimbleful of dust from the floor, and asked: "Who's the cook tonight?"

"Why, I am," murmured a voice from the interior. "You know that without asking. Are you trying to start something? Why, you miserable half-baked whelp of a left-handed prairie schooner, I was a cook before you were a bellhop."

Various comments, mostly of a ribald nature, were fired at the cook. The complacent Sam met and defeated them all in detail with startling personal allusions.

"Pink, you through shaving?" he demanded.

"Yeah," Pink was putting his things away.

"Pull off my boots for me, like a good fellow." Sam stretched out his legs, wincing. "I walked too far yesterday."

Pink knelt down and unlaced the high hunting boots and drew them off. Sam groaned contentedly, stretching his stockinged feet before the fire.

"Say, Pink, my shoes are upstairs in my room."

"Get them yourself, you fool," said Pink cheerfully.

"I'll get them," said the spindle-shanked little gentleman with the torpedo beard.

Nate paused in the act of picking up a stack of dishes and looked significantly at Jake. The quick steps of the little man on the stairs suggested that he had worn patent-leather shoes from boyhood. He was back in a moment; he fell on his knees before the grateful Sam, drew on his shoes for him and tied them carefully. The big man stretched one foot to test it.

"You clumsy ass! You've twisted the tongue in that one," he said. Horace, contrite, made haste to repair the fault.

Jake had hung up his apron. He started out, and Nate

made haste to follow. As they fell in step the arctic chill caused both of them to turn up their collars.

"I don't get this at all," said Nate with a baffled air. "I got your wire and I came—hotfoot. That's all I've been told. It's your party, isn't it?" He looked keenly at the older man. Jake shook his head.

"No," he said.

They walked on across the road to the water mill, where Jake had a little hydroelectric unit as a plaything.

"Then I can say something?" asked Nate. The older man smiled.

"I'll say it for you," he said. "This bunch have come sneaking in here singly, like crows to pick a dead horse. There wasn't a man at the table last night at dinner that Sam hadn't dealt a cold deck to at one time or another. And we were as happy as lambs! That's what you want to say, isn't it?"

Nate nodded, a red glint in his eye.

"He cold-decked our outfit in the Atcheson Extension Plan," he said. His jaws shut with a snap. "I've always said I'd get him, and I will. I'd never met him. I almost fell dead when I dropped in on you all last night and found him there damning everything. I've heard that his wife calls him Damn-it, for a pet name."

Jake chuckled. They were in the little generating room, and he inspected the telltales with the casualness of a switchboard attendant. He inspected the commutator, gave a turn to the belt tightener and adjusted the rheostat. Nate followed him with a curious smile.

"Queer job for you to do yourself," he said. "You've got fifty-thousand-a-year men to do this sort of thing."

"No," said Jake. "It takes ten thousand kilowatts to start them. This is ten. I do it myself and I get a lot of fun out of it. And it rather helps along the impression around here that I am a tinker, one of those cheerful idiots who knows something about everything and not much about anything."

"They don't know who you are?"

"No. And it's rather a pleasant sensation, if you get what I mean."

Nate nodded. He got it. He smiled grimly. He knew that this quiet, settled person who shingled his own barn and knew the technic of dishwashing had been shot at now and then by anarchists purely on the ground of abstract theory. And there was a chain of newspapers that opposed everything he did, as a policy.

"I don't like sitting down at the same table with him," said Nate, "but I'll do what you say, Jake." He had an unpleasant scowl. "What do you want me to do?"

"Get him, by all means," said the profound Jake. "Most of us have, one time or another. Life's a game of freeze out for Sam. I've seen him borrow chips to get back into the game. "Only"—he laid his hand on Nate's arm—"delay the execution. This is a truce. We're here to talk of upper brackets, not to even up old scores. Didn't you see the sena——" He disguised the slip with a cough. "Didn't you see Horace go fetch his shoes for him, like a pet dog?"

Nate assented savagely.

"Well, if Horace can afford to do it we can," Jake said.

Nate said suddenly, in a low tone, "The bee's bitten him, hasn't it? I'd heard so."

Jake nodded.

"Yes—name's coming before the convention. Well, we all have our dreams. Just remember," advised Jake, "that Sam has never been out of his own front yard before without his Jap. He's crooked, yes. But he knows more about tax-exempt bonds than any other man on earth;

that's what he deals from the bottom of the deck," he
said dryly. "We had to have Sam, so we'll have to pull
off his boots for him while he is here. Horace's one ambition is to write a perfect tax bill. And it is his party! Now
do you get the drift?"

"From the start," Jake explained, "we agreed we had to
be alone. No servants. A clever flunky could sell us out
for a million. I ask you, what would the national committee pay for a snapshot of this bunch planning a tax
bill?"

"Wall Street sharks!"

"It's got to be good! It's got to be a bill that will elect a
president. But it is eternally damned if we are known as
the authors."

A wagon wheel creaked frostily on the early morning
air. It stopped abruptly, Jake looked out.

"Hello, Orlo!" he cried, coming out.

" 'Lo, Jake," said Orlo. It was Orlo Sage, the local constable. He reclined with the easy grace of a woodsman
on the bolster, a bag of grain for upholstery. He was
going up "west"—he indicated the general direction with
a jerk of his head—to get his horses shod, and to stop
by to see what Jake was doing here at this time of year.

"How'd you know I was here?" asked Jake.

"I saw someone was drawing water," said Orlo. By
such simple tokens Orlo knew what was going on all about
him. When Jake opened the bulkhead gate of his pond
to draw water for his turbine, he advertised to all the
world downstream that he was here.

"This fellow is all right," Jake was whispering in an
aside to Nate, "but we've got to give him some good
excuse why we are here." They moved across the wet
grass. "Orlo, shake hands with Nate," he said, resting
himself against a wagon wheel that moved uneasily back

and forth as the horses stretched to pick grass. "I've got a good bunch with me this time, Orlo," said Jake. He considered for a moment. "You've got that coon dog yet, haven't you?"

"Nope," said Orlo with significant brevity. He looked up quickly. "Percy Manchester has got a dandy," he said.

"I thought Percy was hiding out, Orlo. Wasn't he wanted for stealing that lumber?"

"Well," considered the constable, "he thinks he's hiding out. He's over in back, behind the coal kilns. He's out of mischief, so I don't bother him. I'll send his woman around if you want I should."

"Would Percy come along?" asked Jake.

"Sure. Else the dog won't work. You have to pay him something—five or ten dollars maybe." Orlo stopped. "I'll come along too," he added, "if it's dark enough so I couldn't see to read a warrant." He grinned. "It's the dangdest coon dog you ever saw, Jake. Ain't that just like it, a dog like that holing up with a skunk like Percy?" He sat up suddenly and clucked, and his team wheeled into the road and started forward. "I'll tell the Miner boy to go get her and send her around," he said over his shoulder.

It was ten when the two men rejoined the group in the house. The others were already seated about the long table, and Jake and Nate fell into their waiting chairs.

"I would suggest," said Horace, affixing his nose glasses and instantly becoming a statesman in spite of his *petit fours,* "that we will begin by setting down the points on which we are in unanimous agreement. In other words," he added slyly, "we won't have to argue with Sam at this session."

"Where do you get the 'we'?" demanded the mild-mannered Sam. Even in his most violent blasphemies he never raised his voice, or changed his face. He broke off the head of a split of champagne against the mantelshelf and drank from a glass. They worked for two hours with that prodigious suavity of logic that is a gift of the gods to the few. The clock was striking noon, in tune to a distant sawmill whistle, when the sen—when Horace gathered together the loose leaves they had written and arranged them in an orderly sheaf. They pushed their chairs back, refilled their pipes. Nate, the younger man, who was sitting among these giants for the first time in flattered inclusion in this circle, found himself amazed at the pleasant amity of the scene. Knowing them and their bloody wars, one had to be a part of it to believe it. It was a tribute to the sagacity of the little man in the torpedo beard. By his genius for regrouping essential details, what might have been monuments of difference had become mere trifles.

And even Jake, who probably had a more solemn realization of the difficulties of the task before them than anyone else at the table, felt the glow of elation. Nevertheless, even at that instant, a presage of impending evil seemed to obtrude itself on his complacency, for the sound of the softly creaking hinges of the woodshed door brought him to his feet in nervous alarm. Someone in bare feet was crossing the kitchen floor.

II

Sam had risen to get another split of champagne from the window ledge, and he knocked off its head dexterously. As he poured the beautifully effervescent stuff into a tumbler, he invited the others, but they declined.

"Why, damn it! I can drink alone and be in better company," he said in his bland tones. He was raising the glass to his lips when his eye caught the figure of the barefoot woman peering in. She had paused at the open kitchen

door and was gazing through with the curiosity of a wild
thing. Her hair was raven black, and a hard knot of it
that hung over one ear caught and reflected a glittering
splash of light from the window. She was startlingly pic-
turesque, beautiful, in that velvety-eyed, creamy way of
the gamins Raphael found in the gutters as models for his
cherubs. She had on a voluminous kilt skirt and a shawl
of many colors, which she wore falling jauntily off one
shoulder. And beneath the skirt her bare legs showed as
smooth and round and solid as marble, but not so cold
and white; warm, instead, with tints of the sun.

With the glass midway to his lips, Sam stared at her.
His eyes narrowed as they fed avidly on the primitive lure
of the picture.

"Come here, Salammbô," he commanded her. She advanced at once to his side, staring boldly at the others as
if daring them to forbid it. "Drink," he said. "It is good."
And he thrust the goblet into her hand.

"No, no, Sam!" exclaimed Jake. "Sorry, old chap, but
that won't do——"

"Who's doing this?" inquired Sam amiably, thrusting
Jake back with one hand. "Drink! Drink!" he laughed.
She lifted the glass, peering over it, with a certain defiance
of the others, for an instant between the cup and the lip.
She swallowed the half of it in a gulp, and rising on tiptoe she drew herself together with her elbows shivering
deliciously, and showing a row of hard short teeth.

Jake took her brusquely by an elbow and led her to the
kitchen.

"What do you want?" he demanded. She held herself
silent, sulky.

"That stuff will make you sick," he was saying. "It
is cider with pop in it."

"Champagne," she corrected him, with a sneering smile.

She smiled without dimples. Her cheek bones were too high for dimples.

Then he suddenly recollected.

"Oh, you must be Percy's wife," he said. "Where will he meet us?"

She leaned toward him and whispered, showing her short teeth again.

"At the keel—tain o'clock," she said.

"How much money?"

"Tain dollar, plees."

Jake thought better than to haggle over the sum. He had only eight dollars, he said, counting some silver. Her slight contemptuous shrug was her only reply. He went inside to borrow two dollars. He counted the money into her hand, and she put it in her bosom, all the time her eyes on him like those of a wondering child. Suddenly closing one fist as if on a dagger, her eyes blazing fiercely, she rasped a question.

"You no catch heem?" she demanded.

"No. We catch heem dog," Jake assured her. "Good-by."

"Goo'-by," she said, and with a flash of her eyes and a flirt of her skirts, she turned to go.

"Oh, Salammbô," said Sam, coming out. The girl turned, looking at him boldly enough for a moment; then her eyes fell and her long lashes brushed her luscious olive cheek, and she wrote bashfully with a little round toe on the floor. It was bad business. Jake, disquieted, ran an arm through Sam's to draw him into the other room, but the big man pulled away.

"Now, young fellow, I'm the cook and bottle washer this evening," he said pointedly. "Don't—butt—in! I'm marketing." He sat down astride the kitchen table. "Come here, Salammbô!"

She approached as before and stood beside him, assum-

ing again the air of the nut-brown maid. His eyes appraised her, and she, sensing the intimate scrutiny, flashed a look up at him and bent her head again, with that faint dimpleless smile of hers. Sam began to tell her what he wanted, in pidgin. She would have understood it simply enough had he used the king's English, but with pidgin he must help out with gestures. He was indicating something about as big as a new baby, and evidently quite as naked. Its head would be thrown back, and its hands—or feet— curled up under its chin. And in its mouth would be an apple—he took an apple from the dish and illustrated. And in its nose would be a spray of something—he picked up a sprig of mint and balanced it on his upper lip as he threw his head back. She laughed soundlessly at this pantomime. His watch fob attracted her childish curiosity, and the creature took it up in her fingers. Sam took out his bill fold. It held only yellow money—new, crisp yellow money. He conferred one crackling slip upon her with a gesture to impress her with its trifling amount. With a dart of her eyes and a flirt of her skirts she was out of the door. It was odd to think of that flaunting savage as the mate of the wretched little jailbird hiding out in the woods up there behind the old kilns.

"Sam, if you wouldn't show your money——" Jake had begun, when the big man cut him short.

"Why, you fool!" he cried. "I'm buying dinner, ain't I? You eat what I provide—and shut up."

Jake gave him a level look.

"And you are my guest," he said in a low tone. "There are certain responsibilities in that relationship which must be observed as our safeguard. Don't risk our anonymity with champagne and yellow money."

Sam's slow smile had a touch of derision.

"Oh, Jake, you'll always be an amateur," he said.

The high, the middle and the low impulses that actuated this man were always a source of wonder to the even, contemplative Jake. In a deal or a poker game Sam ruined his opponents with hilarious glee. He drank men to death who tried to play boon companion with him. And as for his amours——

"Thank God for the women!" one of his bitterest opponents had said. "Had he no distractions, there wouldn't be any Wall Street." The man who said that was cursing the crystal clarity of the mind that could get ahead of him at all times.

"It is fortunate," said the sen—Horace, who wiped the dishes after lunch with a prim old maid's nicety, "that we are in accord. I thought it would take a week. I believe we will get out of here tomorrow morning."

This was the unspoken hope of all. Should Sam lose interest in the upper brackets, the potentialities of the situation were enough to daunt the staunchest of them.

But when they sat down for the afternoon conference, it was Sam, with a devastating acuity, who began to uncover flaws. On paper the thing was perfect. But his mind followed through. He possessed that rare faculty of putting theory to the test of practice in his imagination, trying it out as it were; and returning to the charge with what seemed almost an empirical knowledge. Where this morning it was simple, this afternoon it was hopeless. There was no argument. Sam dominated them completely. He could think not only in terms of himself, unscrupulous, the plutocrat; but in terms of the multitude, of the little man who had only suspicion and envy to inform his logic. It was an amazing spectacle of the great gambler revealing the marked cards with which he dealt—a magician turning back his sleeves. There was a depressing silence, as if the spirit of the group had been hammered into submission. They must begin all over, work from the bottom up.

It was four o'clock when the woodshed door creaked in its sly way on its hinges and the pad of bare feet sounded on the scoured maple floor of the kitchen. An uneasy glance traveled around the circle and rested on the big man, who was still demolishing axioms of taxation with his marginal notes, which he wrote in an almost microscopic hand. It wasn't the woman. It was the Miner boy, barefoot and hatless, a jaunty little fellow with a loaded gunny sack slung over one shoulder. And with the surety of an animal picking a master, he went to Sam and whispered to him, grinning, and calling him Sam.

"Well, fellows," said Sam, rising and putting an arm about the proud boy, "me and my pard take charge from now on. Everybody chase himself—don't come sneaking back till you hear the dinner bell."

Sam went out to rummage in a scrap pile that was behind the woodshed, and reappeared armed with an old grindstone mandrel that he swung menacingly by its crooked handle.

"Chase yourselves!" he said. He locked himself and the boy in the kitchen, and large sounds of sudden industry sifted through the door—the placid profanities of the man and the vivid eagerness of the boy. That boy's fortune was made, though he little suspected it. That is, if Sam took a liking to him, and he seemed to have done so. Sam, child of nature that he was, would probably take the boy back to town with him and ease him into a career with a prodigal godfatherliness that would read like a fairy story.

Jake nodded over this twist of chance as he ran out the car. The exiles motored away silently, along leaf-strewn wheel tracks under the bare boughs of the November woods. This was the country of the gentle New England poets, and their pleasant cadences whispered again in the bright sky, the crisp air and the dun colors of the plaid hillsides. They were coming home, in the evening, a single clear star peering at them over the scarp of the mountain. White smoke pointed skyward from the chimneys. The sen—Horace was moved to quote, loosely:

"I knew, by the smoke that so gracefully curl'd . . .
And I said, 'If there's peace to be found in the world . . .
It is here.'"

There was no dinner bell. But the complete Sam was blowing lustily on a large conch that bathed the hills in sonorous echoes. He left off to spell the Miner boy with the cocktail shaker. Shaking a cocktail was a rite with Sam which must be continued until his fingers frosted. The pièce de résistance was a roast suckling pig, turning on a spit—the old grindstone mandrel—over a glowing bed of hickory embers. It was laid out on a huge trencher board —a slab of oak from the mill—with embrasures of yams, carrots, salsify, peas and parsley, roasted chestnuts and apples. And in its parted mouth resided a rosy apple, and from its pink snout emerged festive sprays of mint and winterberry. The broad table lay white and glistening with linen and silver, and the flames of tall candles danced a little minuet in the mellow light of the tinseled log on the hearth. Oh, it was peace and perfection! Even Horace, with all his qualms, the man who had most to lose, found himself warming to the cheer and plenty. It was good to be alone by themselves with no smug servile lackeys peering over their shoulders with saturnine docility.

"This kid," said Sam, "doesn't know it, but he is going back to town with his Uncle Dudley and see the elephants."

He had the boy seated beside him, and he patted him

affectionately. The boy drank it all in industriously, his bright little eyes blazing with the fires of the moment, little dreaming what the future might hold in store for him.

"Now, damn it!" said Sam, rising with the carvers. "I want everybody to eat! Eat!" he repeated. "Never mind the bouquets! Just eat!"

He was carving. The air grew indolently heavy with the aroma of the burnt offering of poetic meats. It was like a family festival.

For years afterward Horace still retained the picture of Sam and the boy seated there at the head of the table as if they were the only two beings on the face of the whole world—the infinite charm of the man for the child. The sen—Horace found himself vaguely speculating what were the beginnings of this man. Merciless, undisciplined, a man who was a law unto himself. And yet with a magnetism that was incomparable.

Sam was drinking a good deal—not for him, but a good deal for anyone else. The boy watched him, half furtive, half in awe. Sam's poker face never changed. The tones of his voice never altered. He never paused for a word or a thought. Toward nine, replete, he folded his hands across his apron, which he still wore tied around his neck, and slept cherubically, his back to the fire, in his Windsor chair.

The others quietly removed the feast and talked in whispers, nodded among themselves to the soft clink and tinkle of the dishes and silver. It was ten when Orlo came for them, his car shivering in death agony at the gate. Jason was with him, a neighbor, his inseparable. They had on coonskin caps and sheepskin coats, and they carried lanterns and guns. They came into the kitchen, nodding and laughing, and tilted themselves in chairs against the wall while they waited. The Miner boy buttonholed Orlo and told him in whispers of the feast, now and then nodding through the open door to indicate the wonderful Sam, who still slept.

Sam woke up suddenly, staring.

"Damn it! Who's stomping on the tin roof?" he asked. He started up, but his instep gave way and he settled on the couch with a groan; he made another effort to walk, but couldn't. He had overdone it yesterday in the woods. He sat down, sagged; and then, like a weary child, he was asleep again. Jake shook his head; it would be cruel to urge him to go. They replenished the fire, and they slipped out one by one. The cars rolled up the road to the old kilns where they were to find Percy and his dog. Percy came slinking out of the shadows like a reprimanded ghost, his mean-looking cur shivering at heel. Percy was a miserable wretch, not half so bad a bad man as he prided himself on being. He lived mentally in an eternity of boisterous deeds, while he hovered in hiding back there in the forest, priding himself in the belief that the whole world sought but could not apprehend him. He glanced apprehensively at Orlo, but Orlo obviously had laid aside his constabulary attributes for the coon hunt.

III

The dog that men came hundreds of miles to hunt behind had been running silent for some time now, and they sat down in a stand of oak to wait for it to come in. The bright moon shone down on the pale circle of their lanterns through the bare branches. Percy began to tell about himself, stepping out into the lantern light. All evening he had been suspicious of Orlo. Now he came out in the open, and strutted and crowed like a rooster as he vaunted himself and his exploits. He was telling about the time he dived through a window into the river, carrying glass and sash with him, when officers from Barrington came to a dance at the Town Hall to take him. His monologue would have made him a star overnight on Broadway. But in the midst of his gasconade an owl hooted dismally off in the hollow forest, and the wretched creature, robbed of his moment of glory, was suddenly quenched; Percy faded into the shadows beyond the lanterns.

A huddled figure in sheepskin alongside Jake—it was Jason—buried his face in his hands and replied to the hoot of the owl with another so natural that the circle started in amazement.

They could hear someone coming through the brush.

"Who do you suppose that is, up here at this time of night?" asked Jake.

"It's Orlo," said Jason, speaking low at Jake's shoulder.

"Orlo! Why, he's here, isn't he?"

"Not for the last hour," said Jason.

"I didn't know he'd left!"

"He didn't want you should," replied Jason laconically. Then with a note of sharpness Jason called, "Percy!" There was no reply. Percy of the ecstatic fears had rubbed himself out of the picture.

An indrawn silence held the hunters.

"What's up?" whispered Jake.

"I don't know," replied Jason. In a lower tone: "He went down to see," he said.

The crashing of the brush came on. Then a tall figure walked out into the cathedral-like aisle of tree trunks where they sat. The circle of lanterns arose as if the darkness had suddenly become buoyant.

"Who was that big fellow we left behind at the house?" said Orlo. He was standing by Jake.

"Sam, you mean?" It was Jake who said it.

Orlo took a lantern from some ghostly hand and held it up to the staring faces.

"Where's Percy?" he asked shortly.

"Faded," said Jason.

"That Hunky woman stuck him with a knife," said Orlo.

"Sam!" It was the sen—Horace.

Someone cursed in seething anathema, blind rage.

"Bad, Orlo?" asked Jake quietly.

"He's dead," said Orlo. And before the frozen circle of lanterns began to sway again, he turned away abruptly, saying, "Follow me, you fellows."

They fell in behind him mutely. He plunged into the brush where alders whipped their faces and bog holes sucked at their footsteps. Here there were no stars to guide them, but they thrashed ahead by ear. They came out on an old meadow, and crossed it as if fearful of the moonlight. Then again in the cover, and in another moment they were scrambling down an almost precipitous declivity. They came up at the house, with a start of surprise, when they had thought themselves miles away. In the unfamiliar darkness they did not fully realize where they were until they were entering the kitchen. Nothing there. Only homely peaceful quiet, the soft play of firelight, the old clock with its sedate tread, the thin whine of the kettle on a muted string.

"Wh-where is he?" Jake's voice was deep.

"Up above," said Orlo.

When all eyes turned to the stairs he said, "No, no. At her shack—up the river road."

"Sam—he went up there?" It was unbelievable.

"She come for him," said Orlo. He went on: "I found her wheel tracks back of the mill. She was hiding there when we left." He jerked his head in one of his vague

geographical gestures. "The Miner boy followed them,"
he said. "He heard it. He come for me. Didn't you hear
the owl hoot when we stopped at the spring?"

So that was it, the Miner boy. They were standing there
in the glow of the fire. The candles that had lighted the
feast were burned out long ago. Jake turned on the lights,
and in the swift luminescence these men did not look at
each other. They weren't thinking of Sam. They were
thinking of themselves.

The senator—it was his party, after all was said and
done—the senator was the first to break the spell. He
began gathering up the loose sheets of the afternoon conference. He was a person of niceties, his every act trimmed
as meticulously as his correct torpedo beard. He arranged
the sheets deliberately by number, tapped them into a
neat sheaf. One was missing; and he went down on his
hands and knees looking for it: it was lying under the
buffet and he dragged it out and opened the sheaf to
insert it again. Some microscopic marginal note in Birkenhead's handwriting caught his eye; and even at that moment its value attracted him, and he adjusted his glasses
at the proper angle and held it up to the light to read it.
Nothing was so important now to save out of this red ruin
as this manuscript, Sam's legacy; a stark revelation of a
mind that had the curious faculty of projecting itself ahead
of theory, and looking back while others still groped blindly
forward.

The senator's bag lay open in one corner. He began to
throw in his things. Orlo, the constable, regarded him
oddly. A sort of traumatic apathy held the others. It was
not death, nor the manner of it, that daunted them. It was
the audacity of death in striking here and now.

"Uncle Charlie is trailing her," said Orlo gruffly; and

they started at the sound of his voice. Uncle Charlie was one of his competents. He shook his head. "He won't get her! That woman can live in a hollow tree!"

"We don't want her, Orlo," said Jake with finality.

Before the startled Orlo could reply Jake was saying, "Senator, you can take Pink with you." Orlo's eye flickered at the title. "Drop him off at that milk stop on the Naugatuck Division. You can go on through alone. Frank, you drop Scotty at Canaan. There is an early train on the Housatonic. You take the first right-hand turn. You'll be across the state line by daylight." Thus, like a general to whom every foot of the strategic terrain was an open page, he dispersed his army along rivers. "Better figure on not arriving in town all at once," he added.

"I am going through to Boston," said the senator, shutting his bag with a click.

"I ought to be in Buffalo tomor—tonight," Scotty said; he corrected himself, looking up at the clock. It was half-past four.

"That's all right, isn't it, Orlo?" Jake asked.

"It's all right if you stay behind, Jake," said Orlo.

Jake turned to Nate, but Nate intercepted him.

"I'll stick on the job with you if you don't mind," he said shortly.

"Who was the big fellow?—that's what I want to know first," said Orlo.

"Man named Birkenhead," said Jake.

Jason said, "Not Cutthroat Birkenhead?"

Jake pierced him with a look.

"Samuel Cuthburt Birkenhead," he said.

There was a dead silence.

"What's your name, Jake?" asked Orlo. "It isn't Drummond," he added.

"No, Orlo," said Jake. "I bought this place in my wife's

name—a place I could come to, to get away from things. I am J. Hanson Watkins."

Jason's chair came down on all fours, and Orlo regarded him in surprise.

"Now, who are these others, Mr. Watkins?" he asked.

"My name is Jake, to you—if you don't mind, Orlo," said Jake. He named the fugitives, one by one. "Senator Horace Calvert, J. Beverly Storm, Franklin Hodenius, Scott Hammill, and Nathaniel Edgerton," he added, reaching out and patting the younger man on a shoulder.

No one was thinking of the dead man. Hurrying feet tapped the floor boards overhead. Men grabbing their belongings—barons of coal, iron, oil and money.

"Sorry, Jake ——" began the senator. Jake checked him with uplifted hand.

"We must get these lights out before people begin to go by," he said; and lifting his voice he cried, "Move fast, you fellows!" There was no leave-taking.

The four left behind sat motionless until the drone of the cars died on the still air. Then Jake, Nate, Orlo and Jason—they climbed into Orlo's car. It was astonishing how stealthily the old rattletrap could move when called on for caution. They avoided the main road, going around by the precipitous hill of Beech Plain. They came on Cold Spring by the pond road and hid the car behind the ruins of the old charcoal kilns. A dog rushed them, retreated for fresh courage, came on again. Its essay ended in an agonized howl, and the Miner boy came to meet them, armed with a billet of stove wood. He had Percy back of the shack, laid low with that same bludgeon when the shivering ecstatic creature crept up like a ghoul to see what was to be seen in the light of the moon.

Jake had gone inside. He came out almost immediately.

"Percy," he said, bending over the cowering shape in

the woodshed. Percy cautiously opened his ratlike eyes. What he saw was a peaceable-looking stout man squatting beside him, counting yellow money from a bill fold.

"There is eight hundred dollars, Percy," said Jake. "Bring me his watch and his cuff liks and his stickpin by noon, today, and it's all yours." He lifted the cowering bad man to a half-sitting posture, shook him roughly. "Now let's see if that dog of yours is worth its salt." The startled Percy, hardly believing he was free, slunk into the shadows.

Jake turned to Orlo.

"Orlo, is there any reason why Sam wouldn't be as dead down at my house as up here?" he asked. "We can move him, can't we?"

Orlo shook his head.

"No, Jake," said Orlo, and his no was absolute. "I'll telephone for the medical officer as soon as it gets light. He's just over in Tyrington."

"Tyrington?" said Jake with a gleam of hope. "Tyrington?" He seized Orlo by an arm. "We will go get him, Orlo. We'll leave Jason and Nate here on watch."

He drew Orlo to the car. They started out on the state road now, a winding luminous stretch of macadam along the river that slowly revealed itself from the depths of night as the east took on the tints of morning. They drove in silence. There were a number of things Jake might have said. But he left them all unsaid. If it had been a matter of money Jake would have summoned golden galleons of it. That wasn't the way out.

After a little while they came to a wide village street, with a double row of bare elms and neat parks swept clean of leaves. At a pillared house standing stark from its hillside, Jake touched Orlo on the arm.

"We'll stop here a minute," he said.

"This is Judge Trainor's," expostulated Orlo. "The judge won't thank you to mix him up in this," he said. Jake climbed down.

"Come along, Orlo," he said. "You are in charge, you know, until the medical officer takes over."

They quietly mounted the broad steps. Jake punched the portentous bell. They listened. After a long wait a frightened servant peered through the chained door. And then the stupefied Orlo held his breath. The judge himself, in his nightshirt. Judge Trainor had sat on the bench for a brief period early in his career. In the late 80's this district had sent him to Congress and had returned him zealously ever since. But he was always "the judge."

"Well, well!" cried the judge, coming to at sight of Jake. He seized his hand, wrung it. He dashed sleep from his eyes. His face lost its surly irritation. This was one of the judge's great friends in the great world he had so long decorated to the everlasting honor of this little community of pleasant hills and streams. "And Orlo!" cried the judge, who knew every maid and man of them by their first names. Jake spoke swiftly the name of Birkenhead; and the judge paused, his face clouding an instant.

"He was up coon hunting with me," said Jake. "It was too much for him, I guess. He keeled over on us—stroke. We carried him to a shack in the woods." Jake shook his head gravely. "He was dead before we laid him down." He paused, looking at Orlo, and there was a heart-beating silence. "There will have to be an autopsy, I suppose," said Jake wearily. "I thought—maybe you would like to put it through for us."

Tremulously the judge assured him that he would indeed. He was gone, and returned again, dressed, in no time. They started out once more, Orlo driving, catching vaguely the voices in rapid flow in the back seat.

The note of agitation in the judge's voice mounted. The talk was of the country, and the President, and business. They roused out Doctor Kirk, the medical officer, carried him off breakfastless. It was the doctor who now occupied the back seat with the judge.

It was ten o'clock, with the warm November sun still pursuing the remnants of the frost shadows in hidden places, when the medical officer came out from the shack, where he had been alone for two hours, and sat down with his blanks. He shook his pen, adjusted his glasses, smoothed his beard, cleared his throat. His lips formed a word.

"Aneurysm," he said to himself, and began to write. He spelled it out painfully as he wrote it—"a-n-e-u-r-y-s-m. Fifty-six years? Native of—what? Vermont? Indeed? Oh, was he? Married. H'm. Attending physician—what's that? Stiloh? Oh, my word! That makes it all right. He is the greatest heart specialist in the country." He pointed at them with his pen. "Thoracic," he explained, in a professionally abstract tone, "at the top of the arch—hidden!" He wrote again. "Heavy drinker," he muttered. He shook his head. "These heavy drinkers——" He affixed his seal, folded the paper, handed it to the mute Orlo. "Lucky chap, to go this way," he muttered in his beard. "He'd been dead on his feet for a year, and didn't know it. Everything gone inside." He shook his grizzled old head. "I don't know how they keep it up."

He got up and buttoned his cloak under his matted beard.

"Well, judge, we'll be going," he said. "Well, well! I never thought I'd have the privilege of shaking hands with you, Mr. Watkins!"

"No thanks, Watkins," the judge was saying. "I am most deeply grateful to have had the opportunity to serve."

The judge turned and rested a hand on Orlo's shoulder, to help his steps to the car.

"You are my great reliance, Orlo," said he gravely. "Men die so selfishly," he said. His voice was lost as Orlo helped him into the car.

Later in the month, Watkins—Jake—was called to appear before the hearing of the committee, in the matter of the upper brackets. It was the same day that Senator Calvert delivered his now famous exposition of the theory of taxation as applied to modern industry. He spoke from notes, tapping them with his ribboned specatcles. He stilled the burst of applause that broke from even those hardened economists and politicians who sat about the table in the committee room.

"I don't want to take credit to myself," he said, "for the good we are so prone to bury with another man's bones. Birkenhead"—he turned his statesmanly head on its pivot, letting the name sink in—"Birkenhead, Samuel Cuthbert Birkenhead!" He drew it out for dramatic effect. He said, "The man was always an enigma to me. There have been certain acts in his life that brought down rebuke from the great masses of the people. But we cannot deny," he said with emphasis, "that he possessed, above all others of his time, the ability to think in terms of mass mind—to see through and beyond theory into practice." He tapped his manuscript with his spectacles and looked for a moment at Jake, who sat far back in the room. "The marginal notes on this draft," he said, "are in the handwriting of Birkenhead. He was patriot enough to set aside his advantage, his prejudices, and give me the benefit of his counsel, a few days before he died."

Republics forget. You may remember that Calvert's

name went before the convention on the strength of his reputed authorship of a perfect tax bill.

Jake took the Miner boy to a military academy up the Hudson one fair afternoon late in the year. Boylike, with air castles rising unseen about him, he was in the middle of a scrimmage on the football field before Jake's car turned to go away.

"He is in the rough," said Jake to the headmaster.

"That's the way we like to get them," said the headmaster.

You see, this isn't the story of the upper brackets, or of a presidential campaign, or of Cutthroat Birkenhead. It is the story of the Miner boy. Sam would have taken him back to town with him, installed him, in his grand way, in a bountiful career and set him on the road to ruin or riches—a few of Sam's boys had the mettle to come through the fire.

But the gods in their circuitous way gave the Miner boy Jake for a godfather instead. And even if anarchists do take a pot shot at Jake now and then on the grounds of abstract theory, there is something homespun and dependable about Jake. His mother worked out, when she was a girl, in a Swede family where she had to iron the dish towels.

VII

BIG TIME

E STRELLE was in the act of receiving a visit of ceremony from M. Brody, of Paris, Inc., the celebrated dressmaker, when Cuyler Braxton came in. Like all women who have just discovered themselves to be in love, she was conscious of a warm flush of delight at sight of him; and her eyes, deeply lustrous at all times, glowed with a sparkling fire that was instantly quenched. She was pleasantly aware of this involuntary revelation and thankful for the dim lights and blue haze that suffused her shop. Also she had a swift conviction that she was looking her best this morning; only yesterday she had avoided young Braxton in the Avenue because she felt she was not quite up to the mark—a very rare occurrence with Estrelle. And thirdly, to make her cup of opportune happiness overflow, Braxton arrived just as the distinguished-looking M. Brody was bending over her extended hand—Brody was lingering over the favor, drawing out the agony, as only a professional Frenchman can.

M. Brody was extremely tall and square, and extravagantly bewhiskered, as it seems all successful men dressmakers must be, at least in Paris. He had a vibrating asleep-in-the-deep bass voice that caused his women customers to shiver with a delicious apprehension when he was according them a fitting. The great of this earth gravitate toward one another like apples in a tub; so Brody, the *doyen* of the French costumers, was making haste to indicate to Estrelle, his peer, that he had been drawn irresistibly toward her instantly on landing from the *Rochambeau* this morning.

"I do myself the 'onaire to make my compliments at your feet the same instant I set foot to shore," said Monsieur Brody in carefully fitted English.

One sensed, without the necessity of looking, the suppressed excitement among the women of the house of Estrelle, Inc., roused not only by his name and fame but also by his heroic proportions, his hirsute splendor and his bucko bass voice—the lowest notes went so deep one could almost count the beats. When he finally relinquished Estrelle's Grecian finger tips and stood erect, it was to be seen he wore his beard cut off spade fashion, at his second shirt stud, and in his lapel appeared the tiny button of some distinguished decoration. Since he had done her the honor of addressing her in her own tongue, she returned the grace by using his; and thus they sparred through several interchanges, to the utter confusion of eavesdroppers.

Cuyler Braxton, from a safe embrasure, did his best to discountenance the dignified Estrelle by signs of exaggerated curiosity, but she was apparently unaware of his presence. Addressing himself, with the air of a salesman, to Mrs. Wight, Estrelle's chief engineer, he asked, "Who is that big fellow with madame?"

"Yes, isn't he!" gushed Mrs. Wight. "It is Brody, the French dressmaker, just through customs with thirty-seven trunks."

Braxton was just discovering he was suffering from a strange affliction of the heart. But instead of indulging himself in the malady, he was concealing it even from himself. He was just beginning his career under his own

power. He had served four years as one of the bright
young internes on the staff of the district attorney, prose-
cuting thieves and murderers; and now he had gone over
to the defense, having learned all the strategy of the attack.

Calls of ceremony are brief, because there are only certain set phrases that can be used. Shortly the listeners
heard the rumble of M. Brody's adieu. Braxton emerged.
Estrelle made a great pretense of nothings.

"Something of importance brings you here?" she asked
with a brittle brightness of expression.

"You will pardon my interruption during your hours of
creation," he said, "but I have a commission to tender;
a good one, if you can accept it. Will you take luncheon
with me?"

"It is so immediate?" She examined some things to go
out.

He lowered his voice. "A trousseau," he said.

Her heart stopped momentarily. Physiologists say this
is impossible, but it constantly happens to persons in love.

"I'll tell you all about it at luncheon. May I come for
you at one?" he said.

At one they drove to Marguery's whose chef wears the
cross with palms for his fish sauce. It chanced that M.
Brody was there, through some queer instinct that sends
these people to just the right places for all occasions. Estrelle flushed becomingly when the great dressmaker arose
and bowed over her hand. As she swept on and by he
bowed again in resignation; then, turning, he bowed to
the gentleman with the air of a fencer putting himself at
the pleasure of an adversary.

"That beard is inflammable," said Braxton, when they
sat down. "What do you suppose he does with it at night?"

"Women are coming to demand their men dressmakers

to be more and more masculine," explained Estrelle, her eyes straying to the broad back of the great Brody. "Who is the bride?"

"Bride?" said Cuyler Braxton, puzzled.

"Yes, for the trousseau."

"Oh!" He laughed. "It's for a murderess."

"A murderess!" she cried, recoiling.

"Hush!" he cautioned. He summoned the hovering waiter, gave their order. "She is a client of mine," he explained, watching her closely. "She will go before a jury. There are certain aspects of—shall we say—appeal, I will want you to help me build up in her." Bemused by his character, he added, "To bring out the personality somewhat obscured by the exterior."

He examined his surroundings under his eyelids.

"It is to be one of those long-drawn-out affairs, full of fever and struggle; the explosion always just about to happen but never quite coming off; with reporters and sob sisters and flashlights and locked-up jurymen. You know—the usual," he said, his face alight with the picture. "I haven't quite decided on my construction yet, but I will want to break it up in, say three acts, with a very definite motif for each act. The general background is to be youth and, of course, the air of innocence. But not to underline the ingénue effect too much."

Their waiter was proffering the relishes for her choosing on a tray of crowded silver as big as a table top. She indicated with the tip of a fork a suspicion of caviar on an ivory heart of lettuce, a burned biscuit, an anchovy for salt, a pimento for hot and an olive for sour.

"Is it a play you are staging?" she said, watching the graceful transfer of relishes.

"That is the idea, of course," said he. He indicated his choice—all salt and sour. The waiter departed.

"Has the crime been committed?" she asked, a little bewildered.

"Oh, yes, all the preliminaries are arranged." He smiled.

"The murderess is apprehended?"

"No. I have her in my custody. I won't surrender her until you have a chance to look her over. We might even manage a try-on or two."

A newsboy dashed by the door. And even in here, where every effort is made to exclude the clamor of the profane world, his eerie cry of grisly jubilance penetrated, rising on the air as he came near and dying off like a dread fire siren as he fled. Everybody sat up. Even the waiters turned their heads to follow the sound. As it died away it was succeeded in this closely velveted interior by a sudden rush of sibilant whispers. The whole town was on edge. It had been presented with another ghastly murder at its breakfast table, another big-time crime.

Newspaper-circulation figures had been mounting like a fever thermometer since dawn. Tons of newsprint had been released from storage by speculators who hoard the precious rolls for just such an event. There is nothing to compare to the ravening hunger of the public for a new crime—that is, if it is a crime that clicks as they say of a play that bursts into overnight success on Broadway. And just as plays that click are preciously few, so the supply of murder—the big-time murder that reaches the point of drama that captures the public mind—never equals the demand.

The great play counterfeits the great emotions; the great murder trial presents the actuality, long drawn out, before our very eyes. It is a slow-motion analysis of the tigerish impulses of poor humanity. And so at the first clang of the police alarm all those forces of publicity that exploit such a spectacle prepare for action. First it will have the mystery to feed on. Then the solution. Then the study of the motive—what makes people do these things— why? Then expiation.

Now, less than six hours after the discovery of the murder of Hector Verblennes, under circumstances that indubitably pointed to a long-run sensation, special news syndicates were forming, photographic picture corporations had filed papers, and psychologists, visiting noblemen, great detectives, prize-fight champions, chorus girls —everybody, anybody whose name had been before the public long enough to make them drawing cards—were being induced by glamour of great returns, to sign contracts to write—or at least sign—exclusive interviews for the hectic days and weeks and months to come.

The newsboy was coming back. "Hoy, ahoy! Murder! Extra!" came the cry, pianissimo, going to forte, fortissimo. Braxton nodded to his waiter, and the creature, at the bidding, darted off like an unhooded falcon, returning instantly with a whole armful. There was a general movement toward the table. These people, superfluously haughty outside, within the seclusion of their haunts can display impetuous curiosity. They crowded about to find out what was new, the waiters forming the outer edge. Nothing was new. The latest edition was merely a rearrangement of type. When the public is in this frame of mind it will buy fresh extras hour after hour and read the same thing over and over again—it is only required to change the make-up.

M. Brody, pushing his way like a swimmer treading water, said, "Pardon, madame, but is it some grand catastroph' what arrives?"

"A new *cause célèbre*—what we call a big-time murder," explained Estrelle, hardly knowing how to convey the intelligence to an alien just landed. But she recollected that the French do the same thing. They want the same tre-

mendous shock, only they make it appear they have more
subtlety about it. The momentary flurry subsided. They
were alone again. She took up her bouillon cup by its two
ears and peered over the top of it at Cuyler Braxton.

"Hector Verblennes!" she whispered, trembling.

Braxton put on the brakes, not by cautioning her with
words but by creating the diversion of food—he dabbled
in his jellied consommé. He was an experienced diner-out.
Most of his thrills came at luncheon. But he never neg-
lected to eat.

Hector Verblennes had begun life as a great musical
coach, which in music is much like saying, in finance, that
So-and-So began life as a bank president. There are few
great coaches, and they have something more than years
of endeavor behind them.

Hector Verblennes, coming to town unknown, went to
the old Mouquin's one night when he knew that Di Passo,
in charge of the auditions of the opera, was to be there, and
sat at the next table. He said, so as to be overheard, "I
can play better than Conraad Bos." The story ran that Di
Passo cried out in rage, "You will have to prove that to
me, my friend." To which Verblennes replied hotly that
he could and would; and they all went over to the bare
stage of the opera like two parties bound for a dueling
ground. And there, so the story ran, Verblennes, without
music, accompanied Di Passo himself in his one song, the
Song of the Flea, so that at the end Di Passo himself, with
the fervor of an artist, took Verblennes in his arms and
thanked him.

This story got abroad. There was a great exile colony
of musicians in town, for it was during the war; and Verblennes became the rage among them—they all had some
rusty spots to polish. And for debuts and auditions no one
else would do, if you had the voice or the fingers or the

bow to command him. There were tens of thousands of students seeking a hearing, and he could pick and choose.

Some stories were whispered about him, but the whispers were hushed when he sat down and struck his piano and nodded to his soloist. His soloist—— He was the star. The audience came to hear him. An artist who couldn't fill Town Hall alone would stand them up in Carnegie if Hector Verblennes were at the piano. Among his eccentricities was to neglect to shave for his biggest concerts. This morning Hector Verblennes was found by a servant, pinned to the floor of his music room by an African assagai, snatched for the purpose from a wall decoration.

Estrelle only tasted her bouillon. Braxton nodded to the waiter; then came some fish with the sauce for which the chef wore the cross with palms. The pause had been good for Estrelle. Her voice no longer trembled.

"You have her in your custody?" she said, at the same time bowing to a friend across the room with a sweet smile.

"Learn to so frame your words," said Cuyler Braxton, with the effect of great caution but not the air of it, "that anyone could overhear without getting your meaning. You and I are among people all the while. We have no moments of privacy. We are shut off from confidences unless we learn this trick. Try it again."

"Was the meeting last night?" she asked.

The dead man had been found at dawn.

"No; the night before," said he. "Easy, easy!" he said, laughing, because she started violently. "That sauce is hot." She shredded her fish with the tine of a fork. "She had come to me directly from there."

"From where?"

"There!"

"What time was it?"

"Three."

"Why you?"

"I have always dabbled in music," he said. "Fortunately she knew of me. She had the deuce of a time getting away from there at that hour," he added lightly, as if the creature had torn away from some hilarious party at a night club. "She must have sat on my doorbell. I sleep like a mummy. I was tired and sore, and she was naturally wrought up. But after a while we got to the end of it, for the time being—for the time being," he repeated grimly. "We shall have to go over it, over and over again. Plays aren't written. They are rewritten—as I believe someone has said before me." He pushed back his things, turned his chair to face the room, flicked the dust off a toe with the end of his napkin.

"Of course she wanted to rush immediately to the front," he said, looking oddly at Estrelle. "Emotion—that sort of thing, you know. My idea was to let it ride, to let it grow cold," he said, with that curious lack of interest in his own words he could assume at times. "Fortunately Sunday intervened. I said nothing about the trousseau. That occurred to me later. There is a concert tomorrow afternoon. If you could run over, it would be a good time to give her the once-over without her realizing the occasion."

"She is going to sing—in public?"

"Life goes on," said Cuyler Braxton, in that judicial tone young lawyers practice. "Why not? It occupies her."

With the greatest difficulty Estrelle asked quietly, "I suppose she must be beautiful?

"I have been thinking about that," he said. "There is youth." Estrelle, alas, had not youth. Style and aplomb, yes; and a glorious radiance, but not youth. Youth comes twice, says Bernard Shaw—at seventeen and at thirty-one —and Estrelle was verging on recovered maidenhood. Her eyes had widened and grown dusky. "There is the air of innocence," resumed Cuyler Braxton, still busy painting his picture, "and a certain pleading prettiness. We shall have to get rid of that." He shook his head disdainfully. "These are all leads for you. The foundation is there—erase here and build up there. To an artist like you it will be joy. . . . But you are not eating your salad."

"No," she said.

"There is some nice runny cheese."

"No."

"Coffee?"

"I think not."

"I have distressed you?"

"Yes. It is like a painted agony. It is terrible." Her well-trained face belied her words.

"For me," he said, smiling, "it is the one thing I have been praying for—something in the big time. And here it comes tumbling into my lap. She is perfectly cast. I believe I could put her on without a rehearsal, if I had to risk it."

There was a pause. "Bring me a sweet," she said; and the *garçon*, his ears sharp enough for that, hastened up with the confectionery epergne. As she toyed with a glazed dainty she found herself examining Cuyler Braxton through the filter of a new understanding; this portrait was strange, the young man in the throes of luck.

Their glance met and held. There comes a time when words fail but the idea goes on. After what seemed an eternity, she asked, "There is no immediate danger then?" She meant was there danger of immediate apprehension.

"As yet, no," he said. "I shall want to stage that very carefully." He was only a stage manager assembling his props. Entirely sunk in it, he added, "Every move has to be calculated. I have seen black turn white in a jury box." He leaned forward. "You realize what it will mean to me? Have I your help?"

"I have a curious feeling that we are being overheard," said Estrelle, her voice hardly more than a whisper. At this instant M. Brody, who had been fidgeting in his chair at the end of the room, suddenly arose and approached. In one hand he carried his coffee cup, in the other his serviette. Except that he was not dressed for it, he looked like some apotheosized head waiter.

Without a by-your-leave he set down his cup and drew up a chair, filling his cup from their silver pot, and he said, *"Une vraie trouvaille, madame. . . .* You speak French, sir?" he said, turning to Cuyler Braxton.

Braxton admitted that he did, and understood some of it, too, having learned the A. E. F. version. M. Brody, who took it all for granted, had something to confide. It was astonishing how secretive he could be. His voice rumbled, shook the sides, scraped the bottom. Incredible as it appeared, madame, m'sieu, as an infant he had been feeble, very little—he illustrated—a *maladie* of nerves— too tight, like a violin string. It caused his beloved parents to despair of saving him for his great career.

For example, he suffered from a morbidly acute sense of hearing. A fly walking across a windowpane was the galloping of a cavalry horse; a train crossing a bridge a mile away was the collision of worlds in space; the dropping of a pin, the tick of a watch, the running of water, gave him exquisite torture; and as for plotters whispering —ha! He laughed—nothing was hidden from him. Even today he finds himself embarrassed by this frightful— *affreux!*—sense of hearing. It remains as the sole souvenir of his *malaise.*

"What do I do with this beard of mine at night? Monsieur, I leave it out with the cat! I am desolated, but I am in possession of your complete conversation."

Cuyler Braxton was taking his change from the silver

salver as he said to M. Brody, without the flicker of an
eyelash. "We count on your discretion. You introduce a
new note." They arose. M. Brody, bowing deep, indicated
that he was wholly their slave. *"Une vraie trouvaille!"*
repeated M. Brody, as he made his adieus for the last time.
A treasure-trove, indeed—a trousseau for a murderess!

II

There was a saying that big-time murders never opened
cold for Deputy Parr, the man hunter. He seemed to have
a way of anticipating them, as if they had calculable orbits.
And it was a fact that he usually was to be found sitting in
the front row when the curtain went up.

Saturday night, for no reason at all, he decided at the last
minute to stay downtown and bunk in the dormitory. Smoking his good-night cigar on the deserted front steps, he
looked up at the sky and remarked to Barney the old door-
man, "The wind is backing, Barney. That's always bad."

Barney dutifully laughed at this moth-eaten wheeze—
they used it when they went fishing off the Hook to explain
lack of interest on the part of the fishes. But later, when he
was sweeping up, Barney said to himself, "Something is
due. The big fellow knows."

But backing or hauling, the wind accomplished nothing,
and there was only the usual run of fry during the night.
Sunday passed, and Sunday night. Monday morning
brought the police slip Parr seemed to have been waiting
for. Parr first got out several pairs of shoes to change during
the day. Then he gathered his searchers—men of science
who would ask nothing more stirring than a lock of hair,
a drop of blood, wax from an ear or a finger nail paring,
over which, in the quiet of their laboratories, they would
make incantations like witch doctors making voodoo over
a pinch of dust from the victim's footprints. These search-

ers took all the romance out of the detective-story business, making clews so ridiculously simple.

When Parr arrived at the scene of the crime the hounds of the press were already there, sniffing at the door crack. The first extra was on the street. The newspapers had already coined their slug for this case—The Assagai Murder. The reporters wanted to get inside.

"Not yet," said Parr.

Conditions were perfect for the experts. Seldom in Parr's experience had the matrix of a crime come to hand so fresh and unbroken. No one had entered the place—not even the manservant who made the discovery. This fellow had climbed up and peered over a transom light and run screaming to the street.

Nothing would be touched now; it would lie in this rigid attitude for hours on end, to be examined from every angle, in every light. Even the dead man would endure it, as if, immovable, he too challenged haste in his own redress.

Parr's first act was to send for his friend and occasional collaborator, Oliver Armiston. The deputy sensed the unfinished here. Some murders end a story, others begin one. This had the earmarks of the latter category. Oliver was already on his way downtown when word reached him.

"You know who he was," said Oliver, coming in on them. Parr nodded. "You know what he was then," said Oliver. Parr nodded. Yes, he knew that, too, in its several implications.

"Some woman," said Oliver, "or some man avenging her."

"Or himself," Parr amended with an odd smile. In his knowledge nothing shoots so wide of the mark as a guess at motive—murder is blind.

"Why the assagai?" mused Oliver. The slender reedlike shaft stood trembling at a breath.

"Merely a gesture," said Parr.

It wasn't an assagai murder, even if the tabloids would have it so for the sake of typography. Verblennes was a strong man. His idea of a joke was to walk off with a telephone booth with someone in it. That needle-like spear would never have put Verblennes out, on his feet. And if he had fallen on it when transfixed, the thing would have been shattered. No, he had been pinned down afterward, like a butterfly specimen.

The music room was, say, forty by twenty-five. It was the loft of what once had been a brick stable; and his apartments in the rear had been the quarters of the coachman's family in less genteel days. In the studio the walls were dressed with weapons, ancient and barbaric—ax, mace, flail; bolo, machete, boomerang; javelin, creese, scimitar, assagai—this one had been snatched from a cluster backing a kafir shield.

Next in importance to the collection of weapons was the radio equipment. One corner—it had the look of a physics laboratory swept under a bench for the time being—was devoted to experimental paraphernalia.

Armiston, after a brief examination, threw over a little knife switch, and instantly a familiar voice, of a determined cheeriness, was saying, "Take a deep breath! Now! Ready! One—two—three——" Armiston was one of the daily doesn'ts and he shut the thing off with a wry face. Under the bench some actuating deviltry suspired with a dwindling sigh. Oliver raised on tiptoe to look out of the rear window.

"Hello! A back yard!" he exclaimed.

Back yards are getting scarce in this part of the midtown section. Here was a whole block interior of back yards—little bandbox gardens, probably fifty in all, opening on a hollow square of houses, mostly private, fronting on four

streets. Fifty doors of escape for an agile, catlike, resource-
ful fugitive.

Patient policemen had been, for the last hour, consuming brain power and shoe leather examining every entry,
every areaway, every roof top and every householder in
this hollow square. They were searching for the needle in
the haystack, which, contrary to the burden of the proverb,
is not at all a rare find in police work. This patient plodding
is usually the stuff which solves murder mysteries.

A telephone rang. It had been taken over by the police
and looped through Central Office, left open as a trap for
the unwary. But this was one of Parr's voodoo experts,
Doctor Horty.

"Could that have been an electrocution, sir?" he asked.

"Certainly; why not?" said Parr affably; and while he
waited he wrote the word for Armiston to stare at.

"The red corpuscles are broken down, sir," said Horty.

"Good!" said Parr, and hung up. That would alter the
aspect of everything. In the first place, they could revise
their theory of time. At first sight—and without the aid of
a skilled physicist and his microscope—it might have occurred since midnight. But if the red corpuscles were
broken down, it might have abided here awaiting the hue
and cry for another twenty-four hours. "Morel," said Parr
to his man Friday, "go around the block again, on the supposition that it was Saturday, not Sunday." He turned to
Oliver. Oliver was down on his knees in the radio corner.
"Is there enough juice there for a fatal dose?" he asked.

Oliver got up. He threw over the knife switch again. The
actuating deviltry under the bench emitted a fine, rising
whine. Oliver threw back the switch. The whine subsided
in diminishing ratio.

"There you are!" he said. "A motor generator. Three
thousand volts. There isn't any antidote for that, if you get

it right." No, it wasn't an assagai murder. Oliver pointed at the switch. "There's your fatal weapon," he said.

There should have been some mark on the man, some burn. But there was none. They found nothing until they came to look elsewhere. Among the trappings on the wall was a pair of hammered copper bracelets, to fit the forearm of a Thor with barbaric splendor. On the edge of one of these was a telltale iris of purple shading to red, and in its center a shiny bit of copper drawn to a polished bead—the unmistakable signature of an electric arc. It was a perfectly logical assumption that these had been used as electrodes for the application of the lethal current—except for one thing. Why, if the strong man was so meek as to permit himself to be harnessed in this wise, if he wore those bracelets—then why the electric current? There were so many simpler ways.

Morel came in at this juncture and reported that at 154, diagonally across the back yards and fronting on the parallel street, a landscape gardener had been called in by the tenant who lived in the basement apartment—even a coachman would have scorned to occupy a basement in the old days. The landscape artist had been given carte blanche to turn the twenty feet of yard into a garden. No idle inch had escaped his art. There was hardly room to walk among the congested flora. However, someone had walked! Someone in a Number 10—or thereabouts—shoe of French cut had come down, with considerable weight, off the fence, and left his imprint in the expensive patented humus that covered the landscape like a quilt.

It was not the footprint of Manuel Sierra, a violinist, who occupied the basement; and certainly not that of his daughter Pepita, aged five, who, with her dog, a smooth fox terrier, had the run of the garden. The Mexican family were

absent—had been, over the week-end—and their windows
and doors were strongly barred, like a jail. But that signi-
fied nothing. This old private house was fitted with a fire
escape to conform to the tenement law, there being a family
to each floor now, with cooking privilege.

On the parlor floor was an old woman dressmaker whose
clientele was entirely of the dowagers of the rich who did
not care for modern fashions. On the second were two
maiden sisters who rarely came out, but sat in the window
all day looking down on the busy street. On the third were
five girls—art students; on the top, an Italian count who
did not pay his bills well. His mail box revealed that this
morning, the sixteenth, he was receiving a first notice from
the electric company and a second from the gas company—
the regular form duns put out by the collections depart-
ments for slow accounts. Morel, watching a mail box
briefly, could give a Bradstreet rating. The Italian count
was not unknown to the police.

"It is Giovanni di Vergonzi, chief," said Morel.

"The confectionery count!" cried Parr, delighted.

Some humus—Morel had it in an envelope—was found
on the top-floor fire-escape landing—it was the patented
stuff put out for rich people's gardens and was identical
with that which held the footprint down below. On the
strength of this Pelts—Morel's partner, who had gathered
these painstaking data—had entered the count's establishment, first making sure no one was home.

He had found the shoes—of acute French pattern—fitting the print in the garden. They contained, or rather
showed traces of, the patent garden mold. They were not
the count's shoes. The count's feet were Number 6's. The
boot soles were polished and pitted by use; also, they were
scratched, as if by sharp claws. Now householders nail

barbed wire on top of their fences to discourage cats and thieves. The boots might have been tight-rope walking the barbs.

All this might or might not hang a man. Police business is to fill the bag and examine the contents at leisure. Pelts, Morel reported, took away the shoes and left a man on guard to note the reaction of the owner. Happily, the janitor being discovered to be a small crook wanted by the police, he was taken away and a police detective given his job. If the owner of the shoes took alarm, then the business of the footprinted flower bed might be worth while. If not, maybe not.

Meantime every other house in the hollow square was being gone over again with fine-tooth detail. Here in the room of the murder all the doors were locked on the inside, and all the transoms held accumulations of undisturbed dust—of which the voodoo doctors had taken samples. The murderer must have gone by the back yards, and if by the back yards, then through or over one of these fifty houses. Police in uniform talked to householders on every doorstep.

Meantime Parr's secret minions, in the guise of gas men, inspectors, window washers, grocer boys and peddlers, were taking more elaborate views inside. A special detail concentrated on Number 154.

Conte Giovanni di Vergonzi was an extremely graceful and well-dressed young man without a single nickel to his illustrious name. Every day supercilious footmen drove up to the door in town cars of Continental make and left dinner cards of prodigious size. Epicures testify that no man, no matter how great his hunger, can eat a quail a day for thirty days. But the count, during this long hard winter, was coming perilously near to doing it.

A confectioner who catered to grand dinner parties paid his rent—or rather, guaranteed it, which was the same thing—and in return the count went to these parties as part of the decorations, being furnished by the confectioner on much the same basis as any other elaborate sweet. For furniture the count was provided by a distinguished hostess with an elaborate assortment, including, besides the necessities, such *outré* impedimenta of our naïve yesterday as ormolu clocks with pastoral scenes; bisque ladies under bell jars, fruits and flowers in porcelain, an Empire bed, and so on. Almost any society matron had tons of this Mauve Decade stuff eating its head off in storage.

If, as the sage says, utility is the soul of beauty, then these stodgy ornaments were beautiful, for the count was pawning them one by one and selling the tickets for pin money—or more truthfully, gin money. Once or twice he had run afoul of the police, as one who collects and sells pawn tickets is apt to do; but it was always explained away by somebody's lawyer as a terrible mistake. Nevertheless, Parr kept his eye on the confectionery count. Some day, somehow, somewhere, the count would come home to roost—to show up in the morning line-up.

Finally the door of the murder scene was thrown open to reporters, and each one with his bone, off they scurried. This early crew were content with fragments. Later in the day the big fellows would come on the scene, taking their time about it, not accepting too much for granted and not telling all they knew, even in print. The early birds rushed to the nearest telephone with such crumbs as Parr saw fit to let fall.

Parr wasn't interested in feeding the public's depraved taste for crime and crime news. He was feeding the criminal. Step by step, as the muddle of clews increased, he would make the fugitive think he was coming nearer and nearer, like the tapping of a blind man's cane. Sometimes when most at sea he so managed this effect that it became horribly cumulative, and the guilty man would reveal himself most unexpectedly.

"Oh! Oh! Electric! Electric murder! Extra!" bellowed the newsboys in the hollow streets. It was then nearly ten o'clock.

Somewhere in some crowd someone's heart skipped a beat at sound of that word "electric"; to someone that word was like the first footfalls of the Gods of the Mountain in the fantastic drama of Dunsany.

Just what was the layout at this hour? Well, from opposite directions, it had not yet occurred to Cuyler Braxton and M. Brody, as by common agreement, to turn their feet toward the shop of Estrelle, Inc. In fact, the *Rochambeau* had only come up the river a little while ago. Linda Surrey, a young music student who was to debut tomorrow and introduce her small vocality to a waiting world, slept late this morning and was not to know until afternoon that there were special extras on the street.

The count, on the other hand, was out early, for him, pawning an alabaster vase in a Third Avenue pawnshop. He was wondering why another customer, a fishy-eyed bulky person, seemed so vulgarly curious about what he was offering. Concluding his transaction, the count went next door, as was his custom, to sell the ticket; then the vulgar person tapped him familiarly on a shoulder, winked and jerked his head with a come-along gesture. The count was being picked up again as a suspicious person and taken to the station house to give an account of himself. This fellow simply didn't like his looks.

Note how this accident snapped one of Parr's carefully forged links. On the way to the station the cry of a newsboy smote their ears. The count turned pale, then of a sudden he went jubilantly crazy. He smote his captor a mighty stroke on his tomato nose. He hurled a paving stone through a show window. He upset an apple cart and beat the poor old apple auntie with a club he took from another policeman. He tore off his own coat, vest, collar, tie, shirt, tore them to bits and jumped on them. Before he was subdued and put in a strait-jacket he was a total stranger, not a confection, and he gave a fictitious name, laughing gayly. If you want to hide from the police, there is no place—except the morgue—like a police cell on a workhouse charge.

Back in the music room of Hector Verblennes the telephone was ringing again. It was another professor of voodoo.

"I have to report on the dust, sir," said the professor. Parr chuckled and listened. "On the ledge of the street-door transom," said the expert, "the dust is new laid."

"New-laid dust!" repeated Parr. Oliver pricked up his ears.

"It contains foreign material—namely, wool lint from a Bokhara rug, silk floss from a Persian prayer carpet, a trace of lubricating oil, copper dust with graphite impregnation, face powder colored with Number 12 saffron."

"There isn't any romance in crime any more," said Parr, hanging up. "That fellow brought his own dust!"

He laughed, looking up at the street-door transom, on the ledge of which somebody had dusted his own dust, like a floor painter painting himself out of a room. "Gad, have we got to begin pyramiding all over again?" cried Parr.

III

Linda Surrey had contracted, several months previously, for her debut at the Orphic Chambers on the afternoon of the seventeenth, and the big-time murder in which she was called on to play a part was one of those purely chance happenings which so frequently intervene to alter the course of an entire career—especially, it seems, among artists. Linda was to live to shudder over the thought of what might have been her fate had it not been for that fortuitous event. So with all of us. The barking of a dog deviated the course of the history of Christendom.

Being alone and unknown and undiscovered—nay, even unsuspected, one might say, among the thousands of students aspiring for a hearing—it was necessary for her to contract for this debut, to go out and buy it, much as one buys a complete funeral or a blue-plate dinner. Everything is furnished by the contractor; hall, heat, light, tickets, programs, flowers—to be run down the aisle after the first encore—and even, or especially, the audience, which must be of a type and bridlewise. This *entrepreneur* of the masses sometimes would go so far as to guarantee good press, but this is too naïve for any but the ultra-credulous.

Monday night she was up till dawn with her nails and hair and putting a last stitch in some things. She lay late and, on rising, broke fast on a glass of water. She vocalized sparingly as she drew on her silk stockings, which were a tan exactly to match the foundation of her complexion, which was not Number 12 saffron. Her coach—she had always dreamed of having Hector Verblennes for this occasion—came in at the last minute to put her over the hurdles and wring the last drop of nectar out of the limp phrases of Schubert, Donizetti and Delibes which were to do duty for the afternoon.

Her parents had come on from Pray's Mills with a little party of neighbors who had helped send her to New York for finishing touches. But wishing to avoid a premature demonstration, Linda had wisely sent them on to the hall alone. She followed in the car Sam Black, the contractor, sent for her.

The atmosphere was perfect. Even Cuyler Braxton, coming in from the street and getting an unprejudiced view of it, had to take off his hat to the impresario. There is something about a music-hall audience that is distinctly *sui generis*. It isn't only that they must be what we call nice people; it is the perfume, the flutter, the chatter, the air of expectancy, the cozy visiting back and forth. Linda Surrey, looking out through the crack of the waiting-room door offstage, was amazed to note how many faces she knew—fellow students. Nevertheless, she got the thrill of it; this house was assembled for her—for her!

"Where do the critics sit?" she asked. All the papers, of course, would send their first-line battleships.

"Eh? Oh, in the empty aisle seats," said Sam Black. "Don't fret, girlie. They'll show up. There's one now—a new one."

A handsome man who looked music to the finger tips was turning down one of the pair of aisle seats reserved for the *Times*. It was Morel, Parr's handsome man.

"Who is the beautiful woman being seated now?"

"That is Estrelle," said Sam proudly.

"Not Estrelle, Inc.?"

"Yes. And M. Brody, of Paris, Inc., is the fellow with her."

Cuyler Braxton came in just as the boy went out to open the piano and light the floor lamp. A hush fell o'er Eden. Linda Surrey, clasping a spray of bridesmaid roses, was greeted with a spatter of applause that rose to a small ovation. She was not at all affected by stage fright. She knew just exactly what she could expect of her voice and of her audience. She nodded to her accompanist, tapped her foot, took the wrist of one hand firmly in the other and began to sing.

This is not a review of the debut. If you will, you may get the flavor of it through the moist eyes of the proud parents, to whom it was wonderful and beautiful; or of the proud neighbors, to whom it was the realization of fondest hopes; or of the papered house, which, you may be sure, played its part to perfection, for they never know whose turn comes next; or of the critics, several of whom looked in—to please Cuyler Braxton—and—for the same reason— either said something kind or nothing at all; or of Estrelle. Estrelle covertly searched for Braxton throughout the program, but did not find him, because he had purposely taken a position behind her where he could note the reaction on her and M. Brody. Estrelle's first and final judgment was that the girl was not quite up to the part Braxton had given her. M. Brody regarded the girl on the stage throughout the performance with the glazed look of a hypnotized bird— if you can imagine a bird with whiskers.

In the end there was the fluttering rush down the aisles, led by the students, in imitation of the oblations at Carnegie Hall, and the final turning off of lights to dismiss the persistent admirers. Then the audience straggled out, leaving the happy debutante to her own people on the darkened stage.

"It was all right, eh?" asked Sam Black of Braxton, in the lobby.

"Fine!" nodded Braxton. Estrelle, in passing, gave him a chilly nod and went to her car. M. Brody was handing her in when Braxton touched him on the elbow and mutely begged him to remain a little longer. The car drove off with Estrelle.

"I'll have to depend on you, I guess," he said. "Women are squeamish. I'd like to have you talk with the girl. Wait."

Shortly he returned with Linda Surrey. She had got rid of her people on the promise to be with them for dinner. It was to be a celebration. Her fingers trembled slightly on

Braxton's arm as he presented the distinguished M. Brody, of Paris, Inc. They all three got into Cuyler's car and were driven into the line waiting to flow into the Avenue. It was here that Morel stepped out of the crowd and with a curt nod to Braxton took his seat beside the chauffeur. Morel and Braxton were not strangers to each other, and to look at them now one might say there was no love lost between them. Braxton shot a look at his two companions.

"Police!" he muttered under his breath; and to Morel he cried, trying to control his tones, "Morel, this is a little bit too cool. You can't exactly board us this way."

Morel turned and surveyed them, and for the moment held his peace in a menacing silence. Then he said in friendly caution, "Easy! You'll have a crowd on your back if you start a row here. I'm trying to save you. I am to take you to the big fellow."

The girl had gone deadly white. There is a saying that at the moment of arrest the guilty one is prepared and blusters it out, whereas the innocent one in invariably crushed at the thought of the ignominy. Morel was watching the girl oddly. Except for the pallor, she gave no sign.

"Me," said M. Brody, putting a leg out, "I depart. It is not of my ball of yarn."

"Sorry," said Morel, "but my orders are to deliver the package unbroken. Tell your troubles to the chief when we arrive."

It looked like an easy get-away, if M. Brody, dressed for an afternoon wedding though he might be, cared to try. Braxton caught something of the thought. He shook his head vigorously, cast his eye to either side significantly. They were invisibly surrounded—the police took no chances. So they drove up the Avenue. In their careful anonymity they rolled along in the parade unmarked, except for a discriminating eye here and there noting the cut of M. Brody's coat. Shortly they passed into a side street and across town, under the Elevated, and pulled up in front of a row of low brick structures. The block looked deserted, an air that some of these side streets—lying like eddies between the two big arteries of traffic—will assume at certain hours of the day. But as they stopped, Braxton became aware the street was not so empty. Men materialized from here or there, managed to be passing when the party got out. Bulls from Central Office looking for trouble. Braxton looked up at the number.

"Morel," he cried angrily, "you can't do this! As counsel I most certainly——"

"You are not here as counsel," said Morel, helping him out. "You are an accessory—and for obstructing justice."

"Me, I am just in from my sheep yesterday!" protested M. Brody from the seat.

"You picked bad company your first day ashore," said Morel. "Come, get out!"

The girl alone made no protest. She meekly permitted herself to be herded into a little hallway. They started to climb. It was one of those old-fashioned box stairways long since outlawed. Their footfalls announced their coming, for a door opened at the top of the first flight and Deputy Parr came out. He stood blocking the passage, to turn them into the room. Then the girl's nerve seemed to break. As if only then she realized where she was, she suddenly threw her arms above her head and uttered a piercing shriek, at the same time toppling over backward. She was saved from a fall by Morel, who caught her and came on, carrying her. Parr scowled at Cuyler Braxton as the young lawyer passed through the doorway. Parr lifted an eyebrow when M. Brody came to a mulish halt at the threshold. M. Brody began explaining about his sheep again—yesterday morning, on his arrival, he had sent his thirty-seven trunks to customs stores and he must go claim them at once!

"Yes, yes," said Parr soothingly; dropping a paw on M. Brody's shoulder, he gently impelled him onward. Morel passed in with the girl, and Parr closed the door behind them. Morel propped the girl in a wing chair by the fire. She lay weeping dry tears into her cupped hands. M. Brody was standing at full height, staring at an imaginary point in the floor, his eyes having taken on their glazed look again. Oliver Armiston lounged against the radio bench in the corner, eying the scene. Braxton seemed to have become suddenly philosophical. He pushed a chair over to Brody, and the man dressmaker, with a start, sat down, his eyes wavering.

The room had been completely set in order again. The matrix of murder having yielded its all, it had been broken up and cast aside. Life here, where a dead man had lain but a few hours before staring at the ceiling, had taken up the broken threads again. Parr's stenographer sat at a table sharpening pencils, of which he already had a full dozen. The words he would shortly take down would be as meaningless to him as the ciphers a bookkeeper enters hour after hour in a bank ledger. The scene had no thrill for him.

The girl lifted her head and examined her surroundings. Her eyes did not go to that imaginary spot on the floor where the assagai had stood. But her gaze nevertheless had the shrinking aspect of a terrible fear. Finally she fixed on Parr as the source of dread and settled down to a slow regard of his every movement. He rolled a cigar and lit it.

"So this is the girl you are measuring for a shroud, eh?" said Parr, inhaling the first puff.

"What makes you say that?" demanded Cuyler Braxton sharply.

"Your waiter at Marguery's was one of my men," said Parr, smiling. "We were there for something else. When we hold a basket, there is no telling whose head will tumble into it." He paused, giving them a little silent treatment, his eye roving from one to another and occasionally to the imaginary spot on the floor. He turned to the girl.

"Now, young lady," he said blandly, "let us have the story of your life." The stenographer's pencil began to move rapidly. "Remember that anything you say may be used against you. We will begin at 3 o'clock Sunday morning and work backward. Now when and under what circumstances did it first occur to you that you would be accused of the murder of Hector Verblennes, and would be in need of counsel and a trousseau?"

The hypnotized eyes of the girl shifted from Parr, when his words ceased, to the stenographer; when the pencil ceased to move she drew a deep breath, as if suddenly awakened from a dream, and stared at Braxton, who shook his head.

"Answer nothing," he said quietly, and relapsed into his waiting attitude, eying Parr narrowly.

"You studied in Paris two years," said Parr.

The girl looked, with fright, at Braxton, who gave no sign. She nodded—yes, she had studied in Paris.

"Verblennes used to go over occasionally when you were there, didn't he?"

"Answer nothing," whispered Braxton.

"You have good cause to remember those visits," said Parr, scowling. No answer. "Was that the motive?" he asked suddenly, leaning forward. She wetted her lips. Still no answer.

"Didn't you implore him, on several occasions, to make amends—to keep his word—to bring you out with great éclat?"

The girl moved uneasily, but a slight gesture from Cuyler Braxton quieted her. She took refuge in a rigidity of pose that was almost cataleptic.

"I will answer for you," said Parr. "That's the only way to get on. Verblennes refused. He laughed at you. Then you found that instead of being one, you were one of twenty, or fifty, or a hundred. He had told you that you would never be a great artist till you had touched life, drunk it to the dregs." She winced. "And you drank it. Love justified everything—so it seems. And then you suddenly wake up to the cold shock of reality. You discover that everything is gone; that it is only a question of time when you will stand before the world—before your friends—before your parents—before the neighbors who think you another Melba—when you stand before them revealed! You haven't even made a beginning, when they think you are arrived!" He rolled back in his chair, smoking. She did not move. "Nothing remained but revenge," he said nasally. "It's the old story. You followed him back here to make a last effort to force his hand."

"Pardon," said Mr. Brody, interrupting. "But it must be much pain to the young lady that me, a stranger, I am present. I go, if you please."

He half arose, but Parr motioned him down. "You go when I tell you, not before," said Parr. "Now, Linda, tell me this: How did you get in here at eleven o'clock Saturday night? Did you have a key? I think you came through a window. That is the only way I can account for your being here, waiting for him. You were here waiting for him, weren't you?"

He paused for a reply. The girl's eyes were immovable. Braxton muttered, "Answer nothing!" Parr turned and pointed to the music shelves in one corner. They were built row on row to the ceiling and were covered with sliding curtains of green baize. He got up and went over and drew back one of them, disclosing an empty nook.

"This is where you waited, isn't it?" he asked, in the form of a statement of fact. "You smoked four cigarettes while you waited. That was complacency!" He opened a drawer of a little table and took out four cigarette butts. "And, as usual, you dropped a comb. You women always leave a comb! Here it is! He took out the comb, a small affair of shell, studded with rhinestones. "And then, with a thoughtfulness characteristic of you amateurs at this sort of thing, you kindly left a perfect thumb print on the brass curtain rod."

He came to one of his vibrant pauses again, eying her for the effect of his words. There seemed to be none.

"I tell you these things," he cried, "in hopes you will tell me some things I want to know. How did Hector get in when he finally came home from his party? He was very drunk. He crawled upstairs on his hands and knees. How did he open the door? Or did you open it for him? Yes, you opened it for him. Didn't you? You got him on his feet. You half dragged him across the room. Then he went down in a heap again. You were wondering what you could do. That wasn't the sweet revenge you had come for. He didn't even know who you were—he fell asleep before he hit the floor. The biggest part of revenge is in the victim's knowledge of what it is all about. Eh? Isn't that true?"

The girl's face was totally devoid of color, but she never stirred under this rain of blows. Cuyler Braxton, watching her when Parr paused, smiled contemptuously.

"Me," said M. Brody, "I am—I suffer, for this young lady. I rise, I walk a little, with your kind permission, sir."

Parr said brusquely, "Go in that inner room and wait."

The deputy held up a finger, challenging the girl's attention again.

"He was lying there. He didn't even know who you were!" he cried. "Then," he said in a hoarse whisper, "you heard somebody coming." Her eyes quailed for an instant. "You couldn't afford to be found here. You pushed the door shut quietly. You locked it. You left the key in the lock so no prying eye could watch. And you waited there in the dark. Somebody was putting a ladder or something up against that door. You got frightened. You crept over there"—he turned and pointed at the music shelves—"and you hid behind that green curtain. Didn't you? Eh, didn't you?"

The girl drew a deep sigh, shuddering at the top of it, as if her calm were false, as if she were only holding back the shrieks by sheer strength of will. M. Brody had gone into the next room, behind the curtained doorway. They could see his one leg swung over the other as he sat down.

"Now you go on," urged Parr. "You tell me. Someone came over that transom. Who was it?"

"Look out!" warned Braxton in a low tone. "He's trying to trick you. Answer nothing."

"I am doing her a great favor," said Parr. "I am trying to show her her position, and beg her to throw herself on my mercy, not on the mercy of the court, if she will only help me a little. She will admit what I have said so far. Then she will tell the jury that at this point the transom was pushed open and a night prowler, whom she could not see very well in the dark, crawled through and came into the room—and—did—the—job—she—had—come—to—do! Before her very eyes, while she crouched behind that curtain. Ha-ha! Braxton, my dear fellow, tell me, does that sound good to you? You have been a prosecutor. Will the jury swallow it? They will not. Now come through! Tell me! Who was this providential monomaniac? What did he use the salt shaker for?"

Everybody started in surprise. Even the foot of M. Brody, visible through the opening, ceased to swing.

"All right," said Parr, "I'll tell you. When this fellow crawled in and saw how things were—poor Hector being comatose with bootleg gin—well, he turned on the light and took his time about things. His first act was to crawl up to his transom again and sprinkle it with his salt shaker— like this." Parr made a rapid movement with one hand, as if sprinkling salt from a shaker. The girl's eyes bulged.

"Yes! Yes! Yes! Yes!" she gasped, amazed. Then, as if she had hung herself by this one admission, she sank forward, her head in her hand, softly moaning, "But what did he do? How did you know?"

"Careful! Careful!" begged Braxton. Parr chuckled.

"Oh, you begin to wake up, eh?" he said. "Well, he was covering his tracks—laying some new dust. This clever fellow brought his own dust with him. Yes, he brought his own dust with him." He laughed. Then with a swift change he half rose, glaring ferociously at her. "Who was he?" he snarled. "You saw him in the light—who was he? That's what you are here to tell me."

Strangely this sudden attack seemed to nerve the girl. She sat upright again, stared, challenging, at him.

"Good!" muttered Braxton jubilantly. "Hold your trap; he's trying to bully you!"

"If she tells me," said Parr, "I'll believe her. If she tells the jury they'll give her the laugh. Even you can't put that over, Braxton, and I've seen you pull some raw stuff on the other side of the fence. Come on, kid, give me a lead. No? Well, I can go a little farther. I'll show you."

He got up and went over to the radio corner. He took down the pair of hammered copper armlets. From under the radio bench he brought out a coil of twisted-pair wire

which he attached to the armlets. He dragged these electrodes to the imaginary spot on the floor in the middle of
the room.

"We put these on the drunken man's arms," he said, and
he went through the motions. The girl was gnawing at her
knuckles. Then she seized her hair by the roots at the temples as if to lift it off her head. But she did not actually
break until, at Parr's signal, Oliver Armiston pushed over
the knife switch once, twice, a third time, the last time holding it down, and the motor generator under the bench,
building deadly voltage as it sped up, gave forth a rising
fine whine that mounted almost to a shriek. Then the girl
shrieked.

"You devil! I'll tell! Oh, oh, oh!" Her voice trailed off
in a diminishing wail of unspeakable anguish.

"There he goes!" cried Oliver in a hoarse whisper.

Everybody turned. The girl became still.

"Well?" cried Parr menacingly. "Well?"

The girl shrieked again, shrinking from him. Then Parr,
with Armiston and Morel, bounded into the back room;
they cautiously peered out of the open window giving on
the nest of back yards. M. Brody, in the dimming light
of evening, was running across the barbed coping of the
fence tops like a tight-rope walker. He dropped down into
the landscaped garden.

"He seems to know his way," said Parr, chuckling.

M. Brody, the gladness of his afternoon raiment sadly
disarranged, was climbing the fire escape. He struggled
frantically with the window leading to the apartment of the
confectionery count on the top floor; he opened it and
sprang inside.

"I thought his nerve was going to hold," said Parr.

"It was the whine of that generator," said Oliver. "It

was like killing his victim all over again. I suppose that whine will haunt him to his dying day—when he takes the juice himself for killing Hector Verblennes."

Parr was watching the top-floor window across the way. In a moment the eager face of little Pelts, his trusty sleuth-hound, peered out, and at sight of his chief he waved a triumphant signal. M. Brody was in chains.

Parr and Braxton gripped each other by the hand. "Good boy!" cried Parr. "It worked."

"I certainly thought she was lying when she came to me with that yarn," said Braxton. "It sounded like the yarn they make up."

"It didn't sound that way to Brody," said Parr grimly.

They went back to the girl. She was plainly badly shaken, now that it was all over. She was white, tremulous, and looked up at them pathetically. Parr brought her a sedative. She got up and patted her dress and hat, took up her purse and gloves and the program she had brought away from her debut. She twisted the program into a rope.

"Did I do well?" she asked, hardly daring to trust her voice.

"Perfect!" ejaculated Parr, watching her narrowly.

"Do I—do I get my Milan scholarship?" Parr nodded. Yes, she got that too. La Scala! He looked at his watch. "You are keeping your parents waiting," he said. "You should be going. Here is Mr. Braxton, ready for you."

Newsboys were bellowing the extra within an hour. M. Brody, of Paris, Inc., had confessed! He had come to this country secretly, on his brother's passport, ten days ago, and had lain in hiding in the rooms of the confectionery count, Di Vergonzi, biding his time. It was an old feud of gallantry between these two professional beaus, and only blood could wipe it out. It was Brody's brother who came in on the *Rochambeau* Monday morning, the day after the crime, with a perfect alibi for him. The innocent brother merely imagined he was being of assistance in another of those affairs of the heart which constantly engaged the great dressmaker. Except for the diseased sense of hearing from which M. Brody suffered, they were alike as twins, so the deception was easy.

The newspapers made much of the footprint, the patent garden mold and the salt shaker, for they dearly love to suspend a mystery on a thread. It was the salt shaker that convicted M. Brody, for he had taken his supply of dust, to cover his tracks, from a vacuum cleaner in the rooms of the count. That was where the trail began. Cuyler Braxton's going to Parr for help wrote the finis.

But Linda Surrey never appeared in the case. Last year, when she came back from Milan as guest artist at the Opera, she had suddenly come into possession of a voice whose depth of understanding bespoke an artist who, in the words of Hector Verblennes, had really touched life.

Estrelle, listening to the applause finally die away, whispered in the ear of Cuyler Braxton, "Did you ever ask her, in so many words, about the assagai?"

He shook his head—no.

VIII

THE RECOIL

PARR, the police deputy, settled himself in his favorite elbow chair and took up a stogy. While he inspected it for wormholes he unbuttoned his ulster. Merely unbuttoning it indicated to his friend and occasional "medicine," Olive Armiston, that the call was an emergency one and would be brief. "To revert," said Parr, "to our original thesis: Every dog has his flea—if he is a normal dog. And every crook has his squealer——"

"If he is a normal crook," slyly inserted Oliver. "Some of our best parlor sociologists will pick you up there, Parr."

"I know it," said the deputy. "One of them came to my office the other day and told me Killer Whalen was an honest man, only misunderstood. Killer's got a record of four misunderstandings and has just taken a plea of manslaughter on a fifth! I said, 'How can you tell he is honest? I'd like to know how.' He said, 'I look them in the eye! They can't lie to me!' " Parr chuckled. "I wish it was as easy as that. Crime," he said, lighting his stogy, "is a perfectly normal act. A crook is a perfectly normal person. The only difference between him and you is that he thinks you are a fool to work for a living when you can pick it up for nothing. Do you remember the Thwing jewel robbery?"

Oliver nodded. Very well. It made good reading, when it flooded the newspapers a few years ago. Thwing was one of those rare personages—in this country—born to the grand manner. He lived formally, never relaxed. He married a Spanish woman of high degree. Her only idea of money was gold coin, which she kept loose in her dressing-table drawer. Her only idea of a safety-deposit vault was the receptacle in the base of her harp. She played the harp well, like all Spanish women with pretty arms. To Oliver, on an occasion, she said: "Oh, yes, the bayadere is very difficult; but not for me, because I have good technic." She kept her jewels in the base of that harp. When she traveled she took the harp with her, because every morning she must run off a few *arpeggios,* much as the rest of us do our daily dozen. In keeping with the grand manner, they traveled in their private car, and the harp was merely another piece of baggage, and no trouble. The jewels rode in the harp, although Madame's maid always believed—until the jewels turned up missing, in a journey to White Sulphur—that she herself invariably carried them in an elaborate jewel box. It was clever, but of a cleverness better suited to dupe a bandit of the Spanish hills than a crook of the international jungle. Parr and the best minds of the police world recognized instantly the earmarks, and rounded up the several crooks clever enough for the job. It was a dry haul. None of the élite claimed the credit. Several lesser lights of the underworld openly boasted of it as theirs, as crooks will, when they have such a chance. For comic relief, a woman squealed on a pickpocket, said he did it. Two cops brought the poor dip in, and Parr, in no mood for trifling, booted the three of them out of his office. There is such a thing as ordinary intelligence, even in a cop.

"Recollect that poor dip?" asked Parr. "He worked the cross-town cars and never lifted more than a ten-spot in his life."

"You turned him loose, didn't you?" said Oliver.

"Certainly," said Parr.

"What about it?"

"He did it!"

"Get out!"

"Absolutely! He saw that harp on a baggage truck, and from habit, frisked it." Parr laughed. "The girl was right. She was sore at him because he wouldn't peddle the stuff and dress her up. But he was too wise! He buried it. We turned him loose, of course. The job was too big for him. Well, lately he's been spreading himself—dressing up and making big bets at New Orleans and Baltimore. We picked him up and asked him how. He blew! Told everything. We've got all the stuff—or traced it."

Everybody in that case made at least one error— Madame, in being too clever; Parr and his international correspondents, in being too wise; and the dip, in being too trusting. Looking back, Oliver thought, in the light of discounted knowledge, it was difficult to see how any one of the three—each according to his lights—could have avoided the error. Nor could any logician plot those errors beforehand. Given a certain set of facts, what error will a given person naturally fall into? Later, that error, when it becomes known, seems the only possible one, and laughably peculiar to the person who committed it—but it can't be forecast!

"This case is finished," thought Oliver, eying his friend Parr. "He didn't come here to tell me this. There is something else."

This surmise immediately proved correct.

"The Culpepper Lea killing," said Parr, shifting his little elephant eyes to Oliver. "Recollect?"

It was only three weeks old, still in print. Oliver nodded, the tips of his fingers—with which he did some of his thinking when he wrote on his typewriter—tingling pleasantly. The Lea killing. Parr hadn't said the Lea murder, a distinction not made in print yet. It was one of those rare crimes which seem to carry an easy boast of the impenetrable, the enigmatic, the inapprehensible. There are crimes like that. Reading the first account of them in the press, many people, from totally different viewpoints, shake their heads and say, "They will never reach a solution in that case. The criminal will never be apprehended." The public, of course, forgets not only the crime itself but its own fresh reaction to it. Parr never forgot. He knew that sooner or later the chickens all come home to roost. There is a steady stream of forgotten crooks coming in through the back door at Central Office. The police never shelve a mystery. Unfinished business, yes, Parr would admit, but he would never admit he was through so long as a perpetrator remained at large. There was always the squealer, or someone to do the wrong thing at the wrong time.

Oliver was thinking something like that now, with a change of tense. He was thinking: "Undoubtedly someone did the wrong thing, somewhere, in that affair too."

For all its vain air of the inscrutable, the facts in the Lea killing were simple enough as they came to the police blotter. In spite of his high-sounding name, Lea had no very distinguished connections. Some of those Culpeppers and Leas of Virginia and North Carolina, who went West with the Argonauts and got into Bret Harte's stories, bred him and gave him his eagle eye and duelist's carriage. But they were too busy to draw a family tree on parchment for him. He was in the consular service, his appointment dating back to the time of political preferment. He saw the world and was thrown among fine people, and was frequently asked about his honored name. In answer he always told a story. In Newport one time, in a hotel dining-room, he heard the head waiter cry out: "Hey, you, Culpepper Lea! Come and take care of this gentleman."

and worked far into the night on them, returning them the next day. His will, insurance papers, everything—all those items a man accumulates through a long and careful life and wishes to preserve against all hazards—all were gone.

"Go back to the other case a minute," said Parr, as he and Oliver went over these known facts again. "Take the jewel case. Madame had the right idea, but it didn't work out. That doesn't vitiate the rightness of it. She was known to travel with an enormous fortune in jewels with her at all times. Very well, what does she do, with the amount of intelligence given her? She handed her jewel case to her maid and told her never to let it out of her sight. The maid, supposing it to contain the precious jewels of her madonna, was naturally nervous and frightened, and showed it. That was what Madame wanted. That would attract attention away from Madame and her harp, and to the girl—who, by the way, was an old woman," put in Parr. "By all the rules, the girl should have been robbed. In time, I dare say, she would have been—if"—Parr smiled feebly—"my pickpocket hadn't intervened."

"What was in that brief case? Is there any way of finding out?" asked Oliver.

"That's not the point!" cried Parr. "Maybe it was empty," he said, his eyes shifting to the old bronze Buddha toasting its shins by the fire. "Empty, like Madame's jewel box. She had been carrying that empty box around all her life. What for? To arouse suspicion."

"Now, Parr," said Oliver, "don't get too wise! You know your failing. You are not going to tell me he exhibited that brief case just to induce some thug to blow him to kingdom come."

"Why not?" asked the deputy. "It would be a perfectly normal act, of a perfectly normal individual."

"To blow him to kingdom come, yes," said Oliver. "But

on the receiving end, no! That might be a subtle form of suicide, yes. But it would be hard to imagine anybody, especially this Culpepper Lea, so desperately subtle—or so subtly desperate—as patiently to go through this stunt of inviting destruction once a week for eight or ten years. If he were set on suicide, he would have done it himself long ago."

"Maybe he did it himself," replied Parr quietly. "I don't know. There were no witnesses. There are several unexplained coincidences. This lot was empty. No one saw him. Now it happens that is a well-trodden path, about as busy as a side-street block here in town. We have checked that block for a week. At no time during the day was that path idle. There was always someone crossing."

"Naturally, a thug or a would-be suicide would wait until he was unobserved," put in Oliver dryly. "That's not a coincidence. That's normal enough. What else?"

"This!" said Parr. He took a package out of a pocket and let it fall, with a clank of metal, on the desk. "Unwrap it!"

Oliver unwrapped the package. It was an old dueling pistol, with an inch of the muzzle blown off, as if from too heavy a charge.

"Ah, the lethal weapon, eh?" cried Oliver.

"I don't know," said Parr bluntly. "Man disposes and luck interposes. It was found in the water. The spot where Culpepper Lea lay when they got to him was within ten feet of the stringpiece of the dock. The billboard intervened—but the billboard stood on stilts four feet off the ground. An assassin could easily have tossed the pistol into the water. Lea himself might have done it as he fell, but I doubt it. There is still a third possibility—the blackest of all. He may have put in an overcharge, so that the recoil hurled it from his hands into the water. That sounds

a little too pat. But pat things happen. Yesterday we had
another gang murder uptown. May their tribe increase!"
said Parr, his face painted with that odd look of wonder
that sometimes came to even this old stager. "The killer
grabbed his overcoat and beat it. He grabbed the wrong
coat. He grabbed the dead man's coat. It happened the
same tailor made the two coats and they were exactly
alike. The gunman's name was in the coat he left behind.
These things happen," said Parr; "which accounts for my
hair being less gray than it might be otherwise."

Oliver nodded and waited. He didn't quite see the drift
of things yet. This killing was out of Parr's bailiwick,
being in Connecticut. The New York police had been
called in on the bank end, and Parr, as usual, had begun
at the source, in the country. Parr looked at his watch.
He was secretly studying Oliver, playing him for some
reaction which obviously had not yet appeared.

"Why do you say 'blackest'?" asked Oliver.

"About the pistol recoiling, you mean? Because my pistol expert downtown has a gun like this; and he finds that,
with a certain overcharge of black powder, the recoil hurls
it twenty or thirty feet. As I say, it is entirely possible that
it was hurled into the water by the recoil. That would be
good luck for somebody, bad for somebody else. Now, my
pet little god of chance, to whom I burn all my joss, interposes. There is fourteen feet of water at low tide. And
several feet of mud. But along comes a steam dredge with
a clamshell bucket, to open up a sewer that has backed up.
The first bucket brings up this gun! Can you beat it? It's
like the killer that left his name for us in his overcoat."
Parr leaned forward, his beady eyes gleaming. "The mate
to this gun, the other one of the pair, is in a case in Culpepper Lea's library," he said. "It was his own gun."

Somehow the clocks in the room—those clocks that had

played their part in a murder once, by the way—somehow all the clocks in the room seemed suddenly to tick louder. The scowl that had been forming on Oliver's face now perceptibly deepened. He turned his head, as a gun turret turns, to lay his gaze on Parr. Parr got up, buttoning his ulster.

"Some of the insurance companies think maybe they will refuse to pay, on the basis of that pistol," said he. "There is two hundred thousand involved, spread out thin among several companies. They say it is too much—there is no evidence of any estate. Their theory—and it's rather a pretty one, I admit—is that all his coming and going was to establish a reputation of being rich enough to justify this amount of insurance. They even make a point of his care with that brief case—exhibitionism, they call it—how he never let go of it, held it on his knee while he sat on a stool at the lunch counter. This pistol, of course, is their trump card. That's what sent them into conference. Oliver, I don't believe that man killed himself. If they are right, he wouldn't have used his own pistol. I think he was murdered. I want you to go up there and look it over. Maybe your eyes can see something we have overlooked. Will you?"

"I'd be very glad to," said Oliver. "What kind of a wife is she?"

"Fine," said Parr. "Fine! Does it look like suicide?"

"Yes," said Armiston. He looked oddly at Parr. "You've got a hunch, chief?"

"Yes," said the deputy.

"Does she know?"

"I assume so, yes," replied Parr. "The implication is there; she can't shut her eyes to it. But the underwriters aren't making any false moves. They can't afford to. They could better afford to err the other way—pay it all. So they will take their time about it. You've got plenty of time. I've told you, purposely, the blackest part of it. This stuff hasn't got to the newspapers yet——"

Parr paused abruptly, staring stupidly at Oliver.

"Wait!" he cried. "There's something else—the blackest part of it! I almost forgot. It's what started the insurance people on the trail. Oliver," he said, sitting down again, "she always went as far as the gate with him when he went away. Just a habit, you know—a mighty nice one! She always looked him over to see if he was all right; then she kissed him good-by. She'd stand there watching him down the street. At the corner he would look back and she'd wave to him again. And then—that morning—to her surprise, he came back and said good-by once more. She said to him, 'Why, you silly-billy, one would think you expected never to see me again.' And he patted her shoulder and started off again, waving to her, as usual, at the corner."

Parr got up and took his hat. He stared at old Buddha, stony confidant of so many tales told in this room. He looked down at Oliver.

"Do you see any holes in it?" he asked, drawing on his gloves.

Oliver nodded.

"Here and there, yes," replied Oliver.

"Will you go up and look it over?"

"I'll run up this afternoon," said Oliver, rising and opening the door to speed the parting guest.

II

The Vachen School For Boys was at Barhampton. The sight of its colonial brick assembly hall, like a Quaker lady with a snood, gave Oliver a start of satisfaction. He turned in, got down, and entered. The head master would be glad to see him. The place wore the musty smell of learning. Oliver tiptoed across the hall, admonished by a thousand echoes. Behind the silences he caught the treble murmurs of responses. Mind is a function of the brain. But what tricks the brain can play. A breath, a whisper, an odor, or a remembered cadence is all the stimulus needed to touch it off, like a hair trigger. Oliver, as he sat down in the office to wait for Vachen, was a boy of fourteen again. With a sigh he brought himself back to the present.

He could see the whole street from the window. It was really two streets, North and South, as they builded in the old days. It had its double row of elms, with wide parking, and the air was hazy and filled with the incense of the fall burning of leaves. The houses, with a show of antiquarian pride, wore dates instead of numbers. They had picket fences that rose in swift little curves to gateposts.

He wondered which was her gate, where the old man had come back to say good-by a second time.

Vachen was a small man, with a bulging bald brow and dark blue eyes and the shy smile of an ascetic caught thinking of worldly things. Studying him now, after a long separation, Oliver found himself again wondering what was the secret of this man's marvelous success with boys.

"Who is Mrs. Culpepper Lea?" asked Oliver.

All the welcome and vivacity of an unexpectedly renewed friendship faded out of the expressive face of the head master.

"Are you writing again?" he asked.

"No," said Oliver. He explained that he had stopped writing thrillers years ago, at the gentle request of the police; he had grown too realistic, and crooks had plagiarized his fiction, even to the point of murder.

"That poor unfortunate," said Vachen, "is being studied like a bug under a bell jar. What is that dreadful fascination about murder that makes the public so demanding? The appetite must be there, else the editors would not go on soiling white paper. They send experts here to see her. It seems, no savant, no matter how distinguished, can resist their blandishments. They get to her by the most ingenious means. Why? Simply because she is a woman in agony whom they wish to dissect in public. It is like those creatures who slice off a monkey's brain bit by bit, heal up the wound, and study the reactions, the reflexes. Why, even the playwrights come here! Ravel came to me the other day and asked me if I couldn't scheme some way of getting her to luncheon with him, where he could study her as he carved. I said, 'Ravel, can't you invent enough horror for your clientele without getting the real thing to pose for you?' He said, 'There is nothing like the real thing.' And now, you, Oliver, come! What do you want?"

He turned away, somewhat abashed at the heat of his outburst, gazing moodily out of the window.

"There she is now," he said, nodding to indicate a woman passing down the street slowly, with two half-grown children, her arms resting lightly on their shoulders. Something in the composition of the picture suggested to Oliver the line, "She wrought needlework, and kept the house"—the matron deified, in a word.

"Was he a man to shoot himself with his own gun?" he asked.

"The missing pistol, you mean."

"Yes."

"Have they found that?"

"Yes, within ten feet of where they found him," said Oliver.

The woman turned in at a gate below; the children went on, walking backward and still talking and calling to her as long as they were in sight.

"So that's what they are driving at," muttered Vachen. "That's why they keep it alive, day after day! The innuendo has always been there, of course. But they have never dared to come out with it in so many words. I wondered why they clung to it so desperately."

"Drama," said Armiston. "That's why Ravel came here. The public is a child. It likes pictures. Anything that makes pictures. This crime is a picture at every turn—the old man clutching his brief case—he invited attack, by the very means he used to avert it!—his career! His face—he looked like a somebody! The public likes its tragedians to look like somebody! His name—where did he get it? It's too good a name to own without some explanation. His wife—she's beautiful. That's enough. Why, if one of us writers is fortunate enough to pick out some combination of romance, mystery and adventure that has a new twist to it, the reading public rewards us with a fortune. They read through dozens of editions; they visualize it on the screen; they bring it to life on the stage! And when these same rare elements combine in real life, they keep it going as long as they can. That's the real thing—as Ravel says."

"That will be printed—about the gun?"

Oliver let a pause intervene before his answer. Then he said quietly: "Not if we can help it. That's why I am here."

" 'We'?" demanded Vachen. "Who are 'we'?"

Oliver told him in detail, painting it at its blackest. There was a pause.

"What's wrong with the picture?" asked Armiston, watching him.

"It's too subtle," said Vachen. "The big scene is founded on a mathematical absurdity. Here, let me show you!"

He took up a stick of chalk, and with a single sweep of his arm drew such a circle as Michelangelo might have drawn. He indicated the center with a cross.

"That's the location of the exploding pistol, on a horizontal plane," he said. "It has 360 degrees of choice—that is, it can fly in any direction from the recoil. If it falls in the water—flies in that direction, it will never be found. So, at least, we will argue for the moment! Well, what chance is there of its falling into the water? About ten degrees of arc, isn't it?" He struck a geometrical chord across a segment of his circle.

"Thirty-five to one against its falling into the water," said Oliver. "That's a little better than one shot at roulette."

"Wait!" said the head master. "That's only as regards the plane. Now, how about the sphere? It must also pick out a vertical arc, to fly between the bottom of the billboard and the ground. Another ten degrees of arc. Imagine a window in a sphere, ten degrees wide and ten high. What proportion does the window bear to the entire surface of the sphere? That's your problem." He made some rapid calculations.

"About one in four hundred," said Vachen. "Does it strike you that a sane man would deliberately plot suicide, to make it look like murder, with that chance against him? The recoil must throw it into the water to make his purpose effective. Thrown in any other direction, it must surely have been found. And it was his gun. There is no doubt about its being his gun! Now, assuming that he was murdered——"

"Wait just a minute," interposed Oliver. His mind had suddenly taken to leaping forward; it was registering decisions of its own, irrespective of his conscious volition. He stared for some time at Vachen without seeing him. Then he took a package out of his ulster pocket. It was the gun, the dueling pistol, with its muzzle blown away by the same charge that sent Culpepper Lea to his doom.

"There is the whole story!" Oliver said. He almost shouted it. He took up the telephone and called Parr by long-distance.

"Pretty soon, ain't it?" said Parr cheerfully.

"Not for us," said Oliver. "Chief, were there any other wounds on him?"

"No. Only the one. You could pass a hat through that."

"His hands were all right?"

"Yes—y-yes," muttered Parr, beginning to get something.

"Are you sure? Are you sure?" Oliver pressed it home. "Parr!" he cried. "Any charge big enough to blow the muzzle off the gun would blow off the finger that pulled the trigger!" There was a silence. "Do you get me, Parr?"

"Abso——" The deputy's voice trailed off queerly. Oliver recognized the symptom—he had seen the brain of the great man hunter come to with a jolt many a time. "Wait a minute!" rumbled Parr's voice in the telephone. Oliver chuckled. "Morel!" yelled the deputy. The voice came to the phone as if being shouted through a metal tube. Oliver could hear Morel's heel taps as he hurried into the room, a hundred miles away. "Morel," Parr was saying, "we've got the guy that croaked Lea. Part of his gun hand was torn off with the same shot. No man could have fired that gun without losing some skin. Start a rabbit drive! Draw a big circle, taking in Connecticut as far east as New Haven. Canvass every doctor, every hospital, every emergency dressing station. Look for a man with a torn hand on that day. Go to it!"

The heel taps started again, diminished, ceased, the door shut.

"Hello, Oliver! Are you there? What is it? What were you saying? Excuse the interruption."

"That's about it, I guess, Parr," said Oliver.

"Yes! I'm firing my pistol expert! I don't know but I'd better fire myself! How'd it come to you? Just one of your thinks?"

"Yes. Wait just a minute! Hold the wire."

Vachen's hand was on Armiston's arm, two fingers digging in. Oliver leaned toward him, and Vachen whispered for several seconds.

"Parr, he's probably left-handed," said Oliver. "I mean the wound would be on the left hand."

"What's that? Come again on that!"

"The house was robbed two nights previously." Oliver nodded at Vachen as he spoke again into the phone. Vachen trembled with suddenly roused excitement. Oliver was thinking what a queer way murderers have of leaving a broad wake of coincidence trailing along behind. Why did this murderer pick out a town where Oliver Armiston happened to have for a friend a mathematically minded and otherwise involved person such as Arthur Vachen? "The house was robbed two nights previously," said Oliver.

"We knew that," said Parr.

"Well, here's something you didn't know," said Oliver: "Entrance was effected through a high ventilating window in a rear hall leading to the library. This window was accessible to a nimble man on the outside by ascending a drain pipe some eight feet up, and working with his left hand. He took out a pane of glass and reached in to unlock the window. He put the glass back again when he went out. He had to hang on with his right hand, as the drain pipe was two feet to the right of the window. Actually there were boot scratches on the paint below that window and gouges in the frame."

But Parr was not listening. He had summoned Morel again. The telephone at Oliver's elbow was repeating like a loud-speaker.

"Morel, here's the lay: This fellow has been tailing Lea for some time," said Parr, the metallic accents heard in every corner of the office. "He wasn't taking any chance. There wasn't any hurry. He could take his time, think it out. Maybe, like some of the rest of us, he was too wise! First, the question as to the location—where he'd plug him. He was probably a sneak working around a bank. That's where he'd pick up Lea—not much chance to knock him off there. So he takes to tailing him. This vacant lot looks good. He decides on that. He sits and waits for things to break right. They don't come. There are always people going back and forth through that lot at the time Lea comes and goes. This gives him an idea! Remember, he's thought too much already! A flash comes to him! Why not make it sure, with Lea's own gun—if he's got a gun? Then there will be no question, no pursuit! Great! We trail Lea home again. We climb up the drain pipe, take out a pane of glass. . . . We forget to look at that. That's one on you, Morel. . . . And lo and behold! We find the gun with its twin, the old dueling pistols! Just what we want! We will shoot and leave the gun on the job. Not a chance in the world of its failing. But we make one mistake. We overload the gun, not knowing much about muzzle loaders. It's blown out of our hand, maybe taking a finger or two with it. But it falls in the water, where we can't get it. But we make our get-away with the loot. Of course we had no way of knowing that steam dredge would come along later and dip up the gun the first dip. If we did know it we'd say, 'Fine! That's all right! There's your suicide!' . . . Morel, forget about your hospitals! Whom have we got wise enough to do that job in just that way?"

There was a telephonic pause. Oliver and Vachen waited breathlessly. Morel was mentally going over his catalogue of experts.

"Southpaw Jake, the Crippler, gets wise like that sometimes," said Morel. "And Lefty Steulan——"

They had forgotten all about Oliver now, left the phones
hanging loose. They were now basically policemen going
over their lists of crooks who could do this, crooks who
could do that, crooks who could do something else. Crooks
always left their earmarks on a job. When a big crime broke,
Parr would chuckle and send out for Mike this, Jake that,
or Bill something else, and say, "This looks like your job!
Show me you didn't do it." That's what Parr would be
doing in this case—sending out for certain left-handed
crafty members of the thieves' fraternity, to count their
fingers, to ask them where they were on the afternoon of
October eighth, when Culpepper Lea was done in. Police
business is very simple with a lead or two to go on. Morel's
voice dropped to a lower level of audibility; the metallic
echoes became more pronounced. Oliver knew what he was
doing. He was going over a rogues'-gallery section that hung
against one wall. He suggested one after another. Some
Parr accepted, some he rejected.

Oliver hung up. He turned to Arthur Vachen with a smile
and a little *c'est ça* gesture.

"It's solved," he said.

"I don't follow," said the head master. "You——"

"Arthur, it was your iteration of that word 'recoil,' " said
Oliver. He picked up the gun. "Look at it! The charge that
blew off that muzzle blew off a trigger finger too! There
isn't a mark on Lea's hands. Arthur, if I should ask you
to send me, from among your graduates, a dozen boys who
could do a hundred yards in ten seconds, you could do it,
couldn't you?"

"Well, say ten and two-fifths, yes," said Vachen.

"That's what Parr is doing right now," said Oliver. "He

says, 'Bring in all the crooks slick enough to cover a stick-up to make it look like suicide.' There are not many crooks wise enough. Not many of them would take the trouble. You know which of your boys could fill a certain job. Parr knows which of his crooks could have done a certain job. There you are!"

Vachen nodded vaguely.

"Meantime, there is the certainty—we say—of the hand—the left hand—being hurt. At this moment the telegraph typewriter is going in every police station in every city, town and village in Connecticut, asking for a report on all men with injured hands, as of that date. It's not a goose chase. A few days ago a man was killed by a hit-and-run driver. A day later the police, going from garage to garage, found the car over in Long Island City. A button off the dead man's coat was found wedged in the headlight clamp. That's police work."

"You believe they will get him?"

"Knowing this man Parr, yes," said Oliver.

"Lea's coming back that morning a second time"—there was a frightened look in Vachen's eyes—"I must confess——"

"That was probably what your behaviorist will call a conditioned reflex," said Oliver with a smile. "Maybe she dressed her hair differently that morning, or wore something new, or maybe the sunlight made her seem especially pretty when he looked back. Coming on top of murder, it, of course, started that bright young insurance investigator off on a tangent. It did me!"

"We'll go over to the house," said Arthur Vachen, getting up.

"For just a moment," said Oliver. "Present me merely as an old college mate."

She seemed waiting at the door, and when Vachen got down at the gate she came out.

"This is the man," said Vachen proudly, "the police stopped writing thrillers because he got too good. Don't you recollect how we used to devour him? He's passing through. I just wanted you to see him. He's coming back to talk to my boys."

And that was all of what originally was to have been a momentous interview. Three days later when a score of "wise" crooks—some with bandaged hands—had been led before Parr and rejected, there came the one whom, strangely, Morel had named first—Southpaw Jake—Jake the Crippler! He had disappeared from his usual haunts— not a good sign for Jake. They found him in Albany and brought him in. He had a bad case of infection in his left hand. But he came in jauntily enough—knowing, of course, in his wise way, that he wasn't there to be asked about the Lea killing. Parr chuckled at sight of him. He opened a drawer and took out the gun and slammed it down on the table. Jake the Crippler froze in his tracks. Now he had the eyes of a trapped rat.

"Would you believe it, Jake?" cried Parr, sudden ferocity in his eyes. "A steam shovel came along and dug it out of the mud for us, without even being asked. How do you think we got you?"

Jake the Crippler shook his head. He was coming to again.

"I said," said Parr, " 'Bring in the wisest crook in the business! It takes a man with brains to think of that stunt!' "

"It was clever, wasn't it?" cried Jake, beaming. "You know, chief, I laid awake nights thinking it out!"

"The breaks were against you, Jake," said Parr, his eyes perceptibly narrowing.

"Yeah. You can't beat the breaks," said Jake. They led him away. The loot was located, through his confession, in the possession of a notorious fence. Practically all the securities were unregistered and would have been lost. They could easily have been sold, when the furor died down, at market price.

IX

GULF STREAM GREEN

JUST after four that afternoon, in the late fall when the baby-calf craze was beginning to wane in the windows of the swagger little shops in the side streets, Leocadie, the diva, descended on Estrelle, Inc., without any warning, like a magnanimous thunderbolt. The mere casting of her shadow by this famous and pampered lady had all the force of a royal command; wherefore Estrelle herself, usually of the most phlegmatic temperament, her girls in the sewing room and the fortunate few of her clientele who happened to be on hand armed with cards for fittings or appointments for preliminary conferences with madame were tossed into a hodgepodge of emotion. Everybody wanted to dress Leocadie for Gilda, Rosina, Mimi, Violetta, Lucia, or even for herself! But it was not permitted. The privilege, each season, was offered among a select list of approved aspirants and farmed out, to the very tint of the finger nails, by her astute manager and farmer general, Wolfbane, sometimes called her bear trainer. "Have I a ring in my nose, then?" the much-exploited Leocadie would sometimes cry in vexation at being so wholly in the hands of her fiduciary committee.

Now Leocadie came to Estrelle's very well wrapped indeed, as if secretly. The very car that bore her was a leased equipage, of the sort one bespeaks by the week or the month, together with one's own chauffeur, monogram and cut flowers. The curtains were drawn, not ostentatiously but adequately, as if the occupant were some un-look-at-able lady of someone's harem.

Getting down, Leocadie first exposed to vulgar public gaze a tiny shoe—by Luze—then, in the order named, a trim ankle, a lean young calf, and a dimpled knee, discreetly enveloped, à la mode—by Steinband. The morning gown she wore—this once and never again—was by The Brothers, Inc., but its advertising value would never be realized, in this instance, because, unlike its predecessors, it was fated never to be passed on to those ultimate consumers, the women who stood by to buy her clothes off her back. It was of Gulf Stream green, the body color itself being invaded by a mauve. Leocadie, in this instance, was literally to create the tint by appearing in it. However, so eager was Leocadie to preserve her incognito that she had covered it completely with an artful domino arrangement which swallowed up gown and figure in an enveloping disguise.

She wore no hat. Her hair—by Wistairn—was lost in a lace mantilla. She looked up and down the swagger street of the grand little shops that beauty commands. The artistes who conducted these shops would tell you they had left the Avenue and come into the side street because the city's great artery had become so commercial. The truth was, the ten-cent stores and armchair cafeterias offered such enormous rents for choice locations that the fashion mongers were driven off to the sidelines.

A number of people were passing. Leocadie drew the lace closer to shade her features. It may have been chance that held back a petal of the lovely lace and that enough of the bepictured face was exposed to be recognized. At any rate, word quickly ran up and down the street and into the Avenue that Leocadie had just stepped from her car at the curb; and hardly had the door been closed upon her

by the ecstatic Estrelle when curiosity seekers came rushing from all directions, blocking the entrance. Riley, the
policeman on post, walked rudely among them, fanning
their knee joints with his stick, until he found who it was;
and then he divided them neatly into two parts and maintained a free path through the center, from Estrelle's door
to the waiting town car.

Inside, everything had come to a violent stop. To her
hypnotized circle of society elect, Estrelle had the sangfroid
to turn and say, with a whimsical smile:

"At ease, please, everybody."

To her workroom, she breathed, through the half-open
door behind the silken curtains, with a touch of asperity:

"As you were."

To Leocadie she turned with a look of beseeching depre-
cation that at once asked forgiveness and bestowed homage; some mortals, naïve and subtle, can confer such an
ineffable compliment with a single glance.

The diva was delighted. She cast a long painted sheep's
eye over one shoulder at the humans clotting the entryway,
some of them pressing their noses against the glass in their
struggle for a single free look at this so-much-advertised
personage. Then Leocadie, with a smile of disarming confidence, put up her hands to Estrelle's shoulders; she said
nasally in what was called her piebald English:

"My goot frainds, they ask me stay off. Or, eef I come,
I bring thees swarm of—how you say?—locust?"

"We will scatter them somehow," replied the exultant
Estrelle, though how, for the moment, she could not
guess. Matters inside being at a standstill—even the most
sophisticated of her grand ladies being unable to resist the
opportunity to stare unabashed at this unexpected close-up
of the diva—Estrelle, with a charming gesture, swept Leocadie into her inner shrine. This had been the commodious

kitchen in the old Van Bibber days. In place of the range under the bricked hood—where at this hour of dusk the butler would be toasting his shins on the oven rail—there now stood a fireplace of Dutch commodiousness, and on the hearth two hickory logs blazed sleepily. Things were set for tea for two. The diva smiled at this, and looked about as if half expecting to find someone, perhaps a lord and master, concealed within. There was no one, but Estrelle blushed.

As the door softly shut, Leocadie said in a low tone in perfect Americanese, and without a touch of the piebald English of a moment before:

"Can you lend me some girl who would be able to wear my clothes? We could send her home in my place to draw off the crowd."

She took a little walk up and down, and came to a halt in front of Estrelle, smiling.

"You understand. To dramatize me! To be me!" she said, touching her bosom with the tips of the fingers of her two hands. She made a little burlesque of herself. Then, ingratiatingly, as if it were the greatest favor, she asked, "You could pin me up in something to hold me together."

Without doubt Estrelle could pin Leocadie up in something, and it would be more than enough to hold her together. And, stop! She had the very girl! And departing hastily, she returned with a statuesque, charming young creature, who did her best to appear nonchalant while Leocadie walked around her.

"*Bien!*" exclaimed the diva, reverting to type. With a single upward sweep of one lovely arm she drew her morning creation—by The Brothers, Inc.—off over her head, and indicated to the model, by dumb show, that it was hers. The girl, palpitating at the mere suggestion, threw off her little frock and stood ready, and Estrelle dropped it down over her shoulders. It settled down like a butterfly, nestling on the svelte young body. Leocadie took Estrelle's hand.

"It is the new Gulf Stream green that I today introduce to the world," she said; and then, with feminine ecstasy, she cried: "She is perfect! My child," she said to the model, "you will accept this from Leocadie!" She rearranged a fold with her own fingers. Even Estrelle was taken aback.

"Oh, it is too much, madame!" she cried.

"It is not enough," said Leocadie. She drew a ring from her finger—a green stone set in gold—and gave it to the model. Together, the two magnificent tiringwomen drew the domino cloak about the dumfounded girl. But the diva must arrange the mantilla herself. Leocadie walked once across the room, then back. The model, trained as a manikin, with a flair for lofty graces, aped her perfectly.

Then the great singer demanded if she could scream. When it was finally ascertained that she could she was instructed to go in the car waiting at the curb to the diva's home, as if it were her own, in the Normanduke; and, as Leocadie, lock herself in her room. This done, she would admit no one, no matter who demanded entry. She was to cry out harshly, *"Va t'en!"* if they persisted, as they surely would; and if they made demonstrations against the door she was to throw up a window violently and scream at the top of her lungs until they desisted. They would desist. All she had to do was to scream loud enough. All this was conducted *sotto voce*.

The poor model looked at Estrelle helplessly. She was to hold fort against all comers, until—Leocadie looked at the clock on the mantel—until 5:30, when she was to bundle herself in her things again, burst out of her room in a terrible tantrum and make off as best she could, always with a scream on tap if anyone dared obstruct her way. Leocadie, with a deprecatory smile, turned to Estrelle.

"You see, madame, it is the only way I endure life—by scaring them. So, when they hem me in, I scream my way out! *Voilà!* It is as good a way as another to exercise a high C."

Everything was now in readiness.

"Give her some money," commanded the diva. Estrelle opened a drawer and invited Leocadie to help herself—a rash gesture, for she took it all and heaped it on the girl. Estrelle's eyes widened, but she made no protest. Up to this moment the affair had the tempo of a great lark. But in the end Leocadie became suddenly grave.

"Your name, my child."

"Berthe—Berthe Tremblay."

"A proud name! You have good parents, I know."

"Alas, madame, they are dead!"

"A husband, then."

The girl shook her head, smiling a little. She had no husband.

"A sweetheart, surely."

The girl shook her head again, this time blushing.

"Oh! *C'est triste!*" But her smile of commiseration was not without its encouragements. "At least you have no one to tell you what you can do and what you can't do, every minute of life. I envy you that!" exclaimed the diva. "If all goes well maybe you can scream for me again some day. Now go. Good courage."

With a little laugh of sheer nervous excitement, Berthe slipped into her part, drew the mantilla tighter with Leocadie's own gesture.

"If you will pardon me, madame," said Berthe, "my carriage is waiting."

Estrelle herself obsequiously conducted the supposed Leocadie, strutting with the grandeur of a camel, towards the entresol. Several ladies being fitted attempted a sally to pay some hastily framed compliments, but Estrelle moved them back. Officer Riley, who had stoutly maintained the passageway through the crowd at the door, marched ahead, and the bogus diva was shut in her town car with an impressive slam. The crowd cheered as the car started off, and the more nimble pursued it. Those who held on to the end of the block, where a pause for traffic was in order, told others whom the tiny coach contained, and the crush augmented. The car had to traverse many city squares before it finally shook off the last of its devotees and regained its incognito. Berthe rode grandly on.

Left alone for the moment, Leocadie, without a gown, true, yet still superbly clothed, moved about Estrelle's private sitting room—to which, as a rule, even the most grand ladies were not admitted—admiring this and that among the trifles that gave the room its undeniable air. A guest was expected. The tea things were set for two. Leocadie smiled wistfully. She rearranged the table, setting it for three, lifting wafer-thin china things from a tiny closet in the chimney corner. She was thus engaged when the door opened and closed softly—Estrelle, her arms full of stuffs with which to pin up the diva.

"Regard!" said the singer, as sure of impunity as a spoiled child. "I have set it for three! May I guess who is expected? Ah, don't blush. He is magnificent! *Tellement gentilhomme!*"

"You know him, madame?"

They spoke of Cuyler Braxton, Estrelle's fiancé, a distinguished young lawyer.

Leocadie said rapturously, "I sing to you two! But you are oblivious—like two love birds!"

"You recognize us?" cried Estrelle incredulously, palpitating.

"*Toujours.* I wait for you. Do you two ever miss one of

my nights? Ah! they say there is something in my voice for lovers. You make it true."

Leocadie paused an instant.

"Madame," she said, in a tone suddenly vibrant with feeling, "I have a confession. I am here, I am come, to see him specially. A great lawyer! I am in desperate need. I need not only the wisdom of a man of law but the understanding of a friend. It must be secret! Madame, I have taken the liberty," she murmured, with a gesture that entreated. "I am in danger."

"Danger, madame! You, in danger!"

The diva had paled.

"I am in fear of death," said Leocadie.

The foreboding in her eyes, the slight shiver and a swift look at the door told more than words. Estrelle moved closer to her.

"I have an anonymous lover," said the diva. "Do you know what that means for a woman in my position?" she continued rapidly. "It means that I am pursued by a madman. I never see him. But always I feel his maniac's eyes staring at me. I am constantly exposed before him. Every moment is a threat. There is no place I can flee from him."

"He sends you messages, writes you letters?"

"Every day. Every hour almost."

"But the police——" suggested Estrelle.

"No, no! Never that!" Leocadie's hand, upraised, was eloquent.

"Your manager, Wolfbane? It must be an old story to him. Who could cope with it better than he?"

"Publicity!" cried Leocadie, her lip curling. "That is all he knows of method. If a sensation arise, turn it into dollars! Advertise it to the world! If the heavens fall and crush me, if I wake with a knife in my heart, turn it into dollars!

That is Wolfbane, the bear trainer." She shook her head. "Anyone but him," she said. She looked down at Estrelle, who clasped her about the waist. She touched Estrelle's hair lightly. "I have long known who you were," she said—"you two who honor me!" She pleaded with a look. "Your *futur* is versed in the pursuit of the wicked. I say, with so much happiness of their own, they cannot refuse me."

"It will be the proud moment of his life to find you have come to him for help, madame!" cried Estrelle. "Any moment and he will be here!"

"Come, we forget my dishabille," said the diva. "A pat and a pin will do very well." She sprang lightly on a podium Estrelle kept here for her vagrant thoughts, as a composer will keep tools within reach to imprison some magic phrase. She caught up a shawl from the soft pile of silks and began to drape the lovely figure. It was a matter of half an hour. The diva, with one white arm falling through the fringe, emerged in a charming tea gown. Both were enchanted. Estrelle found herself questioning whether it was well to expose the impressionable Cuyler Braxton to an even more dazzling Leocadie. Someone tapped discreetly at the door. They both started, recalled. Estrelle cautiously opened. It was one of the girls. It was closing time. She asked timidly for Berthe.

"Berthe?" repeated her mistress, puzzled.

"Yes, madame, we go home together always."

"Oh!" said Estrelle in sudden recollection. She shook her head. "I have something especial for her tonight."

She shut the door, smiling, wondering about Berthe and if she were screaming yet in her rôle as privileged diva. A little later, while the two women were engaged with fabrics and tints, as if with state secrets, there came another tap at the door—something more peremptory. Estrelle's cheeks flamed. It was he. With a gesture she waved the diva from the podium and tripped gayly to the door and threw it wide.

Cuyler Braxton stood there, hat and gloves in one hand, stick in the other. His head was turned for the moment as he listened to some hollow street sounds—boys or men crying dismally against the echoing brownstone walls of this side street. She thought how striking he looked in his momentary unconscious pose. Then he turned to the room. As he stepped across the threshold his eyes fell upon Leocadie. She stood there, one hand lightly touching her marble throat, the other resting on the little table by her side, a half smile on her lips.

Braxton stopped in his tracks. He was a man who had been drilled in the task of controlling himself, and obviously he was controlling himself now only with the greatest effort. He gazed at the diva as if he could not believe his eyes. When he spoke his voice was hushed and unnatural.

"You will forgive me," he said with tremendous calm. He included both women in the bow. "There has been a terrible accident." He stepped into the room and closed the door softly behind him. "Do you mean to say that you have not heard what has just happened?" he demanded.

"We have heard nothing," said Estrelle.

He looked hard at Leocadie again.

"Madame, it is difficult to tell you," he said. "It is almost impossible! Unbelievable! Your name is on everyone's lips. The whole town is alive with it. Don't you know," he went on desperately, "that you are supposed to be dead—murdered?"

Leocadie, immovable as some Greek statue, continued to watch him, spellbound.

"The streets in front of your hotel, madame, are blocked with people," he ran on, keeping down his tone with an effort. "I have just come from there—from the Normanduke. Someone has been murdered in your apartments—

someone who has been identified as you, Leocadie! Thank
God, you are safe!"

Leocadie breathed rather than spoke: "She was crushed?
Some great weight fell on her?"

The lawyer regarded her sharply.

"You do know then, madame?"

"Answer, please." Leocadie swept aside his question.
"She was crushed?"

"Yes," responded Braxton mechanically. "A section of
the cornice became dislodged and fell just as she entered
the room—your room, madame."

"Berthe!" murmured Leocadie.

"It was a most remarkable catastrophe," he ran on again.
"She had just come in from a drive. She hadn't even unfas-
tened her things. Your things, madame! It is incredible!"
he cried. "The identification was without question. She
was clothed in a gown which, the maids say, you wore for
the first time this afternoon!"

Leocadie turned slowly to Estrelle.

"Berthe," she repeated. "It is Berthe! I sent the poor
child to her death just as surely as if I myself had pronounced sentence." She turned on Braxton. "Sir, it was no
accident. It was deliberate murder. I was the intended
victim. Twice I have escaped by what seemed to be miracles. Now, a third time, an unforeseeable sacrifice pre-
serves me!"

"You sent her as your substitute?" the bewildered
Braxton exclaimed.

II

Oliver Armiston's telephone rang at 6:30. It was his
friend, Cuyler Braxton.

"Oliver, for reasons which I can't explain over the wire,"
said the lawyer, "could you come to me at once?"

Oliver had his smile. He was accustomed to the Court of Appeals dignity of his friend, on all occasions.

"Certainly. Where are you?"

"Come two blocks south," said Braxton. "Cross the Avenue. Ascend the third high stoop on the shady side of the street."

"You, who aspire to ascend the bench some day, let me warn you that that block is honeycombed with speakeasies," said Oliver.

"It is honeycombed with get-aways too," replied Cuyler. "It is as safe as a rabbit warren. Come at once. Wait! Tell the boy at the door that Miss Cain of Katonah sent you to see the police puppies."

Ten minutes later the impeccable Oliver Armiston, stick, gloves and topper cap-a-pie, ran trippingly up the steps of the third stoop, counting from the Avenue, in one of those aristocratic brownstone blocks that were destined shortly to be demolished—not, as some cynical ones suggested, to get rid of the speakeasies that infested the neighborhood, but to make room for the new Opera.

True to its ilk, it wore the air of crestfallen vacancy, even when Oliver pushed a muted bell button. He was turning away, thinking he was in error, when a panel at the height of the eye in the door opened; and, to an eye which appeared there, he explained about Miss Cain of Katonah and her litter of puppies. He was instantly admitted. It was a rich interior of the old régime, of several drawing-rooms *en suite,* with a few tables disposed with an artless art of privacy. Low lights, soft carpets, the murmur of talk and the tinkle of ice and spoons. But most astonishing of all was the presence of Antoine, Louis, Ernest, Victor and Armand, each of whom, as occasion permitted, greeted Oliver as only one's own long-lost waiter can bestow a greeting. Civilized man may be able to live without cooks, but no gourmet should dine without his own waiter. Oliver rubbed his hands together, nodding, smiling. Cuyler Braxton was busy for the moment inspecting, under silver and glass *cloches*, a feast laid out on trays. He gave serious approval, and at a signal a line of bus boys lifted the trays to their shoulders and made off single file, like worker ants. Oliver noted that they departed not by the front door but the back.

Braxton slipped an arm round Oliver's shoulders and drew him mysteriously to the deep embrasure of a rear window, where a table awaited them.

"We have no time for preambles, Oliver," began Braxton at once. "I invited you here because at the moment I find myself operating beyond the pale of the law, and require the connivance of the police. You are the one man, I believe, who can command the immediate ear of Deputy Parr."

"Here?" exclaimed Oliver. "Never! He'd come in a wagon!"

"Is it true," pursued the lawyer, letting his cold eye rove about the room as if to fend off any eavesdroppers, "that he has a private wire from your study to his desk?"

It was true, but not a truth for general dissemination. Parr, the man hunter, frequently operated from the unsuspected seclusion of Oliver's study. That was the reason for the police wire in that unsuspected spot. Braxton, as former county prosecutor, had probably got some glimmer of it.

"What's on your mind, Cuyler?" asked Oliver coldly.

"I have been retained," began Braxton, drawling somewhat to mask a certain diffidence, "by Leocadie."

"Ah!" exclaimed Oliver. "She was your client, then?"

"She is," corrected Braxton.

" 'Is'?" questioned Oliver, with suspended fork.

"She has retained me in the matter of—ah—er—in the matter of her—ah—murder."

"Before or after the *fait accompli?*"

"Both, in a manner of speaking," replied the lawyer. "She came to me secretly, at 4:30 this after—that is, to be accurate, I should say she came secretly to a place where she had reason to believe she would find me. Unfortunately I chanced to be elsewhere." Braxton helped himself to an anchovy, which he laid out gravely on a bread stick. "It was not until 5:30 that we finally met," he added, lifting his gaze.

"She was murdered at—at 4:55," said Armiston. He turned up a palm deprecatingly. "I myself saw her a few minutes later."

The lawyer bit thoughtfully into his bread stick.

"You were there, then?" he inquired.

"Yes. Parr sent for me. He didn't like the looks of it. He wanted me to see the matrix of the crime before it was disturbed. It was one of those rare instances in crime, of the police arriving first."

"There was no doubt as to her identity in your mind?" asked Braxton.

"Except," said Oliver curiously, studying the lawyer, "that she carried money. I happen to know that Leocadie never carried money—never touched it. She made a pose of abhorring it—like the dukes of Buckingham—read your history. Money was found in her purse—quite a considerable sum."

"And that induced you to believe that the mutilated remains were other than those of the person identified?" demanded the lawyer in his best court-room manner.

"Not at all," quickly put in Oliver. "It merely rattled me for the moment. There was no doubt as to the identification. Her clothing, for instance. You know she made thousands by merely being seen in dressmakers' creations. This afternoon she wore a dress by The Brothers, Inc., which was to launch a new color—Gulf Stream green. Her maids had put her into that dress not two hours before. No, there was no doubt as to the identity."

"Then you can perhaps appreciate my astonishment, Oliver," said Cuyler Braxton, "in coming directly from the scene of the catastrophe, to confront her, alive, unharmed, ignorant of the fact that her name was on every lip, that extras were boiling up in the streets announcing her tragic death."

"Antoine, the telephone, if you please," said Oliver Armiston. It was instantly placed before him, on a long portable cord, and he lifted the earpiece off the hook, eying the severely juridical Braxton—who had returned gravely to his hors d'œuvres—as he called a number. There was a wait. Oliver, as he looked around the room, touched the hook thrice, then once. It was as if he had tapped off a *v* in Continental Morse, which, in the abbreviated lingo of an operator, was as much as to say: "I have a message to transmit; get ready to take it." Oliver hung up and pushed the telephone to one side. He nodded to Cuyler, as if the first step had been accomplished.

"So you are concealing, with intent to defraud, the live person of a murdered woman, eh?" said Oliver.

"Yes," said Braxton, bowing. "You can estimate, probably, the extreme delicacy of my position."

"My dear fellow, yes!" exclaimed Armiston. "It is absolutely unique!"

"What do we wait for?" demanded Braxton impatiently.

Oliver nodded at the telephone.

"We don't exactly pick things out of the air," he said. "We proceed softly on rubber shoes. A misstep will ruin us. There has never been such an opportunity before. It is a stroke of genius on your part, Cuyler! Imagine, for instance——"

"But, Oliver, I must have Parr at once. Time presses!"

"Never fear," said Oliver. "Let him find us. He has the facilities. We will sit still and wait. You have her near by?"

"Within a stone's throw, yes."

"Safe from discovery?"

"I flatter myself, yes," said the lawyer.

"You assume it to be murder?"

"I know it to be murder!"

"You assume that the murderer is as much in the dark as the rest of us?"

"I know him to be," replied the lawyer. "He is ignorant of the fact that he has killed the wrong woman. That is our opportunity. You can understand the difficulty I encountered in persuading her to lie perdue. She is not the easiest person in the world to conceal. She is a creature utterly above and beyond discipline. I represented to her that, great as she is, we are concerned with something greater even than she! We must apprehend the criminal, the monster who is capable of such a crime! Should she have persisted, I was prepared to take her by force to conceal her."

"As an essential witness to her own murder," put in Oliver, with the shade of a smile.

"There is only one thing she bows to, and that is the stage," said Braxton. "When she sings, she sings! Nothing shall intervene. Fortunately she does not sing tonight. But tomorrow night she sings!"

The grave young lawyer, who up to now had managed to retain his Court of Appeals manner almost if not quite intact, seemed on the point of becoming human; his voice quavered, rose. Oliver touched him on a sleeve to steady him.

"How did you manage to persuade her to give you the twenty-four hours?" he asked.

"It was the girl who went to death in her place. She sent

her. There is nothing Leocadie will not do to avenge that
poor girl."

"She sent her?" repeated Oliver. "Who was she?"

Braxton swiftly sketched the scene of the tragic hoax
in which poor Berthe rode forth so grandly to her death.

"I represented to madame," said Braxton, "what a
weapon she might place in the hands of the police to run
the murderer to earth at once."

"You believe the murderer will not reveal himself by
some false move?"

"He has already done so," said Cuyler coldly. He drew
a paper from his pocket—the latest extra—and his finger
traced out a line of type. It read: "For several months past,
the diva had been pursued by anonymous letters threat-
ening her life."

"Well?" said Oliver.

"It is true," said the lawyer slowly. "But no one knew
it except the writer of those letters."

"It is incredible!" cried Oliver. "Would she conceal such
a thing?"

"As if it were some overwhelming shame," muttered the
lawyer. "She told no one. Now, the murderer believing he
has succeeded," pursued Cuyler, "he has no hesitancy in
revealing his knowledge. He cries it aloud!"

"But why?" protested Oliver. "To the casual eye, it is an
accident. A cornice falls and crushes a woman to death.
What need to explain?"

"There were two previous attempts on her life," explained the lawyer. "Both by falling weights. Both on the
stage. Once, the counterweight of a fly fell. The second
time, a curtain came crashing down. Seeming miracles saved
Leocadie both times. They were hushed up as accidents—
something had slipped a cog. But when it occurs a third
time, and fatally, they become more than mere coincidences.
There must be some plausible explanation. Hence, the mur-

derer glibly says, 'Murder!' Oliver, she has been pursued by a maniac intent on her life. He is perfectly safe. No one but him knows. Her nerve had begun to break. That was why she came for me this afternoon."

"Do you know who told the police about the letters?" asked Oliver.

"There is only one person who could have told," replied Braxton in his cold tone. "Wolfbane—Wolfbane, her manager."

At this moment Antoine, with two bus boys, arrived with the dinner. It was inspected and approved, and savory odors rose up from the serving table. Oliver said carelessly, masking his context from a possible inquisitive ear:

"I confess that name has presented itself to several of us. What I object to now is the utter absence of motive."

Cuyler Braxton said shortly, "Read your Apocrypha— the Book of Tobit."

"That's the book with the dog in it, isn't it?"

"Yes, but the dog doesn't enter here."

Oliver's face suddenly lighted.

"Ah! The Foul Fiend who strangled the Seven Bridegrooms of Sarah!"

"Yes. If he couldn't have her, none else should! . . . I'll have coffee with my dinner, Antoine, please."

A platoon of motorcycles surged by, with a flurry of detonations. Armand, the *maître*, snapped his fingers peremptorily. Instantly his well-trained crew removed every vestige of contraband. He came sauntering over to the table.

"The police are raiding Tony, down the street," he said in a low tone. "They may call here. We can't be too careful."

"Raiding with motorcycles?" said Oliver. "Since when did they raid speakeasies with motorcycles?"

The motorcycle squad was used mostly as a guard for celebrities, not for hammer-and-tongs work. Armand shrugged. It was not for him to reason why or how; all he knew was, best be wary! Was everything perfect, gentlemen, he inquired, and being so assured, he retired to his peephole.

"Still, I don't follow—or at least, I follow reluctantly," said Oliver. "He is a man of wealth, family, social position, everything. His daughters are really in society, which can be said truly of very few of our importations in the grand-opera line. In addition, he is a savant. As a hobby he measures the speed of light and writes papers on it."

"She was a secret obsession with him," said the lawyer. "Impossible of attainment! He removed her to spare himself the torture of her very existence! If she had had lovers he probably would have removed them." He said suddenly, "We must hurry! We have no time to lose!"

"One instant," said Armiston. "Is this merely a handy hypothesis you have put together to fit some loose facts, or do you know absolutely that she suspects him?"

"It is a working hypothesis that fits the known facts," said Cuyler Braxton without heat. "It so accords with the facts that I again urge you to make haste. I must have Parr now! We have no time to lose. We are not dealing with an ordinary intelligence. If he gets an inkling he will slip through our fingers. He undoubtedly has foreseen everything and prepared for it."

"He has foreseen everything," said Oliver, rising, "except that he has murdered the wrong woman."

He lifted off the telephone, sent that slight signal, the telegraphic *v*, again, and put it aside and sat down. No need to give his location. The police would trace the call instantly.

"Set your mind at ease," said Oliver. "No time is being lost." He resumed his dinner. After a time he said: "Do you know Parr and his methods?"

"I know him as a great policeman, if that is what you mean."

"He is more than that," said Oliver. "He is a murder specialist. I think he is marked for murder. He senses it, as a dog will sense the approach of death. There was nothing in that matrix this afternoon to point to murder." Armiston used the word "matrix" as if it were a mold that could reveal every detail of the crime. "She had just come in from a drive," he went on, casting an image, so to speak. "A dozen people had been entering and leaving that room— her secretaries and maids all had access. They opened that door and closed it in exactly the same way that she did. Yet, as she stepped across the threshold, a cornice fell and crushed her. There was no one in the room with her. The police, fortunately, arrived instantly. They had to break down the door. There were only the windows for escape, and no one could have escaped by them—too high. Ceilings fall. There was nothing to suggest murder."

"Except that it had happened, in kind, on two previous occasions, with the same intended victim as its object," put in Braxton.

"That is a chain of fact to which Parr had no access," said Armiston. "What did Parr do? He proceeded—for what reason I do not know—on the theory that it was murder. To verify his own impressions, he sent for me. I was able to go at once. He said, 'Oliver, look at Wolfbane when he doesn't know he is under observation, and tell me what you see.' "

"Good Lord!" exclaimed the cold-blooded Braxton.

"Wait a bit. I told you he is marked for murder—Parr, I mean."

"But what did you see—what did you see?"

"A smirk," said Oliver. "That idiotic smile of satisfaction which won't quite come off. Have you never seen it on a man's face?"

"Yes," said the ex-prosecutor. "Yes!"

Who had not, in his business? Especially in the courts—

that unbidden and unbiddable look of exultation that will suddenly paint itself indelibly on a man's face when, in a moment of flattered self-delusion, he thinks he has removed himself beyond the reach of the law by some particular cleverness of his own.

"Leocadie was worth millions to him alive," ran on Oliver. "Why should he gloat over her death? There was only one answer."

"A very remarkable deduction!"

"For Parr? Yes. And with no motive apparent."

Cuyler Braxton asked, almost in a whisper, "How did he manage it, Oliver? Can you figure it out?"

Armiston knitted his brows.

"Some sort of trigger touched off that cornice," he said. "It was timed for the instant she shut the door."

"But the others. The maids and secretaries were always coming and going. Why didn't it kill one of them?"

"No," said Oliver. "This was some diabolically clever mechanism that discriminated. It waited for her to come."

"And then killed the wrong woman," said Braxton, with just the shade of a smile.

"*Touché!*" conceded Oliver. "Nevertheless, we will meet that objection too."

III

Pelts, a shabby little fellow no one would take for a police detective, edged his way into the room at the Normanduke, where the big fellow sat in close converse with Wolfbane, madame's manager; and since his chief seemed heavily engaged, little Pelts took out a stump of pencil, carefully wetted it, and with those small niceties of a man who had learned to read and write in jail, put down several words on a torn piece of paper. This paper he folded and caused to be passed from hand to hand among the operatives standing about, till it reached the deputy, who was just then remarking, as he pawed over a little of stuff on the table:

"We can find almost anything we want here to support any conceivable contention or hypothesis."

He referred to the wreckage salvaged from the fallen ceiling. The massive cornice that all but obliterated a human being had wrecked everything in its path. Part of the piano was demolished; a highboy that had been a catch-all was ripped open and its contents scattered—a radio, a china closet, some pictures, a metronome.

"There is a spring and some pawls and pinions," said Parr. "Would you say that was the trigger that touched it off?" Who could say? One was confused by riches. As he ceased speaking, Parr glanced down and, with an odd palming motion, accepted Pelts' missive and opened it with the same gesture. Parr was almost a magician with his fingers. Wolfbane peered nearsightedly over the table edge.

"Something?" he inquired, having been encouraged to ask questions.

Parr nodded, gave him a swift shrewd look.

"There is always 'something,' " he remarked in a confidential tone, glancing suspiciously about the room. "Something unforeseen and unforeseeable!" he elucidated in a lower tone. "It is what we call the 'break.' It always comes. It is on its way! That's a thought I leave with you," he said, and he arose. He tossed the pellet that was Pelts' note into the fire and watched it burn. Then he went inside and shut the door.

Pelts, exercising some devil's license of his own, was there waiting for him. On the table was a package. It had just come uptown by special messenger. Reporters had seen it come and asked about it. Even Wolfbane, who had eyes in the back of his head, was worrying about it. They need not have troubled themselves. It was only a pair of fresh shoes for Parr. He changed several times a day. Regaling himself with new footgear, he could say, paraphrasing the philosopher: "Now I am prepared for anything Fate has in store for me."

"Well?" he inquired as he sat down.

Pelts, for answer, unbuttoned one coat, two coats; he unpinned a vest, and from an inner pocket he produced a tissue-paper package which he laid before his chief.

"Stealing hotel silver again, I see," said Parr, gingerly unwrapping the bundle. "Where do these come from?"

"The dressmaker shop," said Pelts, eying a crack in the ceiling. Parr looked at him sharply. He lifted a foot to unlace a shoe. There were possibilities in that shop. Tracing Leocadie back to the last person who had talked to her, it appeared that she had gone out secretly and unaccompanied, using a hired conveyance that her people knew nothing of. She had been driven to the establishment of Estrelle, Inc., a fashionable gown shop in the speakeasy zone. Now, Leocadie did not go to gown shops; they came to her. This was a mere detail of the cunning exploitation to which every great artist is constantly subject, and was of no special significance, except when viewed in the light of murder. This much the police had learned in their simple way, ringing doorbells and asking questions. Most of their time was spent ringing doorbells and asking questions. When they rang Estrelle's bell no one answered. With the fall of night, surveillance settled down about her place, as tenuous, yet as all-pervading as the night itself.

"Spoons!" said Parr, grunting over a shoe.

"Two dinners went in—over the backyard fence," said Pelts.

"Two?"

"Two. I was one of the bus boys when the trays came out," said Pelts.

"And you helped yourself to the spoons?"

"Yes, sir."

The deputy chuckled. He limped to the door, a shoe in one hand, and peered out; everything ceased outside under his fierce glare.

"Lemaire!" he called; and Lemaire, a fingerprint expert, came in. Parr waved him to the spoons. Lemaire examined them, being careful not to touch or to breathe on them. He polished a magnifying glass and explored the surfaces. Lemaire's weakness was fingerprints; he had a camera eye for fingerprints.

"There is madame's print, for one," he said.

Parr paused in the act of pushing a foot into a shoe. He turned and stared at little Pelts, who, faithful one-man dog that he was, was staring wistfully at him, as if half expecting a bone or a kind word.

"That's the only one I recognize, without direct comparison," said the expert. "I'll develop them and let you know in a jiffy."

He gathered up the precious spoons and let himself out. Parr thoughtfully pushed the foot into the shoe.

"Pelts, what time did that tray go in?"

"At a quarter to seven."

"And it came out?"

"At 7:20."

The deputy leaned back and drummed on the desk.

"Pelts," he said softly, "I have told you before, and I tell you now, if you had my good looks you'd have my job some day."

Pelts shifted from one foot to the other. His idea of the end of the world would be to have no Parr to fetch and carry for. Bringing in these spoons was a taste of paradise for Pelts. But he would never admit it by so much as a look. A silence intervened. The door opened softly. Morel entered. Two pairs of eyes turned to survey him. Sensing something, he paused. Morel was the elegant. He was Parr's silk-stocking satellite. He and Pelts fitted so perfectly that at times they seemed to be materialized functions of the great man-hunter's brain.

The man hunter asked, "Has Tony's place down the block been raided lately?"

"The speakeasy? Not that I know of. Armiston, by the way, is in Number 23. He is signaling for you."

"That can wait."

"Do you know who is with him?" asked Morel. "Braxton, the former prosecutor—the one who used to take so many pleas to save the county money."

"Here is what you are to do," said the deputy: "I want you first to pull Tony's. Back up the wagons and make a lot of noise. While the crowd is occupied helping you with catcalls and hard words, go through the block and break in—quietly—at this dressmaker's. You will find there Estrelle, whom you know—she helped us in that assagai murder case—and Leocadie."

Morel's gaze flickered almost imperceptibly. "Yes, sir," he said.

"Madame dined there at seven," said Parr, "and was good enough to send out her fingerprints on the spoons. Otherwise she might deny her identity."

Morel's eyes shifted to the door and back to Parr. Parr sensed the unspoken question. He shook his head.

"No, he doesn't know," he said, his eyes glowing. "I don't believe he's got the slightest suspicion. See if he is still out there. Bring him in."

Morel stepped to the door. Wolfbane must have been on

the alert, because he appeared instantly when Morel raised a finger. He glanced from side to side as he entered, as if testing for a trap. Seeing Parr putting a pair of shoes in a box, he laughed.

"Was that what came in the box?" he asked. "I took it to be something very mysterious."

"There is nothing mysterious about murder. It is usually merely stupid," said the deputy. "You still say, do you, that Leocadie was murdered?"

Wolfbane looked pointedly at Morel and Pelts, as if they were in the way. That little pause saved him the necessity of an answer. At that moment there came an interruption from outside.

A wailing voice cried, "She is here! I know she is here! I must see!"

Morel opened the door, and a young woman almost fell into the room. She looked about her in an agony of apprehension.

"Where is Berthe?" she cried, turning from one to another.

"Berthe? Who is Berthe?" said Parr gently.

"We always go home together! . . . This afternoon the mistress called her—into her sitting room! It was when this great singer, who has been——" Her voice trailed away.

"Mistress?" said Parr, steadying her with his voice. "Who is your mistress? Why do you come here?"

"Madame Estrelle!" said the girl. "Oh, I know that something terrible has happened!" She became inarticulate with weeping.

"Take her away, Morel," commanded Parr. "Humor her. . . . Come, my child, this gentleman will take care of you, help you to find your friend." They closed the door on her. The deputy turned with a wry smile and tapped his forehead. "These poor creatures!" he said. "They turn up from nowhere whenever there is a calamity. I suppose the excitement touches them off."

Wolfbane was still staring after her.

"Do you personally see any of those letters, Wolfbane?" asked Parr.

"No," said the manager.

"How were they delivered?" demanded Parr. "Not by mail."

"I had the impression," said Wolfbane precisely, "that they were cunningly deposited in places where presumably no one but herself would find them."

"Good! Someone inside, eh? That fits in," said Parr. "Things are beginning to break," he said mysteriously. "One of the secretaries doesn't check up so well in her answers." Wolfbane smiled. "I may need you quick. Where can I reach you? Some place where you can avoid reporters, without seeming to."

"My studio and laboratory, in Tenth Avenue," said the manager. "I have bachelor quarters there. When my family is out of town, I stay there—as at present."

"Excellent! Go, now. Be sure no one follows."

The manager obediently departed, two shadows tailing him.

Morel stepped into the room.

"She has identified the body," he said, "as a Berthe Tremblay, a sewing woman employed by Estrelle. The woman had on Leocadie's clothes."

"Have you got her well bottled up?"

"Yes, chief." He added: "Did Wolfbane get it at all?"

"I doubt it. But we move fast now, Morel! . . . Morel!"

"Sir?"

"Take along the motorcycles," rasped Parr. "We will run no risk of her being recognized. We will change our plan of

operation, to save time. Don't break in. Pick up Oliver and
Cuyler Braxton, and go in with them. They know all about
it. Inform them," said Parr with a grim smile, "they have
nothing to tell you. You will do all the telling. They only
function, just now, to prepare madame quietly and swiftly
for removal. All this time there is to be a lot of commotion
from the raid over at Tony's."

"Yes," said the stoical Morel. "Where am I to take them,
and under what supposition? Are they under arrest?"

"For their protection, yes," said Parr. "When I go by,
you will wait twenty minutes. Then you will take the ladies
and follow leisurely."

"With the motorcycle squad?"

"Yes. You will hedge them about, to keep the populace
from being too inquisitive," said Parr.

"To what destination?"

"To mine," explained Parr. "At that hour I go to have
a little heart-to-heart talk with Wolfbane in his studio in
Tenth Avenue. We will be sitting there, smoking and talking, with dim lights. I will complain about my eyes, so he
will lower the lights. I will still be politely incredulous of
his theory of murder. In the midst of it I would like to have
her walk in quietly, alone, and stand there looking at him."

"Leocadie?" Morel's voice betrayed a slight tremor.

"Herself."

"And then?"

"Nothing," said the man hunter. "Under no circumstances must she speak."

"You mean like a ghost?" blurted out Morel.

"A woman reinvoked from the dead," said Parr.

"If she refuses?"

A slight smile touched Parr's lips.

"She will not refuse," he said. "She is an actress. He is a
superstitious man. If he is guilty he will be brought to the

verge of confession. If he is innocent it will be a happy reunion. .... You understand? Start out!"

Morel without a word turned to depart. But at the door he looked back and said:

"There is one thing; that is a factory building, where the studio is. There is a janitor and also an engineer. They are employed by Wolfbane."

"They will be removed by Pelts between the time of my arrival and yours," said Parr. "Pelts will be there to time her entrance to a *t*, so there will be no mistake."

Parr arrived alone a few minutes after nine at Wolfbane's and went up. He had previously telephoned, and the manager, smoking a short light cigar, awaited him at the elevator.

"You have quite an establishment here," said the deputy, looking around. "Would it trouble you to have a little less light? My eyes bother me."

"At heart," said Wolfbane, moving from lamp to lamp and pulling out clusters of lights, "I am a man of science. I spend twenty thousand dollars a year on my laboratory."

"Chemistry?" inquired Parr, sitting down in a gloomy spot and taking out a cigar.

"Physics and mechanics."

"Then probably you can give me some hint as to the mechanism employed by the murderer," said Parr.

"Merely a trigger of some sort. Even a stupid murderer could devise that."

"But this was not stupid," put in Parr. "It waited for its victim. There was no one at hand to touch it off at the right moment. We have satisfied ourselves as to that."

"It is fortunate for you that scientists, as a class, do not major in murder," said Wolfbane, with a dry smile. "They have so many facilities at hand which, though simple enough to them, are utterly incomprehensible to the average intelligence."

"The police, I suppose you mean," said Parr, smoking stolidly.

"Yes," agreed the scientist. "Here, for instance, is a potential murderer," he said, and he turned to his workbench. "A photo-electric cell. Every man of science is at present much interested in its possibilities. It is destined to take the place of millions of men in industry. The possibilities are infinite."

Parr took the contrivance in his hand and examined it. It resembled an ordinary radio vacuum tube. Parr thought of the wreckage in the murder apartment.

"I wonder," mused Parr to himself, "is he so sure of himself he can show me how he did it!" Aloud, he said shortly, "How?"

"It discriminates," replied Wolfbane precisely.

"As to what?"

Parr's eyes explored the gloom of the lower end of the room behind Wolfbane. He thought he detected a movement of a shadow, but he could not be sure.

"Anything you choose," responded the glib Wolfbane. "It is merely a question of the intensity of a beam of light that falls on the target inside that bulb. See. Let me show you how it discriminates between, for instance, different shades of the same color. Green, let us say."

He pushed the bulb into a receptacle in a device that seemed to have been prepared for this demonstration. He held up several cards painted with different shades of green. He passed them one by one rapidly in front of a beam of light. For each one, a mechanical counter clicked audibly and registered. Always the same counter clicked for the

same card. The tiny bulb never made an error. Wolfbane
smoothed his beard, smiling.

"You follow?"

"It is connected electrically to those counting machines?"
asked Parr.

"Yes, it could be connected, through a relay, to a stone
crusher, a trip hammer, a blooming mill——"

"Or a trigger that touched off a cornice——"

"You get the idea," nodded the demonstrator.

"——when a woman dressed in Gulf Stream green passed
under it?" Parr inquired.

Parr's breath was a little short. The shadow behind Wolfbane was Leocadie. She stood pressed against a pillar by
the mantel, listening intently.

"Exactly!" said Wolfbane crisply. His look was so fixed
that the pupils of his eyes seemed to have become pin
points. "Mind, I do not say that is what did happen!" he
cried. "I say that is what could happen. You see how helpless the police would be when pitted against a really learned
murderer. The mechanism obliterates its own identity in the
crash. Constructive murder," he said crisply, pointing at
the mechanism, "is so much more interesting than emo-
tional murder."

Parr sat up. One hand remained by his side. He could
shoot accurately from any position.

"It could not go wrong, you say, Wolfbane?" he asked.

"It discriminates," reiterated the scientist patiently.
"You have seen." He smiled on Parr, shrugged to excuse
ignorance.

Parr leaned forward and said in a hard voice, "Wolfbane, what if the wrong woman wore that dress—that Gulf
Stream green?"

Now suddenly he changed his plan of operations, on the
very battlefield.

"Look behind you, Wolfbane," he said in a low, tense voice.

Wolfbane swung around in his swivel chair.

" 'Cadie!" he gasped convulsively.

He grasped the arms of his chair. His eyes slowly shut. For ten seconds he did not move. Parr indicated to her, by dumb show, not to stir. Wolfbane, recovering himself with no outward evidence of the shock of revelation, excepting only for a pallor, swung back in his chair and faced his desk.

"That is true," he said in a panting voice. He shook his head. He picked up a little square of silk on the desk. "This is the green she wore," he said, and he held it up for Parr to see. At the same instant a terrible reverberating roar rent the stillness of the room. A heavy-calibered pistol had fired from some point in the shadows, and Wolfbane sank back in his chair, drilled through the head. Leocadie screamed. Oliver, Braxton, Morel and Pelts came rushing in.

"Take care!" shouted Parr warningly. "It's a trap! Wait!"

Parr secured his cane, and using the crook to catch a rung of Wolfbane's chair, laboriously worked it to one side out of range of the fiendish device. He picked up the piece of silk—Gulf Stream green—and held it out at arm's length at the end of his stick. As it approached the sensitive photo-electric bulb, the air of the room was shattered a second time by a terrific explosion, and a vicious bullet plowed through the workbench, directly over the spot where Wolfbane had sat.

"Up there in that ventilator, Morel!" cried Parr.

That was where they found a heavy army pistol cleverly hidden and held in a vise; its trigger was operated by a secret electric connection with that cell on the workbench— the cell that discriminated. To the casual eye, the mechanism on the bench looked merely like another radio set. Had Wolfbane been found that way, with no witnesses, it would have looked like another murder.

"He planned to join her, I think," said Oliver.

"He anticipated everything," said Cuyler.

"Except the wrong woman," said Leocadie, drawing a deep breath. "Now she is avenged."

X

THE DOOR KEY

JASON had been cutting down apple trees in the pasture all afternoon, and cording them up to haul in on the first snow. There is no fuel for an open fire like apple. He was felling the trees not because he couldn't take cider or leave it alone himself, but to put teeth in the Eighteenth Amendment as it applied to his cattle. It was the only form of prohibition that really prohibited among his cows. So long as they had any hope of getting it, they stood around all day at this time of year, waiting for an apple to fall; and when it fell, they rushed pell-mell and fought over it. Thus they were not only adding injury to indolence but actually making cider—a lacteal form of it, at least—when they were supposed to be making milk. Even after the later frosts had finished the orchards, they wandered from tree to tree and waited, with a sort of acquired barroom patience, a kind of drunkard's hope. So, no more apple trees in his pasture after today.

He shut the kitchen door and set down his ax. There was an old wrought-iron key on the kitchen table. Someone had left it during the afternoon. He picked it up, puzzled. It was a beautiful thing, ward, stem and bow, wrought lovingly by an ancient smith before the days of beauty as a cult. What his eye saw was not so much the æsthetic as the armorial significance of the key. Whose was it? Somebody among his neighbors had gone away, turned the key in its lock, and left it in Jason's keeping. It was such an uncommon thing for a key to be turned in a lock, that anyone could tell him who it was that had gone away. But he was annoyed not to identify it by the scroll of the bow—one was supposed to know his neighbor's key. He would recollect. He opened the stove and fed it clean hard maple as heavy as coal, and gave it a long drink of kerosene from the can. The flames leaped and roared in the chimney. If his mother had been home, she would have hurried in, crying, "Jason, are you using kerosene on the fire again?" and Jason would have replied, "There was a big motor truck just went by, back-firing. Maybe that's what you smell so strong."

He filled the kettle, pushed back the setting of cheese, and lighted the lamp. He took down the nested milk buckets from the rack behind the stove, and at the rattle of the bails, Tom, the kitchen cat, came down off his chair with a soft thump and stood, looking up lovingly and rubbing his back against Jason's boot buckle. Tom hadn't missed a milking since he was weaned. The pet coon, George, in the wood box, lifted a periscopic nose, but seeing nothing on the horizon as yet to write home about, submerged without a rustle. This coon early in life had consolidated the wild and tame, retained the best points of each. For instance, George accepted cooked food from the kitchen, but still, taking no chances, he washed every mouthful he ate in the brook. George slept with Jason on cold nights, which was all right with Jason, excepting when George got hungry during the night and went fishing, and then came crawling back up the kitchen roof through the window and into bed, cold and wet, and more often than not fetching along a live fish to play with.

Jason was shaking open his lantern when he turned to listen. The door opened and Oliver Armiston came in. Oliver had been watching for the light across the long meadow. Parr, the police deputy, had telephoned that he was coming up on the late train, which meant cooning, eeling or bullheading. The great man hunter craved such diversions when brain-weary. Probably he had just brought to a successful termination another of those sleepless vigils which the papers report naïvely as "the police have obtained a confession," and wanted something to make him dog-tired, so he could remember how to go to sleep again.

It couldn't be cooning—the only coon dog in town belonged to Percy Manchester, the local bad man, and Percy was in jail; they might borrow Percy for the night, but they would have to put him back before daylight, which might be inconvenient. There would be too much moon, also too much water, for spearing eels. All of which meant bullheading at Messenger Pond. This was a matter of sitting up all night in a leaky boat, incased, for warmth, in a none-too-particular horse blanket; and whiling away the gooseflesh hours persuading frozen worms to conform their outlines to the curvature of a No. 6 bass hook, and then arguing with a horned bullhead which would, of course, swallow the hook before consenting to be dragged into the boat. It didn't impress Oliver as art, but he was loyal, and he would stand by; at least to the extent of holding the lantern while Jason dug bait. Jason, however, was delighted. Parr was one of those unfortunates who never relaxed, no matter how much he prided himself on so doing; and to sit up all night with the man hunter on a lonely pond was, to Jason, an inestimable privilege.

"As soon as I get my chores done," said Jason—his eyes swung around to the key on the table, and he said suddenly, "I got to do his too!"

"Whose?" asked Oliver, picking up the key. He hadn't heard of anyone's front door being locked. One usually did hear of a thing like that almost before the key was turned. He balanced it on his fingers—he didn't place the key. During his several summers up here he had acquired an almost heraldic knowledge of his neighbor's door keys.

"Ensign Belding's," said Jason, his eyes narrowing.

Oliver looked up, surprised. He put down the key.

"I thought Ensign Belding lived off the country," he said with a dry smile. "I didn't know he soiled his hands with chores."

Jason held open the door for Oliver and the cat to go out.

"He's milking one cow lately," said Jason vaguely. "She comes over here sometimes. I send her back home with Shep."

"Since when have you two asked favors of each other?" asked Armiston.

"Never," said Jason laconically. He moved across the dooryard to the bars where Shep had the cows waiting; cattle that regarded their approach with looks of gentle reproof. "But that's his key," said Jason. "He must have gone off again." He let down the bars, and the cattle filed in, counted by Shep. "He must have gone in a hurry," said Jason, scratching his head, "else he wouldn't have left his key with me."

There was something inviolable about a key. It meant creatures to be cared for, not petty human differences to be raked over. Ensign Belding didn't spend much time here. It was only the neap tides that brought him back home. But even at these low ebbs of fortune, he still thought himself too much of a gentleman for his old neighbors. One meets out in the world now and then some very devil of a small-town fellow, one wonders what he was as a boy in a country community, and how, amid his cattle and rustics, he acquired his slick sophistication. One wonders more what he still is when he goes creeping back home to lick his wounds. This Ensign Belding would be gone for months, for years. Usually, when he came back, it happened at night; and smoke issuing from the chimney of the stone house on the hill back of the tannery would first apprise the countryside that the owner was in residence, so to speak.

"Has he been alone this time?" asked Oliver, with the rather meticulous intonation of one ashamed to find himself prying into the affairs of a man apart. Oliver sat in the doorway, watching the gorgeousness of coming evening: the iridescent first stars breaking through the purple of the sky, and the deepening sepia of the shadows at the edge of the wood. The moon would rise early.

"I don't know," said Jason softly. He drove milk tumultuously into the resounding bucket. The cows nosed their grain, pulled at wisps of hay, danced little solo steps in the litter; the ties clattered musically and the air hung heavy with the aroma of warm milk. Outside, the maidens and far matrons listened wistfully as they chewed on dry cuds.

"Where does he get the cash to get away with?" asked Armiston. "He's always stony broke when he comes home. That's the only reason he comes back, isn't it?"

"I'll show you, if you'll come over with me," said Jason mysteriously. He moved methodically through the milking, not straight down the line, but in an irregular way, like the firing order of an eight-cylinder engine—there is a certain prestige in a herd, rank must be observed. Soon the separator was whining and pigs squealing and the barn calves thumping buckets, and the cows who had given up their rich burdens sedately withdrew and joined their barren sisters in the barnyard. It was dark in the shadows when they started down the lane to short-cut across the Belding meadow. Shep suddenly ran ahead. It was the little heifer, come over to visit again, standing wistful and lonesome against the bars.

"Here's part of his chores right here!" laughed Jason. "Leave her be, Shep. I'll milk her out on the grass."

He squatted beside the timid creature, but arose at once, muttering angrily. Her quarters were badly caked; she flinched when he touched her. He put her in the barn, stancheled her, and fed and watered and made friends with her; and carefully kneading the udder, he managed to strip her.

"There ought to be a law!" muttered Jason as they started down the lane again. They climbed the wall and went around the hill through the woods, Shep pattering at heel and the swinging lantern calling up a troupe of shadows. They came on the stone house from the rear. There was a light in the kitchen window.

"I won't go in," said Oliver, hanging back.

"Wait for me here," said Jason.

Shortly Jason returned.

"There is no one there," he said. "Come on; I want to show you something."

It had been a pretentious house, and it still wore the air. The long living room, almost empty of even makeshift furniture, was in an advanced stage of deliberate destruction. The mantel had been taken out entire, and only the yawning chimney hole remained to stare accusingly on the desolation. It had been a quaint old piece, that mantel, with carved awning to which clung sooty cupids ardently climbing upward through vines and fig leaves to a shaky temple of love built not on a rock, nor yet on sand, but on a swaying bough. The whole had been brought bit by bit from the Cape by ox cart by one of the early Beldings, who, feeling the oats of prosperity, had bethought himself to go back to Hyannis for the old lares and penates which had been left behind as too bulky to swim the Connecticut River withal.

"Ensign knows his onions," remarked Jason with a smile. He nodded at the wrecked chimney and the fresh plaster on the floor. "You'll find that in some Madison Avenue antique shop before the winter."

He paused, staring down at the print of a high-heeled sandal in the dust. Then he hadn't been alone this time.

The same tale was told all over the house. First the furniture had gone, bit by bit, probably skimmed from the top down. Then an informed vandal, learned in the wants of antiques for the trade, had taken the interior to pieces. Worn threshold sills, hewn beams, door-post capitals, heaven-help-us hinges and escutcheon plates, lintels, pilasters, paneling, mopboard moldings, stair rails, even the odd bevel of a window box. It had all been picked out carefully by someone who, as Jason said, knew his onions. This fellow hadn't come creeping back to lick his wounds; he had come back for nuggets, to dig deeper and deeper into this storehouse of unconsidered trifles of Colonial utility, which, through the ironic orientation of taste that feeds the antique trade, had become, in the eyes of beholders, *objets de vertu*. Door sills worn hollow, with polished nail heads protruding—it was the tread of vanished feet that left the veneer of cost for the collector. The door sill must be hollow, or you are distinctly parvenu.

There was a note on the kitchen table, held down by the lamp. It read:

My dear Jason: I can't imagine myself ever chasing this cow again for her milk. Take her, my boy, as a gift from me, in appreciation of your thoughtfulness in keeping off the place while I am in residence. Please blow out the lamp.   E. B.

Jason put down the note, puzzled.

"I wonder what he wants," he pondered. He looked about the kitchen. He touched the stove. It was chilled, and already damp with the dew of evening; it hadn't held a fire for hours.

"Why didn't he leave that note with the key?" asked Jason. "There are no chores. Why bring me over here?"

"To blow out the lamp," suggested Oliver, with a smile.

"Why light the lamp?"

"To bring you over here to blow it out," said Oliver. "Do your duty, and let's dig bait."

"Look about, first," urged Jason. "There is something he wants me to see; else he wouldn't have worked about in a circle. You don't know Ensign. The only thing he'd give me is a pestilence," he explained, his lip curling.

They moved from room to room, Shep casually sniffing at rat holes, but not otherwise interested. It was certain the place was deserted. Jason blew out the lamp and turned the key in the lock.

"Did you ever do him a favor before?" asked Armiston. These people at times had such singular ways.

"No," said Jason shortly. He looked back in perplexity. "I'm inclined to think I've done him one now—but for the life of me I can't figure out what it is."

They found tire tracks in the drive, with the print of a woman's high-heeled sandal to show where she had stepped into the car. The tracks were lost in the hard road, and it was impossible to tell which way Belding had gone.

II

It was nearing midnight. The three fishermen sat hunched in their horse blankets in that attitude of dogged expectation which only their tribe can achieve. Talk, the hushed, guarded interchange of conspirators who fear eavesdroppers, had for the moment died down. Pipes glowed, but there was no movement. The wind was gone, and there was no sense of mobile water. Parr was conscious

of a pleasing languor which, if not disturbed by some inquisitive bullhead, would very shortly take complete possession of his senses. After all, fishing is not for fish. It is
a good deal like gazing into a crystal ball. It soothes the
attention, it shuts out ulterior sights and sounds, and after
a while, if persisted in religiously, it achieves perfect lethe.
The great man hunter was brain-weary, too tired to sleep.
The silence was lulling him. Late frosts had stilled the
cicada and those other whispery voices of night which are
always present as an undertone in the growing season.
Now they were too far from shore to catch even the rus-
tlings of the forest. The occasional lazy turn of some fish
too near the surface was the only disturbance. Parr nodded.

"Here they come now," said Jason softly, as if speaking
out of a dream.

"Who?" demanded Oliver. The boat stirred momentarily
as their thoughts came to life.

"Listen," cautioned Jason from the depths of his blanket.

The prow of a canoe drifted ghostly out of the blanket
of mists that clung to the surface of the pond, and came to
a stop alongside, with the soft thumping of gunwales.

" 'Lo!"

" 'Lo!"

There was a general exchange of muted grunts, like the
"How" of so many chiefs in solemn council. It was Orlo
Sage, the town Pooh-Bah; the second tattered figure re-
solved itself into none other than Uncle Charlie. The two
were inseparable; especially when the town constable was
exercising his official functions. Whose avuncular connection he was had long since been forgotten; the whole town,
man, boy and woman, knew him by that appellation.

"What were you two doing over to Ensign's?" asked
Orlo.

"Did you see our tracks?" asked Jason quickly.

"Yeah," said Orlo. Oliver tried to think what tracks they could have left that would be so readily readable by night. Another pause. Parr shifted, unhooded himself.

"Well, what of it?" demanded Jason.

"Nothing," Orlo hastened to say. "Only we didn't know Ensign had gone off again."

"Did you want him?"

"No."

"How'd you know he'd gone off?"

"We just been fishing his car out of the river."

To Armiston the essential fact was that the car had to be fished out of the river. Not so with Jason.

He said, surprised: "I didn't know he had a car!"

"Neither did we, till we fished it out," admitted Orlo.

"What makes you think it's his?" asked Jason.

"Remember that carved awning on the mantel his gran'ther fetched up from the Cape?" asked Orlo. "That was tangled up in the steering wheel when we got the car out."

"Maybe the car belonged to the woman," suggested Jason. "She might have come up after him."

"No, I don't think so," said Uncle Charlie. "At least she wasn't doing the driving."

They had not overlooked the print of that high-heeled sandal in the soft mud of the driveway, nor the fact that it was on the right side of the car.

Parr suddenly exclaimed, in some exasperation, "Well, are they dead? Were they drowned?"

"No," said Orlo, disgusted. "If they were, that would end it. They'd be out to sea by now. No one ever went into that river when it was in flood whose body was ever found again. What worries me is why they rolled their car down the hill sixty miles an hour into the mill race."

"Maybe they couldn't help themselves," suggested Oliver.

"They didn't try!" cried Orlo. "They weren't in it!"

"How do you know that? Did you see them?" It was Parr who snapped out the question.

"I didn't need to," said Orlo. "I saw the car after we fished it out. Any fool would know enough to put on brakes, if he had them. Wouldn't he? Well, Ensign had brakes! But he didn't use them. He ain't the one to commit suicide!"

Man can, within the limits of the free will that has been vouchsafed him, like a calf on a tether, decide exactly what he will do in a certain contingency—and do it. But meantime he is surrounded by fellow creatures who are tugging at their own stake chains of volition; what they are going to do, in the fourth-dimensional area called time, to coincide unwittingly with his plans, cannot be foreseen, and can only be guarded against within the region of a gambler's choice. Ensign Belding did not know that Orlo, of all persons in the town, having finished the more pressing of his fall work, was taking the day off to draw a wagonload of milk cans filled with nine-inch trout from the hatchery to put in the river. This was a methodical horse-drawn job, requiring the use of the old and almost abandoned West Street road. Else Ensign would not have chosen this day to leave his front-door key with Jason.

Orlo picked up Uncle Charlie on the way over. It was an all-day job, behind horses that walked three miles an hour. Not a moment dragged. Every so often these two managed to go at a walk over every road in town, no matter how remote. And it was what they observed on these trips that made their administration of the law, as it came down to their fellow citizenry, so mild and unburdensome a thing.

Parr, the man hunter of the metropolis, taking his quantum of sunshine on the Avenue, with an unseen scout ahead and an unseen scout behind, performed much the same office for his constituents.

At the foot of Pray's Hill, by the old silk mill, abandoned fifty years gone by, but still standing foursquare to wind and weather, they pulled up short and stared. Ensign's car had taken the curve at the base at what must have been locomotive speed. It mowed off the posts of the guard rail as if by some gigantic bush scythe. The river was at flood, and the turgid waters of the old tail race boiled with swirling eddies.

Orlo and Uncle Charlie got down without haste. This thing had happened hours before. Yet, in spite of the irresistible force that had snipped off the fence posts, there was a tameness about the wheel tracks of this madly rushing car where they crossed the soft shoulders of the road.

"The wheels weren't locked," observed Orlo.

"Better empty the trout first," advised Uncle Charlie.

They carried the forty-quart cans, one by one, to the race and completely submerged them before upending them. Even if Ensign were pinned under the car in the river, haste would not help him now, and these two practical messengers first attended to their trout. When the last can was emptied, they took ax, crowbar and chain; they never traveled without these tools, with which they were more versatile than a burglar with his jimmy. They first cut a pole in the woods and punched the boiling waters of the race. The car hadn't traveled far after it struck the water. They located it on the bottom and got the chain around it; and, urging the team into its collars, they had it out on the bank. They had no doubt whose it was when they saw the mantel awning.

"There is a sharp curve at the foot of the hill," put in

Parr, who had forgotten bullheads and his craving for sleep. Orlo nodded.

"Someone must have steered around the curve," said Parr.

"They did," agreed Orlo.

"And got out at sixty miles an hour?"

"They got out," admitted Orlo, unruffled.

"That sounds like bareback stuff," remarked Parr, with just a trace of sarcasm. "Must have been the lady."

"No," said Orlo blandly. "He was doing the driving."

"But how?" persisted the police deputy. He was a hundred miles from his own bailiwick, but he was taking charge. And furthermore, Orlo and Uncle Charlie were reporting to him, and to him only.

"He went out on a limb," said Orlo.

"At sixty miles an hour?" said Parr incredulously. "Was he an acrobat?"

"He was," said the imperturbable Orlo. "I'll show you the limb. And I'll show you a hunk of skin he ripped off his arm!"

"Who is this Ensign Belding?" demanded the deputy.

They told him what they knew. It was not much. They were surprised themselves at how little they really knew of Ensign. The police deputy nodded thoughtfully over the story.

"It's a get-away, of some sort," he said softly. He turned to Orlo. "He just came back occasionally to hide, didn't he?"

Orlo shook his head, perplexed, and looked at Uncle Charlie. He had never thought of Ensign as being in hiding when he was here. It was possible. It was even a brilliant conception, all things considered. Oliver was thinking, what an odd twist it would be if this fellow, for all his bad manners and pin-money antiques, should really turn out to be

some big fish in Parr's world—bandit, thug, sharper, gambler—if he should be uncovered because he forgot to set
the brakes for the sharp eyes of a rustic constable—or because Parr himself happened to be going by. Such things
are what crooks call breaks. Breaks keep the jails full.

"He has faked a drowning, of course," said Parr. The
body never would have turned up—if there had been a
body. The torrent of the river in flood would have taken
care of that.

"It is not life insurance," went on the deputy. He had
the trick of classifying human beings by category; filing
human foibles by card-index system. Fake drownings usually are life-insurance frauds. Hundreds of original thinkers
every year conceive the brilliant idea of pretending to be
lost by drowning, so they won't have to produce their own
dead body to collect. The idea is *passé,* but they don't
know it.

"He has played out his string," said Parr, falling into
the argot. "He is making a get-away, so he can turn up as
somebody else. Let's go look-see!"

He took down his rod; Jason drew in the anchor, and
Oliver slipped in the thole pins. They moved off through the
blanket of cottony mist, on whose surface, chest high, the
moon played a silvery light. When the prows unerringly
found shore through some ghostly knowledge of their own,
Orlo lifted up his voice in the plaint of a tree toad—a tree
toad sadly out of season—yet a second answered from
somewhere in the gloaming, and Percy Manchester, the
town bad man, and his wonderful coon dog stepped out,
shivering with dread, into the moonlight. Orlo had taken
him out of jail and brought him along, thinking they might
need the dog.

An hour later, Parr, studying a thumb print through a
magnifying glass, was describing it by telephone. He was

rather rusty on this science, having delegated it, among his multitudinous functions, to men of science who had time to make a life-work of it. Nevertheless, like the youthful De Maupassant differentiating between seemingly identical stones under the guidance of Flaubert, his master, the police deputy did convey in words the salients of these whorls and apices in such a manner as to isolate them from every other thumb print in the world since the dawn of time. There is nothing on earth identical with any other thing, to the eye taught to observe.

A voice in far-off Centre Street, headquarters of the New York police, said quite audibly to all in the hushed kitchen:

"Shall I call you back, sir, or will you hold the wire?"

"I'll hold the wire," said Parr.

They waited.

"This stuff," said Parr, of the thumb print of Ensign Belding, "is not so difficult as you might think." With the point of a pencil he traced the lines. "If he has ever been finger-printed, it is only necessary to look in the right pigeonhole. There is a process of elimination that gradually narrows down. We haven't a clearing house for the whole country yet. We will have some day. But we cops," he added, his little eyes twinkling, "collect choice specimens among ourselves. We add to our collection by swapping back and forth, like we used to swap birds' eggs and postage stamps when we were boys. I have a notion he may be a choice one," he added vaguely. The big fellow nodded. He had been sleepless for upward of three days. With an effort he gave heed to the phone.

"It is Chappie Van Sittart," said the voice at the other end.

"Well! Well!" cried Parr, beaming on the company. "It's Chappie Van Sittart! He is an acrobat, Orlo, I grant you!"

The name meant nothing to them—not even to Oliver.

If they had hived in the Ritz, at White Sulphur or Deau-
ville, or ever made a smoking-room passage on a four-day
boat, they would have heard of this elegant athlete, lady
killer, gambler. It was his forte so to involve his victims
that they couldn't complain. He talked a good deal of his
honor, and freely offered satisfaction to anyone who wanted
it. But such was his prowess that the point was never
pressed. There had never been a formal charge sustained
against him, but his career was such that Parr had caused
him to be brought in occasionally for the morning line-up,
so his bright young men could file the handsome face for
future reference. Parr laughed.

"I never suspected he was a local product," he said. "You
ought to be proud of him!" He turned to the phone. "Do we
want him?"

Apparently not. The voice said casually he would ask
Chicago and Washington and Asheville—it was the fashionable hour at Asheville just now, and that is where Chappie
would most likely be wanted, if at all. Unless, as Parr had
suggested in the boat, the man had run out his string in this
line, and wasn't following the migratory swells this fall.
While he waited, Parr made pencil markings on the table;
his heavy eyelids drooped, fell lower and lower, closed; he
slumped over the table, his head pillowed on his arms, and
he was sound asleep. Jason softly got up and fed the fire.
Silence reigned. The big fellow slept and it was not etiquette
to withdraw. They were frankly disappointed. Now that it
transpired that their neighbor was the glamorous Chappie
Van Sittart, important enough to come under the cogni-
zance of the great Mr. Parr, they would have liked to have
him do something worthy of his fame. Pushing an automobile overboard was not a heinous crime. It is being done
every day to ease the used-car market. Jason grinned. After
a time the telephone dangling at Parr's elbow babbled inco-
herently. Jason picked it up and gave heed. The voice said

there didn't seem to be anything; no one in police circles had any immediate call for Chappie. Sorry.

"All right; I'll tell him," said Jason.

Armiston pushed back his chair to rise, when the door softly opened, and the agitated face of Percy, the town bad man, appeared. He craftily examined the interior. Percy was always suffering delicious apprehensions for the imaginary feats of crime he had executed. Every now and then— as now—Orlo locked him up just to soothe his vanity. Orlo stepped to the door and bent down. Percy whispered. He had followed Ensign's tracks from the top of the hill over to the Hollow on the east branch of the little river. There he had lost them in the hard road.

"Was anybody with him?"

The bad man shook his head.

"How did he go?"

"Walked."

He probably caught a bus; there were dozens of them. Well, thought Orlo, good riddance for all time.

"What's that?" said Orlo, cocking an ear.

A distant murmur was on the night wind. Percy whispered. His dog had three coons in a tree, in the apple orchard on the mountain. He eyed Orlo apprehensively. Orlo let himself out, and when he was wholly out, he turned and beckoned to the others. They joined him. It was lèse-majesté to abandon the big fellow, but no one dared to awaken him. They slunk off into the shadows, led by Percy, who now and again raised his voice in the plaintive peep of a tree toad, to keep them at his heels in the dark. Ahead and away up on the mountain, the dog barked dismally, urging them to hurry, hurry.

III

Morel, the fashion plate, who, with little Pelts, the shabby, formed the close-fitting shadow that never left the

deputy, night or day, placed before his chief two photographs. One was a rogues' gallery likeness of Chappie Van
Sittart; a truly handsome fellow even under these unflat-
tering conditions. The other was a rotogravure likeness
from a Sunday newspaper of Captain Boylin-Eckford,
snapped by some press hound at Palm Beach. After Parr
had studied them, Morel took them away, and in their
place laid two enlargements; of the face in each case. To
these portraits he applied a pair of calipers, with which he
made certain esoteric comparisons. Physiognomists, and
especially anthropologists, study and differentiate among
human heads in much the same way as Parr studied and
indicated the points of variance in that fingerprint he sent
by telephone. No two faces are alike and no one will ever
be mistaken for another when subjected to Morel's calipers.
However, parenthetically, few of us carry calipers.

"It sounds good," agreed Parr. He had great admiration
for Morel, who had spent two years abroad in Bertillon
work.

"I'd like to send our own photographer down there for a
full face and a better three-quarters," said Morel.

So it happened that a fortunate photographer, of police
ilk, was given a Palm Beach vacation. Weeks later satis-
factory photographs arrived of Captain Boylin-Eckford at
play. These views, being duly subjected to calipers, were
filed with the Van Sittart *dossier* until such time as the migratory swells started north. They would pause at Beaufort,
James River, White Sulphur and Asheville. But eventually
they got back to town, sun-bronzed, in time to shop for the
spring flight to London.

One afternoon, at the Sherry Netherlands, Morel, in an
afternoon costume that might have been meant for one of
the walking gentlemen in charge, tapped Captain Boylin-
Eckford politely on the shoulder as he sat at table with his

elegant friends. The captain shivered with irritated apprehension and turned an angry face on Morel.

"Don't do that, I beg of you!" he commanded crisply.
"What is it, fellow?"

Morel said, not moving his lips, but with perfect manner,
that the captain's car waited at the curb on the street side.
The British officer considered for a moment; he arose, still
cogitating; he bowed deprecatingly to his friends and followed Morel out. Such things are bores, but they require
attention. It was not the captain's car but a police car,
as he saw at a glance. They drove downtown.

"What do they want now?" demanded the irritated officer, who seemed to know how to take this sort of thing
philosophically. Morel shook his head, smiling—he was
merely the messenger boy.

He took the Britisher in to Parr. There was nothing
about the trappings to suggest a jail. It was like the office
of a business man—a big one.

"Well, captain!" said the deputy, with a specious genial-
ity that probably would not last long. The captain bowed
and waited.

"Or Mr. Van Sittart, if you prefer," said Parr amiably.

The philosophical gentleman shrugged a graceful
shoulder.

"Or Ensign Belding, if you like that better!" said Parr,
a bark to his tones and a glitter in his eye.

Ensign Belding was not prepared for that, as he was for
the other. He blanched. He even took a step backward,
made to feel for the knob of the door behind him, before
he recollected himself. He shook his head, recovering his
sang-froid.

"No, I am afraid not, sir," he said.

Parr opened a drawer and took out a door key—Ensign
Belding's front-door key—and placed it on the blotter

before him. Ensign Belding's eyes followed the act as if magnetized. It seemed impossible to drag his gaze from that key.

"So," said Parr easily. "Draw back your sleeve. Let me see your left arm."

The prisoner flinched; his easy athletic poise grew swiftly tense. It was Morel who took his left arm and with a single gesture pulled up the sleeve, revealing the deep scar of a torn muscle, just above the wrist.

There was a pause.

"You follow me now, don't you?" asked the deputy. He motioned to a chair. "Sit down and think it over," he said. Parr looked at him as though he were a piece of wood. The prisoner felt his palate go dry, his fingers closed convulsively; and it was only by a great exertion of his will that he prevented his eyes from shutting—that primordial gesture of utter despair. He was a brave man ordinarily. He had steeled himself against this sort of thing; he could carry it off magnificently, as a rule. But when they dragged back his sleeve to lay bare that livid scar—when they called him Ensign Belding—and that key——

"Sit down," said Parr; and he obeyed, trying, between shame and desperation, to get hold of himself, to recover his poise. Actually it was shame to think they could disarm him with a single word. But here was Parr at his elbow.

Parr was saying, in a low impersonal tone: "What do you want to do, eh? Do you want to go through with it from beginning to end? Or do you want to take a plea and cut out the agony? You are somebody now, as Captain Boylin-Eckford. Your new crowd hasn't got on to you yet." Parr's tone was still as smooth as a purring cat. "I can put you away as Ensign Belding, and no one will be the wiser. You'll get maybe twenty years, ten off for good behavior, and a chance with the soft-headed parole board. Then you can come out like a new penny and start all over from scratch." Parr stopped. The man was kneading his knuckles white, bowing his head under the words. If it hadn't been for the ironic certainty in the tones, he might have cried out, put on his magnificent manner. But there was no uncertainty. Parr knew what he was talking about. Parr winked at Morel, and Morel moved his head in a barely perceptible affirmation.

"If you want to take a chance on a first-degree charge," said Parr, his eyes narrowing and his tones harder, "go to it! I admit I'm not sure we can make a first-degree charge stick. But I'll bet you the rope around your neck that you won't get less than manslaughter. If you stick out for it, I promise you will get the works. If you take a plea you will get the minimum sentence. Think it over."

There was another pause. Parr took his eyes off the man now, to lessen the tension. Ensign Belding wetted his lips. He picked with shaky fingers some imaginary lint on his beautifully tailored sleeve. He began to speak, painfully at first, but gaining some courage at the sound of his own voice.

"I seem—to be here—under some horrible misconception—as to my identity," he said, looking timidly at Morel as if the error lay, quite excusably, with him. "You speak of a plea and manslaughter—and first degree—and"—he paused, to hearten himself—"you speak of a rope about my neck—as if I had committed some heinous abysmal crime—as if I had m-murdered my brother—whereas I am merely a poor miscast devil of a card sharp, trying to pick a living—God knows it is precarious enough—out of a parcel of idiots suffering from overstuffing of wealth. It is useless to deny it. You know me for what I am. But as for this m-murder—this scar on my wrist——" He pushed back the sleeve and stared at the scar.

"Maybe you'd like to see what we've got pickled in alcohol in there," said Parr carelessly, jerking a thumb over his shoulder.

The hectic spot of color that had crept into the lost man's cheeks as some measure of courage flowed again was suddenly washed out. He became a rigid automaton, watching Parr. Parr knew everything.

"Ensign," said Parr, "you know the electric lights went out that evening. Or maybe you don't know it! They did. You thought, when you lifted yourself out of the car on that limb, and sent your lady fair crashing through the fence into the river—you thought she would be carried out to sea—and that would be the last you'd ever see of her. Well, she wasn't carried out to sea!" snarled Parr, rising. "Ensign, something stopped the turbines at the electric-light plant down the river that night. What do you suppose it was? They had to shut down and dig it out, bit by bit. Come!" he cried with a sudden ferocity, and he seized the man by both arms and dragged him to his feet. "Come! Let me show you!"

But Ensign Belding, fighting with the strength of frenzy, shrieked, "No! No! No! Never! I did it! I did it, yes. But I—I can't look!"

Parr loosed his hold. "Why—why did you do it?" demanded the deputy. "What did she ever do to you?"

"She followed me there! She threatened to expose me! She was desperate! There was nothing I could do to silence her—nothing but that!"

He covered his face with his hands and fell back in his chair.

"Take him away," said Parr.

When the door shut, Parr moved a large screen. Behind it at a table two men had been sitting—one a stenographer, the other, Oliver Armiston. The stenographer arose, put his sheets in order and, with a bow to the deputy, walked out, closing the door.

"The electric lights didn't go out that night, Parr," said Oliver.

"I know it," said Parr.

Oliver looked frightened.

"But the bones——"

"What bones?" asked Parr.

"Why, the stuff you said they dug out of the wheel—the stuff you offered to show him when he began to shriek——"

"There are no bones, Oliver," said Parr.

"No murdered woman?"

"Not that we have ever been able to find," said the deputy. "I took a long chance. The shot went home." He shrugged. "Well, that's one rascal out of the way for the rest of his natural life," he said. "Oliver," he cried suddenly, "the only sign of a woman we were ever able to materialize in this whole affair was, first, that footprint in the sitting room, and, second, the footprint in the driveway where she stepped into the car. She never got out of that car. Recollect?"

"Yes," breathed Oliver. "Yes!"

It was true. Except for those two footprints, they never found another vestige of the woman that night.

"We made inquiries," said Parr. "It was her car. She was one of his old gang. She has never been seen since that night. She had something on him; she had him with his back to the wall. Oliver, is there any doubt in your mind that he killed her or how he did it?"

"No, I have just heard him confess," cried Armiston, bewildered. "But, Parr, if he hadn't broken down, if he hadn't confessed—if he had said, 'All right, let me see what you've got pickled in alcohol.' What then? What would you have done?"

"Nothing," said the deputy. He laughed harshly. "I'd have turned him loose! What else could I have done? You can't convict a murderer, no matter what you believe, on the strength of a couple of footprints. Were you watching him? When did he break?"

"When you put that key on the table," said Armiston. He shivered slightly, as from a draft. He was thinking of that cant line, "The police obtained a confession"; he wondered how many newspaper readers, over their morning coffee, had any conception of the drama behind those words—how, in this instance, the mere sight of a key—the key to his own front door—was sufficient to start a train of thought that left the victim helpless and pleading for mercy.

THE END